Still Life
with
Devils

A Novel by
Deborah Grabien

F

Still Life with Devils

Copyright © 2007 by Deborah Grabien

This is a work of fiction. Names, characters, places and incidents are the product of the author's imagination and any resemblance to any organization, event, or person, living or dead, is purely coincidental.

Published by
Drollerie Press
Once upon a time...

www.drolleriepress.com

Library of Congress Control Number: 2007932580
ISBN-13: 978-0-9798-0810-4
ISBN-10: 0-9798081-0-3

Cover art and design by Deena Fisher. The cover font for title and author of *Still Life with Devils* is *Techno*. The devils marking the end of each chapter are taken from the *Mythologicals One* font by the incredibly creative Manfreid Klein. All other text is *Georgia*.

Dedication

With heartfelt thanks to Lieutenant Jerry McCarthy of the San Francisco Police Department's Homicide Division, for his generosity, cooperation, and patience in answering the undoubtedly silly questions of a civilian.

For Jeanne Posey, a very good painter indeed.

Prologue

Theresa Gabriel, eight months pregnant, was on her way home.

Despite her advanced pregnancy, she was walking as fast as she could. She had good reasons to hurry. The grocery bag she carried was heavy. The fog was in, curling around her ankles, obscuring the lights of Fulton Street. Also, it was nearly full dark. Common sense should have prevented her taking this short cut through the western end of Golden Gate Park, especially at night.

None of those reasons—there were others, less benign—had been enough to outweigh the fact that she'd run out of eggs.

This wasn't as silly as it sounded. Tonight was the Gabriels' fifth wedding anniversary, and Jerry Gabriel was a fan of his wife's cooking. Theresa had planned to surprise him with his favorite dinner, a soufflé, but she'd run out of eggs. And she couldn't make a soufflé without eggs.

She hitched the grocery bag higher, wincing at the pain of a stitch in her side. Her bright red jacket was a splash of color against the thickening darkness. Jerry would be home in an hour. She kept walking.

The bag, which contained not only eggs but milk and wine, was putting a cramp in her shoulder. She stopped and set it down, panting. Maybe she should have taken the car. But driving a sports car at eight months pregnant wasn't easy. The last time she'd tried to wedge herself into the low-slung seats, she'd hurt her back and it had taken her nearly ten minutes to extricate herself. Besides, the doctor had told her that walking was good exercise.

She wiped her sweaty palms on her jacket, and decided it was time she stopped coddling herself with these little rest stops. Home was five minutes away; she could see the lights of her own kitchen windows through the trees.

Theresa bent to retrieve the makings of Jerry's favorite dinner. As her hand closed on the bag, something rustled in the thick shrubbery to her left. A shape materialized out of the fog and the encroaching night. A black-gloved hand, holding something thick and heavy, came down hard.

The single well-placed blow to the back of her skull took her down into the darkness. She fell face-down, one arm hitting the grocery bag, smashing the eggs that had brought her out to meet her own ending.

Theresa Gabriel had no time to understand how and why death had come to her. She had no time, either, to realize that of all the reasons to have avoided this excursion, the most basic had never even occurred to her.

The weapon that had taken her down was slipped into a deep pocket. In that same pocket was a long length of clear nylon cord. It was carefully, lovingly taken in hand.

The killer cast one considering glance around, at the deserted path, the deepening fog, the lack of traffic. They might have been alone together, hunter and prey, alone in a damp chilly universe.

The nylon cord went easily, too easily, around Theresa Gabriel's neck. The ends were crossed, tightened, and mercilessly held in place while the dying body bucked feebly, fighting for air and life.

But that battle was lost before it began. In moments, the cord pushed Theresa over the edge of nature's waiting dark place, and into the world of light.

The killer straightened, breathing heavily, a slight figure in black cotton trousers and jacket. These articles of clothing were cheap and nondescript, obtainable anywhere in Chinatown. San Francisco was full of people who wore these things, right down to the cotton shoes with the plastic soles. The only odd touch was a fisherman's cap, angled low.

For a moment the shadowy figure stood, staring down at its sacrifice to mortality. But the pause was brief; there were still things to be done.

Swiftly, and with curious grace, hands slipped beneath Theresa Gabriel's limp shoulders, pulling until the dead woman lay on her back, her head pointing toward the apartment she would never see again. Living hands manipulated dead ones, and folded them across the swollen stomach. Then, the ritual of death and victory complete, the dark form stood up.

The air was foggy, growing darker with every passing moment. Hunter and trophy were alone together.

The killer walked away, back turned, as if that now death had been given, the abandoned envelope of skin and bone was pointless, worthy not even of contempt. On the ruined body of Theresa Gabriel, partially concealed by the shadows of tree and sky, the fog settled like a cool wet shroud.

Chapter One

"Damn!"

Leo Chant fumbled with her keys as the last light faded. She was hurrying, trying futilely to manipulate the double bolts and the heavy door. The city of San Francisco was wrapped in fog. Evening had come on, the normal vivid colors lost under a dense layer of grey that sat, unmoving, across the city's face. The tops of Coit Tower and the Transamerica Pyramid were invisible; the city lay marooned in its own sightless universe.

"Come on, move it, open up now open come on... ."

Leo despised fear; not even to herself did she admit that a woman might have good reasons for wanting to get indoors quickly in an inner city neighborhood. Her brother Cassius, a cop of thirteen years' experience, had long ago given up regaling her with his opinion of the South of Market area as a place to live. He knew his sister Leontyne. As close as they were, her mind was her own, and he had never once changed it for her.

Tonight the door took longer than usual, the task made more difficult by the fog. Leo had not expected to get home this late, or this thick, paralyzing darkness, claustrophobic as cotton wool. She swore, set her artist's portfolio and a bag of groceries on the pavement, and wrestled with the locks. After a moment they yielded, and, with a breath of relief, she stepped into a home designed to meet an artist's fondest dreams.

Leo's sanctuary had been built some years back, not as a residence but as a compactly sized warehouse, designed for storing beer, street drugs, or crates of the cheap clothes made by the illegal immigrants the city sheltered.

Just before the city's dot-com industry in the South of Market area had sent real estate prices through the roof, and long before the subsequent economic collapse had turned those same companies into picturesquely named memories on ghostly billboards, the building's cash-crunched owner had tried to burn it to the ground three times, and failed each time.

Something about the place had appealed to Leo. It refused to be destroyed, no one wanted it, and the insurance company had correctly fingered the three fires as arson and insurance fraud. Bankrupt and prison-bound, the owner had signed title over to his brother and his brother had sold it to Leo for pennies on the dollar, with the proviso that she was buying it in its "contractor's special" condition. This meant that she would have to make the necessary repairs herself, and at her own expense. Seeing the potential and correctly guessing the direction in which the city's real estate values were heading, Leo had jumped at the deal and dug into her savings.

The warehouse was a long room, forty feet by seventy. Its vast bathroom was badly plumbed and equipped with only an ancient toilet and a tiny sink. The walls bore the scars of the arsonist's kiss; the skylight was nothing more than shards of glass that threatened to fall at the rumble of every passing truck. Only the warehouse's windows, each fitted with a roll-down metal shutter, had remained intact.

Leo had co-opted the whole of her enormous acquaintance, several of whom were architects and interior designers. They stripped wood, laid natural brick flooring, installed tiers of subtle track lighting that could be raised and lowered and focused at a touch. The new skylight was protected by a sophisticated burglar alarm; the redesigned bathroom was a sybarite's dream. The fire-scarred barn had been transformed, into something as luxurious as it was functional. Leo Chant, at thirty-seven, liked her creature comforts.

She entered her alarm code and flipped the switch that controlled the lights. At once the room was bathed with a soft phosphorescence that lit every corner. There were no shadows in Leo's nest, and no place to hide. The central heating, left on low this chilly October day, kept the place at a livable temperature.

My God, she thought, home alone with nothing to do. The evening was her own, there was nothing to press her and, for once, no deadlines to meet. And she was home.

She headed into the bathroom, just long enough to grab a hand towel from the rack and rub the fog out of her hair. She spared a thought for the 1990s, when women of color had wasted time and energy on elaborate cornrows, or beaded dreadlocks, and grinned. Leo had never fallen for that one; her hair was as close to a buzz cut as a black woman could get. With her bones and beautifully shaped skull, the look was as effective as it was low-maintenance.

An hour later, she'd eaten dinner and was considering a bath. It occurred to her that she hadn't checked her messages. The phone and answering machine lived on a table at the far end of the room. Since there was nothing else to engage her attention there, she constantly forgot about the phone, sometimes collecting messages four days old and then only when the instrument rang and jarred her memory.

The light was blinking, showing four messages. She ran the tape back.

Beep. A resonant male voice, hurried and harassed.

"Hi Leo, it's Cass. Can you ask Mara over for dinner tomorrow night? There's been another murder and it looks like a couple of all-nighters at the station. I'd ask Mom, but they've been getting on each other's nerves and I think they could both use a break. Give me a call if there's any problem. 'Bye. Oh, sorry, it's Tuesday, ten-forty PM."

Something cold moved down Leo's back. While she avoided the news whenever possible, she knew as much and probably more about the serial killings frightening the city than the most avid media hound. Her brother, after all, was in charge of the investigation. There was a dark, nauseating flavor to these killings of pregnant women, bitterly underscored by the panic and tension that built with every new death. Cassy's message brought the total to six, and what the police had in the way of evidence, Cassy had told her a few weeks earlier, wasn't worth the price of a postage stamp.

There was another issue, more insidious. The city had seen nothing like this since the Zebra killings, many years earlier. There was no reference point to help them cope with the mounting fear. If this crazy bastard wasn't caught soon, something was going to snap... .

Leo took herself in hand. She wasn't pregnant. There was nothing to fear and nothing she could do to help, either. She reactivated the tape.

Beep. "Good morning Miss Chant, this is Susan Ortiz at *Inside Look*. I know I said two weeks for those book sketches, but the printer's union is threatening to strike and we may need them by Monday morning. Call me if that's a problem. It's Wednesday, noon. You have the number."

"Damn it! Susan, you bitch, don't do this to me!" So much for not worrying about deadlines. Leo jabbed viciously at the button and moved on, to message number three.

Beep. A languid female voice, pitched low and sensual.

"Aunt Leo? It's Mara, Wednesday afternoon, I don't know what time it is because I'm in a phone booth, I forgot to charge my cell phone. Look, I know Dad called you, but don't worry about having me over, I can arrange something with a friend. Just because Dad gets frazzled doesn't mean you have to get frazzled, too. Go take a hot bath and curse at your deadlines, or whatever. Talk to you, 'bye."

Leo's eyebrows went up. Her niece had this unnerving habit of leaving soothing, sleepy little messages that recommended courses of action long decided on by Leo herself. It could get on a person's nerves. Leo decided to leave Mara to her own devices; there were times when a fourteen-year-old girl, even one as self-contained and "old soul" as Mara, was too much to cope with.

The fourth caller had left no message, hanging up before Leo's taped demand for a name, date, and number could cycle through. Leo erased the tape, sighed, and checked the clock.

It was nearly eight, which meant that Susan Ortiz would have left her office hours ago. Six illustrations by Monday morning, Leo thought bitterly. Bang goes my nice relaxing weekend. Damn that stupid magazine. *Is that a problem?* Now, how could that much work in five, no, *four* days, possibly be a problem? Damn, damn, damn. She wandered the long room aimlessly, glancing around without seeing, trying to capture the calm that had been shattered by the intrusion of the real world.

She stopped, her eye caught by a stack of canvases in one corner. Those were the still-life oils for the Kepple Gallery showing. A good show. She'd not only sold three canvases, she'd spent an uproarious weekend with Davis Grieg, the gallery owner. He was not ideal, being too neurotic and too yuppie and too white generally, but he was a good connection and a basically nice guy and not too bad in other respects, if only he would stop taking everything, including himself, so seriously.

Leo grinned at the memory. Carla Morisco, the other featured artist at the Kepple show, had made a few pointedly funny comments about sleeping with the enemy, and the two painters had shared a good giggle over it.

Those pictures, now. There they stood, painted surfaces against the wall. Leo stared at their blank, uninformative backs. What were they again, the few that hadn't sold?

A still-life of nuts, the bowl and table extremely realistic, the nuts impressionist; she'd been experimenting with multiple styles in a single context, not entirely successfully. Another painting, a vibrant white wicker cage with exotic birds flaunting their colors. Why hadn't that one sold? Perhaps the vicious tilt of the beaks, the attack stance of the winged furies, had frightened the buyers off. Two others were smaller and less memorable.

Leo made up her mind quickly. She flipped through the stack and found the canvas of the Rembrandt table and bowl with the Monet almonds. Pulling it free of the others, she set it on the easel directly under the skylight.

She checked the door, making sure that the bolts were shot and the chain in place. The iron-shuttered windows, always left down when Leo was out, protected her from prying eyes. Breathing slowly and deeply, she walked to the painting and sat in the hard wooden chair that she always kept in front of the easel.

She fixed her eyes on the painted bowl, the dense lines of her own vision catching and holding her. There was a liveliness to this piece, something both restful and alert; you could almost smell a September day. The background was a soft wallpaper effect, the painting lit from an unseen window somewhere. Colors. Yellow ocher, French ultramarine, a streak of Payne's gray that had blended with the yellows and whites, speckling the lit side of the bowl, echoing, singing, resonating with a kind of visual laughter. Sunlight, and the smell of fruit outside that hidden window...

Leo Chant, staring wide-eyed, motionless, and barely breathing, walked out of her body and into her painting.

Lieutenant Cassius Chant, Cass or Cassy to his friends and colleagues, rubbed his eyes and tried to focus on one of the nastiest photographs he'd ever seen.

The insides of his lids felt gritty, and focussing was getting harder every day. Six killings in ten weeks made for sore eyes when you were in charge of the city's Homicide Division. Killing in any form was an affront. But this kind, pregnant women nailed by a lone operator with a screw loose, was nightmarish. One death, three deaths, and suddenly the deaths themselves became almost incidental to other things: the pressure, the media, the mounting panic registered by the upsurge of scared calls to the police department and the increase of petty crimes all over town.

The photo was only one of a dismal series. Some had been taken at the crime scene in Golden Gate Park, others on a mortuary slab. The face was blank and pop-eyed, crumpled like a tissue, hideous with the blue lividity of suffocation and early mortification.

"Nice night for it."

Cassy looked up. Jim Delgado, one of the fourteen homicide inspectors under his command, was leaning against the door frame, a cup of coffee in each hand. His thin build usually seemed too slight to hold the energy packed inside. Tonight, he appeared to need the door frame just to hold him upright; the wilt was visible, and growing worse every day. Energy was just one of the minor casualties inflicted by the killer known strictly to Homicide as Captain Nemo.

"Not for Theresa Gabriel." Cass dropped the photos and closed his eyes, resisting the urge to knuckle them. "Not for the baby, either. I thought you were off duty tonight. Where's Shansky?"

"In bed with the flu. So are Soufriere and Jackson, which, in case you're wondering, is why I'm here. I'm not on duty, but at least I'm healthy. 'Tis the season for vitamin C and chicken soup. You know something? Captain Nemo is beginning to get on my nerves. I never thought I'd find myself hankering after a nice old-fashioned gang killing."

"Or even a drive-by. I know what you mean. Is that coffee for me? Nice guy, and a mind-reader, no less."

Delgado passed over a cup. "Hell, I'm just sucking up. The way I see it, if I'm nice enough to the head honcho, he'll see about transferring me to Lost Luggage or Missing Parakeets or something less stressful."

"We don't even have a division for—" Cassy caught Jim's eye and grinned. "Nobody's transferring anywhere, not with half the department down with

the flu. Anyway, you want out of this hell-hole, don't be so good at your job."
He swallowed a mouthful of coffee. "Thanks. I needed that."

"You needed that more than you think. Rumor has it the chief wants to
throw a little party, you know? A conference for the Dogs of War."

This euphemism, coined by Homicide's receptionist Elena Gonzales,
referred to the media at large. Cassy groaned.

"Jesus, Jim, what does he want to tell them? That there's been another
killing? They already know that, it rated a special bulletin during *Survivor
XXVIII* or whatever crapola show was on last night. That we don't know
what sex, age, color or species Nemo is? Hell, they know that, too. I can just
hear him, or is it only me who's supposed to host this party?" His voice took
on a pompous overtone, unctuous, bitterly edged in sarcasm. "'Members
of the press, on behalf of the commissioner and the mayor's office, I'm
here tonight to announce a major breakthrough in the Maternity Murders.
We have determined beyond any possible doubt that the perpetrator of
these heinous crimes is, in fact, a carbon-based life form. I can't praise the
forensics people highly enough for their unflagging energy, their tireless
efforts, their unceasing cooperation, their brilliant insight, their—'"

"Hey! Loot!" Delgado was startled. Cassy's voice had begun to spiral out
of control. "Hey, whoa, easy. Calm down, Lieutenant. Chill. Just breathe."

"Right." Cassy let his breath out. "Right. Jim, do you know what I'd like
to do right now? More than anything?"

"Go fishing," Delgado said immediately. He was a passionate, obsessive
devotee of the sport. "Someplace where they don't speak any English
and no one ever heard of the Maternity Murders. Antarctica, maybe. Or
Cameroon."

"Nope. I'd like to find the guy that came up with this 'no smoking in the
workplace' shit and get him addicted to nicotine. You know? Just tie him
to a chair and blow smoke at him—twenty-four-seven—for a few weeks.
Then I want to put his interfering, self-righteous ass in charge of this
investigation. After that, I'll just sit back and see how he handles this kind
of pressure without something to fall back on."

Delgado, who didn't smoke but wasn't too bothered by people who did,
grinned. He'd heard Cass sing this particular tune before. "I know, I know.
Serve the bastard right. I hate busybodies too. Meantime, why not go take
a breather outside? Or should that be a choker outside?"

The phone rang before Cassy could annihilate him. "Homicide, Chant speaking."

"Daddy?"

At the sound of that slow, easy voice, Cassy relaxed. It was hard to admit, but it was true; if Nemo killed nothing but pregnant women forever after, he would be frightened for his daughter. Maybe every parent in town felt that way. Or every parent on earth.

"Mara, honey. How you do?"

"I do fine." This ritual greeting dated back to Mara's first experiments with speech. Although she had outgrown her eccentric use of verbs, the greeting remained as a private joke between them, as intimate as a goodnight kiss. "I'm over at Shelly's house, for dinner and homework."

"Who the hell is—oh, you mean Shelly Wilson. The girl with the weird hair, sticks out in front, like a quail?"

Mara snorted. The elegant exhale was idiosyncratic; she'd never giggled in her life, at least not within her father's hearing. The snort was uniquely Mara's. Another enigma, another mystery. He sometimes wondered if she was really a teenage girl.

"Yes, Father dear, a quail. Anyway, I'm having dinner here and then her mother's driving me home. And she'll get out of the car with me, and walk me inside, and help me turn on the lights, and make sure there's no one hiding in the closet. And don't worry, she definitely isn't pregnant."

"That's not funny. In case you hadn't noticed, there's a psychopath running around town, killing women—"

"Pregnant women. Very pregnant women. And I can assure you, in no uncertain—"

"*Mara.*" The snap in his voice was a warning, and Mara stopped teasing. She never pushed too far unless she considered the issue a matter of moral importance. It was something that Cassy, as a single father, had reason to be grateful for. There had been no tantrums from Mara, no spoiled sulks, not even as a toddler. His mother, a firm disciplinarian who had helped raise the girl from infancy, summed it up perfectly: Mara always knew when enough was enough.

"All right, Daddy. I won't tease anymore. And I was only teasing, you know. I don't really think all these precautions are silly. Believe me, I take them as seriously as you do. I mean, suppose I was wearing one of my big oversized sweaters, and he saw me in profile, and thought—"

"Hush. You just *hush*." Cassy saw Delgado, who had been idly flipping through a stack of reports, turn to stare at him. He caught the look on Cassy's face and hastily turned away. Cassy had heard the naked emotion in his own voice. It couldn't be helped; the picture Mara had conjured up was horrifying.

He swallowed hard, suddenly furious with his exquisite, inexplicable daughter. Why did he have to love her so much, when just a little less feeling would have made his life so much easier? He pushed the anger away.

"I'm glad to hear you're taking it seriously. You call me once you're home, okay?" A sudden thought occurred to him. "Hold it. How come you're not at Leo's? I left a message on her machine, asking her to invite you over."

"I'm not there because I left her one, too, telling her I was going over to Shelly's and she didn't have to worry about it. Don't get antsy, Daddy, I'm fine. And I promise I'll call when I get home."

"Good. In the meantime, give me the number at Shelly's, and yes, I know you have a perfectly good cell phone, it costs me enough every month. Oh, wait, never mind, it's here in my rolodex. If you get scared, you call me. Okay?"

"Okay." The smooth, calm voice never flickered; heaven only knew what was going on inside her head. She was about as easy to read as a lead-lined coffin. "See you 'bye."

Cassy hung up. At his elbow, the stack of reports, the photos, the memos from the assistant district attorney's office, made an unwieldy pile. His head ached, and his hands were damp and unsteady. Hell, he thought, too much tension is a bitch and no mistake. It was definitely time for a smoke and a breath of night air.

"Did I hear you mention Leo?"

Cassy, reaching for his jacket, turned to Delgado. He had not missed Jim's tone, offhand and too casual. Jim's admiration for Leo had been noted and remarked on by everyone except Leo herself. "Probably. Why?"

"Just wondering how she was. She hasn't been in here for a while. Those head shots she drew, when Friedman was on vacation last year, they were great."

"Nothing for her to draw on this one, or for Friedman either," Cass said grimly. He saw something on Delgado's face, an unspoken sentiment wanting out, and paused at the office door. "Spit it out, Jim. What's on your mind?"

"Oh, nothing." He met Cassy's eye, and his ears turned red. "Oh, hell, and you called me a mind-reader! It's just that, you're pretty worried about Mara—"

"Of course I'm worried about Mara," he snapped. "Wouldn't you be worried about your daughter with this crap going on?"

"If I had one, you're damned straight I'd be worried. But Leo's even smaller than Mara is. Hell, she just tops my shoulder, and I'm not starting at center for the Lakers any time soon. Don't you get worried about her, too?"

Cassy considered him, a reluctant grin dawning.

"Jim, if there's one person on earth I don't need to worry about, it's my sister. I know artists are supposed to be weird, but not Leo. Leo's depressingly normal. Nothing ever happens to her; she's too real to *be* real. Look, I'm going outside for a smoke. I'll be back in five if anyone calls."

He went quickly through the pebbled glass doors, leaving Delgado staring after him.

Usually, when Leo walked into her own fourth dimension, it was as easy as passing through mist. So it was tonight; there was nothing different, nothing alarming, nothing new.

It didn't always work. Leo had learned years before that she could not walk into a picture without a scene. A nude with no background, an anatomy sketch, a page full of hands or feet or noses, were locked doors granting her no entry. But a landscape, a still life, anything where she had painted a setting, was open country.

Her body stayed behind, limp and relaxed. Since no one knew of her strange ability, she'd never had to explain either the mechanics or the sensations involved in this psychic travelling. Had she been asked, she would have found herself hard-pressed.

She might have said that she could enter no work that had not come from her own hand. She might have said that the hands of her mind, or her consciousness, clasped a thin colorless cord, a cord that linked spirit to body and acted like a velvet-covered rope in a theatre queue, keeping her attached to the essential something that was Leontyne Chant. She might have added something about the way her senses worked in the shadowlands of painted reality; that while all five served her in that odd place, sounds were muffled and booming, colors filmed over, smells fleeting. Beyond that, she would have had no words.

Tonight the cord lay against her, a tow-rope back and forth between dimensions of an artist's reality. She could feel herself, both ends of herself. She was present faintly, distantly, both in the silent, unblinking shell that waited passively in a hard-backed chair, and present, too, in the painted kitchen where freshly picked almonds lay in a bright bowl, waiting for a hand to come and take them. The hand would never come, for Leo had not painted it. And yet, following the line of power between self and self, Leo herself could taste them.

She did what she always did on these journeys. First she found a center, a focal point, and established her spirit there. From there she could stand safely and allow, without fear, the bombardment of her senses. Tonight she knew at once that this would be a pleasurable hour. The bowl, the almonds, the wallpaper dappled with day, were all benign.

She hovered in her own painting like a ghost, waiting.

Sound came first. It washed over her as if from a vast distance, a soft muffled whispering she identified as a tiny breeze. It held its own reality, that gentle blowing breath of air, and hard on its heels came smell: warm, tantalizing and familiar, something that did not come from the painting itself.

Wrapped in a peace outside of temporal considerations, Leo was puzzled. She forced away the impatience, the wanting to know. She never strained toward knowledge or forced her own understanding at these moments. It could not be done safely; she had tried it once and found herself back in her body, lying bruised and nauseous on the studio floor, sweating with cramps and fever. Passivity was another condition of this odd talent; she was welcome to what was offered, but must not ask for more. Sometimes the anomaly would resolve into firm identification, sometimes not.

Tonight the elusive scent clarified. Apricots, she thought distantly, that's the smell of apricots. So there's a garden or an orchard outside that window I suggested but never painted. Would I smell them so strongly if they were alive and growing, still on the tree? Probably not. So the fruit had been picked, or fallen from the boughs, hitting the ground, splitting the rich skin, staining the fertile earth of the orchard with juice, delighting the birds...

Another sound, close yet far away. Singing. A human voice? No, she thought, birdsong. Birds in the orchard, pecking, shrilling, offering thanks for nature's gift.

Something moving across her skin, warmth followed by a short quick chill. The breeze that could be implied but never painted had found the backs of her hands, laced her briefly within itself, moved on.

The almonds, misty and sketchily painted, beckoned to Leo. She thought about them, and felt her mouth water. She summoned them from their charming vivid bowl, tasting one, delighting in her detachment at their firm texture, their crunch, the oil, was it oil paint or almond oil that left a faint spectral touch against her palate...?

When she finally felt the tug of her body, the sudden jolting of a small pain somewhere within herself, she had reached a level of tranquility incomprehensible to another mind. With no regret, no sense of loss, she gave herself to the imperative wrench of the weightless, colorless cord that linked her to the physical world. It was time to go.

A tremble, a sudden thickness behind her eyes. The cord was solid against her, tangible in its meaning.

She faded, dissolved, and followed it home.

Leo found herself sitting in the wooden chair, her right hand cupping her left elbow, rubbing the ache and the tingle away. As she'd stood and crunched nuts in another place, leaving her body behind, her arm had fallen asleep.

Secure and serene on the wooden easel, the almonds rested in their bowl, dappled with sun, kept fresh by the breeze from the hidden window. Somewhere in the painted reality that was only one small dimension in Leo Chants's universe, birds sang and ate apricots.

Chapter Two

In Cassy Chant's flat, a young girl was engaged in a ritual of her own.

Mara Chant's beauty was unexpected. A mixture of races in a single package often produces an orchid instead of a rose, rare and exotic. Still, while potential can be there from birth, the thing itself usually remains latent until the protective gloss of maturity is attained. It is rarely found in children. When it is, it is often unnerving, something to disturb.

Mara at fourteen was a taller version of Mara at birth. The stillness, the hint of something hidden beyond the grace and self-possession, had been there with her first breath and had barely altered since. Watching her learn to crawl had made her family obscurely uneasy; watching her first steps had startled them into silence. Even her father, who worshipped her, had taken few baby pictures to mark the passage of her days. Perhaps he had known that there would be few changes to record.

She sat in her room, her eyes closed, a green pastel pencil in one hand and a sheet of drawing paper on the floor in front of her. There were three other pencils on the floor beside her: scarlet, black, cerulean blue. In the course of this ritual she would use them all, never once opening her eyes to see what she made. Vision would not have served her in any case; the room was dark.

There was music playing, a CD of her father's: Miles Davis, *Sketches of Spain*. Mara's taste in music was as unlikely as her quietude and her physical grace. Her friends, going from pop to heavy metal to hip-hop, had given up trying to convert her to their way of hearing. She listened almost exclusively to instrumental jazz, with the occasional classical or ethnic piece—the *Carmina Burana*, Irish folk music—thrown in as what she called leavening for the dough. *Sketches of Spain* was her personal favorite; it bore, to Mara's ear, a mythic quality.

Now, as the acrid notes of the trumpet soared in the darkness, she allowed the music into herself and let it guide her hand. She never looked at what she drew until it was done, never went back to what she had made, never changed, never repaired mistakes or imperfections. No photographic record of her life's passage was necessary; it lay here, hidden among her things. Her genius was instinctive, and it was secret. No one knew she could create, much less create blindly, as a kind of reflex.

Her hand moved across the paper, leaving a short tight sweep of color that, as it took flight, its creator could only sense. In this one thing, Mara Chant renounced her self-possession. She gave herself up to whatever wanted in, wanted out, letting it use her, doing her best to distill its essence and then forgetting it for a time. Her work, in its own way, was an act of simple faith.

Tonight the instinct was imperative, the direct opposite of the roaring flights of sound coming from the speakers behind her. One by one, the four pastel pencils moved across the heavy vellum. As Miles Davis sketched Spain, his listener's eyes remained deliberately sightless.

Music and art finished together. Mara laid her pencil down. Whatever had carried her was fading out, gently and without pain, leaving her limp and a bit empty.

She tucked her legs into a full lotus, breathing deeply and evenly. Her body was still, quiet, a dusky splash against the dark room. After a few minutes she rose to her feet, turned the bedside lamp on, and looked at her work.

There were technical mistakes, of course, lines that didn't quite meet, colors that jumped each other's borders, shapes without precision. But the picture was there, the essence of the thing itself, a man on horseback holding a spear. She studied it dispassionately for a few minutes, realizing with a distant surprise that the shapes were familiar, evocative of something she knew.

After a while it came to her. The horse was a donkey, the spear was a broom. This was Don Quixote on the creature with the odd name; what was it, Rozinante? There were yellow lights on the beast's skin, and something savage about the rider's profile. Sketches of Spain, indeed.

Because the pastels would smear without attention, she gently blended a few dominant lines with one finger and blew the rainbow dust from its surface. Then she put it away with a stack dating back some six years, in the bottom of her old toy chest, laying it flat and covering it with a sheet of wax paper. In a week, a year, a decade, she might take it out and study it more thoroughly, getting to know its curves and edges and deeper meanings. For now, the doing was enough.

"Sixth Death in Maternity Murders."

Physical exhaustion was nothing new to Cassy. As the youngest man ever to attain his position, and the first African-American, it was an old companion. He had reached his rank, a coveted and respected one, through talent, intuition, and mind-breaking hard work.

In his time, he'd handled gang warfare, drive-by killings, householders surprised and shot by burglars who seemed to feel that they'd been forced into crime by the inconsiderate presence of a homeowner who should have stayed at the movies. He'd coped with drug dealers, and cautioned their customers. Too often, he'd read their rights to sullen teenagers whose distraught parents sat beside them, wondering what had gone wrong. It was never easy, and it never got easier.

This was something new, at least to Cassy. There were a handful of older men under his command who remembered the Zebra and Zodiac killings, thirty years earlier; to them, the rage was familiar, a taste of sickness they could identify. Cass himself had been a child at the time, and he barely remembered the fear that had taken hold as the shootings escalated into double digits. Those cases had been so long ago that the frustration of those who had worked the killings, at once cerebral and visceral, came back with surprise.

The fear engendered by this new wave of murders came as a shock to Cassy. In a city where so many died of so many causes every day, he found it inexplicable that not only the civilians but the police themselves should be breathing a miasma of superstitious terror. Death, after all, was nothing new to urban America.

Cassy thought about it now, trying to make sense of what seemed a ridiculous chain of reactions. Not ten weeks ago, there had been a gang eruption over a crack deal in the Bayview neighborhood, some poor fool apparently trying a shakedown with eight friends at his back. A firefight had broken out, and the cops had picked up twelve bodies, three of them under fifteen, all riddled with semi-automatic weapons fire. The papers had given it a smallish box on page two—right under a half-page interview with Jack Peralta, one of the Maternity Murder victim's husbands. Twice the number of the serial killer's total in one sitting, and no one even bothered to shrug.

This morning, the newspaper headline from the previous day sat on Cassy's desk. He could have dropped it into the recycling bin since he knew the pertinent sections by heart. Yet something, some streak of stubbornness, kept it there.

"Lieutenant?"

Cassy realized that he'd been sitting back with his eyes closed, very near to sleep. He straightened his back.

"Jim, Luis. Top of the morning."

"Afternoon, you mean. It's just after twelve." Luis Valenzuela had a huge, booming voice. His temper was legendary at Homicide; so was the softness of his heart. "You look wasted."

"Thanks for the update." Even to his own ears, Cassy sounded glum, bordering on petulant. Childish, he thought impatiently, and shook it off. "I could use some sleep, say about a week's worth. What's up?"

"Reports from the lab." Delgado tossed the stack onto Cassy's desk. There was something different about Delgado today, a kind of excitement, a stiffening of last night's wilt. Cassy let the papers lay where they'd fallen and cocked an eyebrow.

"Something?"

"Could be." Valenzuela had it too, whatever it was. "Three footprints and some fibers. I'd call that something, considering what Nemo's left for us so far."

"Hot damn!" It was the first break they'd had, the first physical traces that this killer was something other than an incubus conjured up from San Francisco's foggy nights. So far, Nemo had been either very lucky or very careful. Maybe he was getting careless with success; maybe the luck was deserting him at last. Cassy shot a hand out, scattering the reports and the newspaper.

"Where?"

"Right on top, photos attached. No, here, the ones with the paper clips." Delgado's thin fingers found and pulled. Cassy glanced down and took a deep breath.

"Okay, baby, okay. Here we go, maybe. Could somebody rustle me up a cup of tea? Hot, strong, really sweet?"

"Tea? You want tea?" Luis exchanged a startled glance with Jim. "*Sweet* tea? You mean, like, with sugar in it? Damn, boss, I've never seen you drink that stuff. Thought you were strictly a coffee type."

"You thought right. Now find me some tea, please." As Luis went to relay the order to Elena, Cassy took up one of the two reports and began to read.

The information was brief and simple, couched in the usual style of the lab down the hall. Some minute fibers had been caught in the armpits of Theresa Gabriel's jacket, possibly indicating that the killer had moved the body after death. The fibers were black cotton, came from a well-worn garment—possibly the cuff of a jacket or shirt, probably not a glove—and showed traces of laundry detergent and fabric softener. Since Mrs. Gabriel had been wearing a brightly colored sweater and red wool jacket, the fibers had not come from her.

"Black cotton. Helpful." The sarcasm in Cassy's tone was misleading; any information, even as vague as this, *was* helpful, and he knew it. Like his subordinates, he was aware of an upsurge, a flash of hope. He was just superstitious enough not to show it.

"Check out the other one, the report on the footprints." There was urgency in Delgado's voice. Cassy read for a moment, looked at the accompanying photograph, and made a noise in his throat. Slowly, a small tight smile settled on his face. It was the expression of the hunter sighting prey, the fisherman feeling a bite on his line, resettling his patience, able to wait.

"Well, well, well," No wonder the others had been excited. "Not much, but I'll sure as hell take it. Clumsy bastard, isn't he? It's about time he screwed up."

"You got that right." Luis's mouth twitched. It came to Cassy that he was not alone in his hatred for Nemo. The others were taking this as personally as he was. Luis went on with real satisfaction. "Nice to know the son of a bitch can make mistakes. Truth is, I was starting to wonder."

This time, the hatred in his voice was naked and raw. It was disturbing in the cluttered office, and he intercepted the look the others gave him with a flushed face.

"I interviewed Jerry Gabriel last night," he said coldly. "The husband, you know? I asked him what the hell she was doing, wandering in the park after dark when everyone knows how dangerous it is. You know what he said? He told me she'd gone out to get some stuff for a special dinner. Last night was their fifth wedding anniversary."

"Jesus." Delgado closed his eyes momentarily. "Oh, Jesus."

"Yeah. His wife's mother is staying with him, I guess to make sure he doesn't do something stupid, like buying himself a gun and eating it. I talked to him in between sedatives. You know something? I don't like watching grown men struggling not to cry themselves sick." Luis's cannonball voice had lost its body, becoming high and savage. "Not at all."

"Maybe it would be better if they did cry."

Elena, edging between them with a tray, offered this opinion calmly. She was logical, frighteningly intelligent, and opinionated. "If men wouldn't keep their feelings locked up and act as if emotions were something to be ashamed of, maybe they wouldn't be so tight-assed all the time." She met Valenzuela's look and added, with steel in her voice, "And then maybe women wouldn't get killed so often. You know?"

"Thanks, Elena, this is just what I wanted." Cass took the tray; it held a pot of tea, an egg salad sandwich, and, unexpectedly, an assortment of fancy cookies. "You think we're tense? Tight-assed? You don't think maybe we've got a reason to be tense right now? Here, have a cookie."

"Thanks. Do I think you're tense? You tell me." Elena spoke simply and reasonably. "Look, I'm talking about the real world here. Truth is, in the real world? Relaxed people don't kill other people. Nobody gets a hot oil massage, follows it with yoga, and then says hmm, what to do, oh I know, I think I'll go shoot someone with a high-powered rifle and then maybe knock over a convenience store. Do the math."

"Point," Cassy muttered through bites of the sandwich. "The lady's got a point there, people."

"Of course I do. Women don't lock the heavy stuff up, and we aren't ashamed of it. So we don't get all bitched up inside, like you do. That's why women commit fewer violent crimes than men do." She threw a challenging glance around the room. "Don't they? You know the statistics as well as anyone."

"No. No, you're right. No argument here."

Elena nodded, acknowledging Cassy's agreement. She took a second cookie, offered the tray to Delgado and Valenzuela, and spoke with her mouth full. "So what's in the second report that made you folks so happy?"

Cassy immediately pushed the report toward her. No one stood on ceremony with Elena; she had more brains and more intuition than the rest of the department put together, and they all knew it. "Footprints, lady. Pretty photogenic little footprints. Only small segments, true, because there were fallen leaves in the dirt, and leaves don't take prints. Still, three good clear impressions, even if they're only partials, are better than a poke in the eye with a sharp stick, which is pretty much what we've had so far. Look at those babies. Aren't they nice?"

Elena looked at the photos for a few moments, chewing slowly on her cookie. She put the photos back down, reached for the reports, and read them through. When she was done, the others watched her, waiting for her reaction. Elena never missed the obvious, and rarely missed the obscure.

"Black cotton fibers," she said thoughtfully. "Rubber soles on the shoes, striations consistent with the martial arts practice or espadrille buckle shoes sold in Chinatown."

The others stayed quiet, watching her. Her eyes had narrowed, darkening with concentration.

"Those fibers. Could they maybe have come off one of those kung-fu jackets, the black cotton ones that they wear down in Chinatown? I mean, is this dude going around town snuffing pregnant women, and he's all dressed up for karate practice? Or maybe he thinks he's some damned ninja, or something?"

"Somebody give the woman another cookie." Cassy was grinning now. "She got it in one."

Elena considered this in silence. She had wiry black hair, lots of it, worn pulled back from her face. Sometimes, when thinking hard or in the grip of a strong emotional reaction, the others swore they could see electricity crackling through her hair. It was crackling now. Finally, she looked up and spoke.

"Well, it's something. Problem is, they must sell thousands of those shoes and jackets every year. I hate to bust your bubble, but I don't see how you can use it, unless you throw it to the Dogs of War like a bone or something." She caught the grins, and her eyebrows disappeared halfway up into her hairline. "What did I do, hit the bull's-eye?"

"You sure did." Cassy reached for the phone. "If we can't hang a name on Captain Nemo with this stuff, at least we can make the public feel better."

"...so then, not three minutes after Grieg manages to smooth down the reviewer, what does that lunatic cubist do but call the guy an ignorant barbarian? Man, talk about the shit hitting the fan! The whole place was in an uproar."

Jim Delgado grinned. It was Saturday afternoon, he had a rare morning off, and he was still amazed at his own daring. Waking up exhausted and depressed, he had done what he'd wanted to do for months; pick up the phone, call information, and call his superior officer's slightly batty but definitely sexy big sister. Probably, he thought, his conversation with Cass had triggered this unaccustomed display of courage. He had half expected himself to hang up if Leo answered the phone, and half expected her to either not recognize his name or brush him off.

To his delight, he'd been wrong on all counts. His courage had held, he'd been identified with his first words, and she'd sounded pleased to hear from him. Not only that, she'd announced that she'd been working for two days on a set of illustrations for reviews of boring-ass books that she had zero intention of ever reading, that her eyes hurt and she was tired of drawing anything, and of her own company too. She'd added that if he came over he could butter toast and she'd even make the coffee.

Somehow, he'd managed a coherent reply, got himself cleaned and dressed, and made it to Harrison Street in under a half hour. He'd even had the forethought to stop off for a dozen donuts along the way.

The station house joke, that everyone knew about Jim's attraction for Leo but Leo herself, was true. Delgado, who was not without insight, admitted to himself that he used her relationship with his boss as an excuse to steer clear of her. He found her energy daunting, and the sense of freedom she exuded downright terrifying. She moved in a different, unfamiliar universe; she was the only artist he knew, and the most direct woman he'd ever met. She would have said she made no compromises; Delgado privately felt that she took no prisoners. For all that, she was catnip to him, and he ruefully admitted it.

He was not without women in his life. In a city where the women greatly outnumbered the heterosexual men, Jim Delgado spent Saturday nights without a date either by choice or because his job demanded it. He had looks, physical energy, and brains. His only physical drawback, a height that meant most of the women he dated were taller than he was, led to his one personality kink, a tendency to get snappish and defensive about the subject.

Along with the pros and cons, he also had his share of healthy masculine conceit. But his conceit deserted him when confronted with Leo Chant.

"...but that's reviewers all over. They've got about as much self-awareness as a sack full of wet gophers, and they know less about art. Want some more coffee?"

"Love it. No, you keep your feet up, I'll get it." Jerked out of his reverie, Delgado realized that he'd been listening with half an ear, and that Leo, awake and vigorous, had been talking for some time. He himself was tired, jaded, a bit dislocated. Even being in Leo's company was not enough to shake off his depression. Maybe the flu making the rounds at the Hall of Justice had finally caught up with him.

She realized it, of course; there was never hiding anything from Leo's eye. She got up, carrying plates to the kitchen counter and stacking them up. The glance she shot him was keen and considering.

"Short on sleep?"

"Huh." He carefully measured coffee into the filter. "An understatement for the ages, Leo. Since this damned thing started I've averaged maybe three hours a night. And Cassy's worse off than me. He's on the hot seat."

Leo, who had purposely kept off the Maternity Murders, scraped plates into the garbage disposal. Jim was a nice guy. It would probably help him to talk about it. The fact that she was curious about the official progress was, she told herself virtuously, merely coincidental.

"I've barely spoken to him recently," she said thoughtfully. "And since I never watch the news and hardly ever read the papers, well... ."

"Lucky, lucky woman," Delgado said enviously. "I wish I could ignore it, or at least concentrate on something else. Unfortunately, it's my damned job."

"Accept my sympathies."

"I will. I do."

"You know something?" Leo watched his face. "It just occurs to me that I don't know anything about you. I mean, I know that you work with my brother—"

"Nope," he corrected her. "I work *for* your brother."

She ignored this. "—and you like to fish, Cassy mentioned that to me once. But that's all I know. Come on, clue me in. Who, precisely, is Jim Delgado?"

"Well." Was she trying to take his mind off Nemo, or was she really curious? Did it matter? "You want a personal resume? James Anthony Delgado, thirty-six. Education, unimpressive but sufficient. Height, short— I'm barely departmental regulation."

"Your height looks fine to me," she interrupted. "I get pretty damned sick of getting introduced to average guys, so-called, and barely hitting the lower half of their ribcage. It sucks. I always wondered why no one ever gave me shit for being four foot eleven?"

"Even money?" Delgado heard his own voice, dry and ironic, and pushed his defensiveness away. "You scare the crap out of people. I just wish to hell I'd been able to scare some myself. Anyway, that's my guess, and I'm sticking to it."

"Good." She sounded appreciative. "I like scaring the crap out of people. Sorry, I interrupted you. Tell me more."

"Hair, black." He was relaxing into her mood. "Only child of Anthony and Mary Delgado, which since we're talking about Italian Catholics, usually needs explaining. The only child part, I mean."

"Not to me," Leo said appreciatively. "But I thought Delgado was a Spanish name, not an Italian one?"

"My grandfather was Della'guardinia. They shortened it for him at school."

"And who shall blame them? Go on—more, please."

"Okay. Born in Oakland, California. Religion, not much of anything. Political views, center to slightly left thereof. Annual income, less than a union janitor and *don't* get me started on that one unless you want to see me foam at the mouth. Occupation, homicide cop who's being driven nuts by this Maternity Murder thing." Abruptly his good humor deserted him. "There was another one the other night."

She nodded. "The Gabriel woman? I know. Cass left a message on my machine, asking me to have Mara over because he wasn't going to make it home."

"He does worry about that kid, doesn't he?" Delgado's eyes were fixed on the kettle. "Can I ask you something?"

"Sure." Leo perched on a kitchen stool. "Ask away."

"Okay." For some reason, Jim felt an odd reluctance to bring up the subject. He took a breath. "Is your incredibly gorgeous niece completely human? Adopted from a Martian supermodel agency, maybe? How does she come to look—and act—like that? My best guess is that she's part Asian somewhere, but how—?"

"Ah. I see. Her mother." Leo's voice had flattened out.

The kettle boiled, sending a wailing cloud of steam into the studio, and Leo moved to attend to it. When she spoke again, her voice was neutral. "You want to know about my completely unbeloved former sister in law, Tam Lin Chant, formerly Tam Lin Chiu."

"Is that being nosy? Delgado watched her. "Because I'm not trying to be, Leo. Problem is, I'm a detective. It comes with the turf. Besides - oh hell, I'll admit it. I want to know."

"Color me not particularly shocked," Leo said drily. "I guess Cass never told you how he came to be the best single father in the Bay Area."

"Not a word. He doesn't talk much about his own affairs, Leo. The strong private type."

"Yeah, I know." Leo did not sound happy. "Just like his sister. Oh, shit. Look, Jim, this is a tough one. Usually I respect his privacy, but you've got to work with him, and you ought to know where the swamp is if you're going to avoid sinking up to your eyebrows in it. Here, grab the rest of those Krispy Kremes and come sit."

The coffee had finished dripping. Silently Leo handed Delgado his cup and led him over to the sofa.

"It was like this." Her black eyes were smoky, looking back into an unpleasant distance. "Cass was barely twenty, but he was already close to getting his degree in criminology. He was a phenomenal student, we're talking prodigy levels. This was over at Berkeley. He met an exchange student from China, going to Berkeley. A very pretty girl. That was Tam Lin Chiu."

Her face was impassive, impossible to read. But her voice gave her away; the venom was electric and, at this distance in time, almost indecent. "Hey," he said, startled.

Her eyes swiveled towards him. "It shows, doesn't it? I hated that girl on first sight. All the little hairs at the base of my neck stood straight up and sounded the alarm: it was like they were bleeping out *heartbreaker, bitch, user.* She was maybe eighteen, slender as a reed, drop-dead gorgeous. You know what I mean? She was gorgeous in that innocent doe-eyed way a lot of Asian women have. Man, when they're beautiful, they don't do it halfway. Hell, look at my niece."

She laughed, totally without mirth, a dead echo in the comfortable room. "As a matter of fact, Tam didn't do anything halfway. Her philosophy of life was simple. One for all and all for Tam, and everything she wanted was hers to take. Spoiled to death—probably the result of all that gorgeous. Well, for a little while, she decided she wanted Cass Chant."

Delgado blinked at her. "What did she do?"

"Swallowed him. *Vamped* him. Ate him alive." To Delgado's horror, her eyes were wet. "If she'd loved him, if she'd even liked him, I wouldn't have minded. But she didn't love anything or anyone; she wasn't capable of it. She was just playing, experimenting, trying out the product to see whether it was worth keeping. She was purely selfish, the kind of woman that woman-haters use as an excuse to hate the rest of us. A complete bitch. Maybe vampire would be a better word for her better than vamp."

She lifted a hand and dashed the tears away.

"You know," she said bitterly, "I can't even really remember what she looked like, not clearly anyway. I can't remember what she sounded like, except that you would have expected one of those high chirpy voices and hers was low and sexy. I can't even remember if she was as slinky-swoony femme as my memory says she was. All I remember is that I knew she would hurt him. To tell you the truth, I only met her three times in my life.

I refused to go to the wedding at City Hall."

"I'm so sorry." The words were quiet and, Jim felt, completely inadequate.

She looked down at her hands. "Cass didn't speak to me for a year. We'd grown up like twins. He protected me from his friends and I stood up for him to my mother. The first three paintings I sold, the money went toward his tuition at Berkeley, and I was damned glad to do it."

"But if you were so close...?"

"I was a threat, don't you see? A threat to Tam. And whatever Tam wanted, Tam got. She wanted me out of my brother's life. So he wrote me off for *ten months*. Not just me, either. My mother, who'd raised us by herself after my father died, she got cut off, too."

"Okay." Delgado laid his hands over hers, feeling them knotted like old oak. "Okay, Leo. Relax."

She fetched a deep breath and sighed. "It's cool. I just don't think about this too often, and I never talk about it. That's why it gives me the shakes."

"Do you want to tell me the rest?"

"There's not much more to tell. She got knocked up—that's why she lowered herself and consented to marry him. Three days after Mara was born, Tam disappeared from the hospital, went home while Cass was in class, packed everything she owned and a lot of stuff she didn't, and vanished into thin air. She left Cass a note, said she was going to home to China, she was going to wipe him out of her mind, feel free to divorce her. She took Cassy's pride, his money, and pretty much everything else. About the only thing she didn't take back to China with her was Mara."

There was a sickness in the pit of Delgado's stomach. The ugly story was made worse by his affection for Cass, as a co-worker and as a friend. And Leo's pain and rage had sounded down fourteen years like the echo of a wolf's cry.

Some of this must have shown on his face, for Leo, recollecting herself, took a visible grip on her self-control. She got off the couch, and was reaching for the empty cups when the phone rang.

"That may be for me," Delgado said quickly. "Sorry, but I had to leave this number. I'm on call, and my cell's got a dead battery—I forgot to charge it."

"No problem." She reached the instrument on the fourth ring, one ring too late to get it before the answering machine turned on.

Cassy's voice, urgent and imperative, flooded the room. "Leo? If you're there, pick up the damned phone, I need you and Delgado, too. We've just had killing number seven, and this time we've got a witness and a possible make on Captain Nemo. Friedman's in bed delirious with flu and I need some sketches. Leo? Leo! Goddamn it, answer the phone!"

Chapter Three

San Francisco is known for its fog. No other city on earth is so defined by a trick of the weather, or as remembered for it. Seasons have no effect on the city's fog patterns. Cool air sweeps triumphantly through the Golden Gate, blanketing the water, swirling around bridge towers, obscuring landmarks, faces in the crowd. Sometimes it cloaks, and sometimes it merely touches with chilly fingers. Only locations seem predictable; that the downtown areas will clear earlier in the day than the coast is a safe bet.

At seven-thirty on a late October morning, the downtown area was still encased. This morning had seen long mobile wraiths, peculiar shapes drifting like uneasy abstracts in the wind that rode the hills. The financial district, deserted on a Saturday morning, showed office towers in odd segmented strips, the higher and lower levels banked in fog while the midsection stood clear. Just to the northwest, in Chinatown, pagodas and wrought-iron gates showed glistening patches of color and texture through their dulling haze.

Joseph Ching turned down Spofford Street and moved towards Washington. He was hurrying as best he could. Since he was nearly eighty, his progress was slow. Moreover, the morning was cold, and his jacket was buttoned around him like a baby's bunting. This restricted his motion further; as a result, he was trotting. Every morning for the past forty years he had taken this route, from his apartment on Sacramento Street through the twisting alleys of Chinatown, down to the little grassy area called Portsmouth Square.

Joseph Ching believed that these morning forays had kept him alive so long, alive in defiance of a faulty heart and a pair of eyes that no longer worked very well. He had been one of the founders of the current group of citizens, all races and ages and sexes, who met in the square between half past seven and eight-fifteen, rain or shine.

They came to practice *tai chi.* Three of the current group were corporate executives, two Asian, one black. They never missed a meeting, understanding that the sense of calm and physical well-being given them by their morning ritual would keep them alive and sane, as it had done for Joseph Ching. Even in the wake of several crippling earthquakes, Joseph had come without missing a day since nineteen-fifty.

Today, however, he was late. It wasn't Joseph's fault that he had overslept. A neighbor, an old man who suffered from the same heart problem as Joseph himself, had been taken away in an ambulance in the small hours. Joseph had held the man's hand, offering what strength and comfort he could. The attack had been mild, but still frightening; Joseph, feeling the proximity of the dragons that watched over his own mortality, had lain sleepless until almost four.

He emerged from Spofford Street, turning east on Washington and pausing, for a precious moment, to steady his irregular breath. Leaning against the shuttered facade of a novelty store, a hand pressed to his aching side, he thought that one of age's penalties was the unforgiving nature of time. Oversleeping by fifteen minutes would have made no difference thirty years ago. He could have dressed quickly, sprinted through this maze of streets instead of shambling. At fifty, fifteen minutes was barely noticeable; at eighty, that quarter-hour might as well have been a year.

He regained his breath and checked his watch. It was seven-thirty exactly, and he was going to be late. Ah well, it couldn't be helped; they would begin without him. That young lawyer, Sarah Gold, could lead the movements almost as well as he could himself.

Once Ching accepted the situation, he relaxed into a slower pace. He could see the patched splendor of the city's financial nerve center. He could even catch tantalizing glimpses of Portsmouth Square, a scant block away.

At the corner of Washington and Waverly Place, Joseph Ching stopped in his tracks.

He didn't know what had caught his awareness and sharpened it.

It hadn't been sound; that alone would have made no impression, for Chinatown was never silent. At that precise moment, less than two blocks away at the other end of Waverly Place, three men were noisily unloading a shipment of rice flour for the restaurant at that corner.

It had not been motion, either. The fog still moved here, curling around doorways and his ankles with wet little touches.

Not sound, not motion. All Joseph Ching knew was that his heart suddenly stopped, clutched, started again; that his stomach suddenly sickened and tightened; that everything learned throughout eighty years in the world suddenly took dark wings and snapped them across his spirit, frightened it, and then forced it around in concentration.

Slowly, painfully, Joseph turned his head.

Between the blank, featureless walls of Waverly Place, two shapes were etched in bas-relief. One lay supine, its hands open on the pavement that glittered with dew and the detritus from the restaurant kitchens. There was something misshapen about the outline. It seemed wrong, badly made, distorted by a huge humping curve at the middle.

The second, dressed completely in black and bent at the waist, was in the act of handling that unwieldy figure. Looking like a dark extension of its motionless target, it pushed and tugged until the swollen stomach was parallel to the wall, and the skull pointed toward the southern end of the alley.

Joseph Ching knew, and understood.

He opened his mouth to cry out. Then he shut it again, managing no more than a whistling exhalation of terror forced through nostrils flaring with shock and horror.

The short, shrill breath was enough. The figure in black, whipcord thin and obviously agile even while standing still, stiffened like a hunting dog scenting a deer. It straightened, seeming to Joseph Ching's confused and age-rotted vision to move at blurred speed.

The head turned quickly to the south, and saw the oblivious men unloading their sacks. To the east and west were towering walls, blocking the way, reaching skyward. There was no way out; killer and victim waited in a canyon whose walls were concrete and men.

The figure in black turned back to the watcher on Washington Street. Then it bent its head, hunching its shoulders to hide its face, and charged straight at Joseph.

The thought came to Joseph, briefly and without passion, that here was death. He knew what he had seen; he knew, too, that the killer could not afford to leave him alive.

His mind was clear and very calm. His body, however, reacted of its own accord, the heart rate accelerating wildly, fibrillating out of control. His body was failing him. He was dying, bursting, unable to breathe.

In less than five seconds, the killer reached him. Joseph had a confused impression of a thin, muscular shape, of no obvious age, with a fisherman's cap pulled down over half the face.

A hand shot out and pushed him hard, sending him staggering. Then the killer turned west, streaking up the steep hill with the strength and power of a trained athlete, and disappeared into the fog.

Joseph Ching fell. Sounds washed him: the snapping open of windows, cries, pounding feet that stopped as they came to what lay in the alley.

The last man kept coming. He reached Joseph's side, slipping a powerfully muscled arm to raise the old man out of the puddles, exclaiming, feeling his pulse.

"Heart," Joseph whispered in Chinese. He had come to America sixty years ago and he spoke English reasonably well, but the frightened face above his own was Chinese and, in times of fear, memory becomes touchstone and touchstone instinct. "I must go to the hospital, my heart is bad. Please call an ambulance." He remembered the silent figure on the ground, the push from the killer's hand, his *tai chi* group who would be wondering why he had not come, and added, painfully, "And get a policeman."

The black-and-white dispatched by Cass arrived at Leo's place within six minutes. The driver, who was young and excited, managed to keep quiet. Luis Valenzuela, in the front passenger seat, offered details, the most important being that they were headed not to Room 450 at the Hall of Justice, but to Chinatown Community Hospital. Joseph Ching, the witness, had suffered a heart attack. He was resting comfortably, out of danger. He wanted to talk to the police, as soon as he woke from the sedative and his doctor allowed it. Which, Valenzuela remarked, was just as well, because the police sure as hell wanted to talk to him.

They made the trip with the siren blaring. Leo, who had done Identikit pictures before, understood the urgency. The mask of the beast was still fresh in the old man's mind; the passage of time, even too much thought, would blunt the edges of that mask, dulling it, allowing uncertainties to creep in.

"Almost there." Delgado pitched his voice to sound above the siren. "Is Lieutenant Chant at the hospital, Luis?"

"When I left he was sitting next to Ching's bed, cursing about the 'no smoking' rule and refusing to budge. He got there minutes after the paramedics called in from Chinatown." Delgado caught a fleeting grin in the rear-view mirror. "He's had a morning from hell, what with being dragged out of bed and half the department down with the flu. Another morning like this and I'll need some sick leave myself."

"Who—who was the victim?" Leo was uninterested in the circumstances causing such excitement in her escort. She was angry in a muddled, primitive way, reacting to the same mental movies that had haunted her during the earlier killings. Who was she, this poor fool lying in a doorway, beneath a tree, half-hidden by garbage cans, in an alley...

"There's no positive ID yet, Ms. Chant. At least there hadn't been last I heard."

They pulled up to the red zone at the hospital's front entrance. The driver, who had been silent, caught Leo's eye in the rear-view mirror and smiled. She smiled back, and then realized that he looked familiar.

"I think I know you, don't I?"

"Yes, ma'am. We met earlier this year. That was the night your burglar alarm kept going off. It was pretty late and you probably don't remember me. I'm on your beat."

The memory distracted Leo momentarily. "Oh, yes, the cat-fight up on the roof. That would have been funny, if it hadn't been so annoying. It never occurred to me the alarm system was so sensitive."

"Or that a pair of cats could weigh so much? A lot of people don't know half of what their alarm systems can do." Valenzuela got out and opened the door for Leo; on the other side, Delgado was already out and waiting impatiently.

Leo shot a quick, penetrating look at Delgado's profile. She recognized the tension she saw; that taut, concentrated expression was just the way she herself looked when studying herself in the mirror during a self-portrait exercise.

"Delgado and Valenzuela, Homicide." Jim flashed his badge at the policeman guarding the old man's room. The hospital was bristling with police; whatever Ching had seen, Cassy was obviously taking no chance on his not living to tell the story.

If the hospital was overrun with the law, they were outnumbered by the media. There were reporters out front, in the lobby, herded into waiting areas. Cameras in hand, microphones stuck into averted faces—they were vultures, Leo thought, feeders on death, with hooded eyes and predatory teeth. Knowledge that the comparison was unfair did nothing to mitigate her disgust. There was a feeling in the air, an excitement and fear that spoke of events extraordinary even for a place whose business was life and death.

Leo loathed it. She thought of Homicide's staff sergeant and artist, down with the flu, and nearly cursed him out loud. Twenty minutes ago she'd been eating a donut and scraping plates. She'd also been rejoicing because she wasn't obliged to pick up a pencil for the rest of the weekend unless she wanted to. No doubt about it, Leo thought ruefully, life has one sick sense of humor. In the words of another artist, this is not the vision I had... .

"Yo, Leo? You okay?"

Jerked out of her reverie, Leo realized that she'd stopped moving and that Delgado was watching her with a mixture of impatience and concern. He was waiting for her to follow him. The relaxation of an hour ago was gone, replaced by the pronounced look of the hunter. It showed as a dark eager flag across tightened cheekbones, narrowed eyes, mouth thinned into bloodless pallor. She turned away from him, the thought clear in her mind: *I don't want to go in there.*

Her own cowardice infuriated her. What would the morning's horror have etched on the face in the bed, on her brother's face? She didn't want to know. This bit of self-knowledge left her furious and astounded at herself, for knowing and interpreting was the artist's purpose in the world. She shook herself mentally, hoisted the battered leather sack she used for carrying art supplies higher on her shoulder, and followed Delgado.

Joseph Ching lay on his back, covered to mid-torso by the regulation blanket. He was breathing deeply and regularly, the finely wrinkled porcelain skin of his race and age lightly flushed. Leo looked at his face, ignoring the tubes and charts and other impedimenta of the patient's routine, and felt a tingling in her fingertips. He would be wonderful to draw. Translating the serenity and wisdom lying like a fine mist across his features would be like somehow giving herself a long massage. But she wasn't here to draw him, and whatever she translated this morning would not be calm.

"Leo, honey, thanks for coming. I owe you one." Cassy got up and gave her a quick hard pull around the shoulders. She pulled her gaze from the sleeper and, turning to face her brother, blinked with shock. The last time she'd seen him there had been four murders. He'd looked tired, played out. But he'd been Cass, her brother, recognizable in every way.

Now he wasn't. He no longer looked tired, but he looked different. She searched his face, trying to pin down where the difference lay. He'd contracted, lost the protective coverings. This was Cass to the ultimate power, the essential man himself, powered by heaven alone knew what. Brother to the *nth* degree.

It was too much of Cass Chant. If the eyes which had seen murder done could sleep peacefully, if the morning's horrors were hidden by Joseph Ching's antique-ivory lids, there was no peace for the man in charge. Here were those horrors, superimposed on a face she loved.

"Jesus," she said, before she could stop herself. She felt like biting her tongue out. Whatever Cass needed right now, it wasn't for his sister to be telling him how bad he looked.

Cass took no offense. The smile he offered her was small, but genuine.

"I know, I look like three miles of bad road. You feel like painting me in this condition?"

"Not today, bro." The suggestion was obscene. It would have been like drawing a torture victim, stripping flesh and bone away. Leo almost shuddered, controlled herself, and glanced at the man in the bed. "How is he?"

"Ching? He's fine, just sleeping off the meds they gave him for his heart. Incredible stamina, considering what he's been through and the fact that he's eighty this year."

"What happened?" Delgado was unable to keep silent any longer. "Do we know anything yet?"

"Some of it. We haven't been able to talk with Ching yet, but there were three other witnesses, or nearly witnesses." Cass regarded their dropped jaws with grim satisfaction. "That's right, broad daylight in Chinatown, four witnesses. Maybe he's just conceited, or maybe he thinks he's invincible. Of course he hasn't had much reason to worry up to now." Cass offered them a nasty little grin, and added softly, dangerously, "That may change."

"What happened?"

"From what I've got so far, it was like this: Ching was on his way to a *tai chi* session in Portsmouth Square when all hell broke loose. The delivery guys at the other end of the alley say that Nemo actually ran straight at him and knocked him down. And look at him! He has a heart attack, calmly requests an ambulance and the cops, passes out, and is currently sleeping like a lamb. He's expected to fully recover; the doctor says there's no further damage to the heart. Man, I wish I was that healthy now, never mind at eighty. Maybe I ought to take up *tai chi*."

"Wow." Leo looked at Joseph Ching. As she did, he sighed, murmured, and turned his head slightly on the pillow, as if seeking a cool spot. Leo instinctively lowered her voice. "So you're positive it was the Maternity Murderer? And *what* did you call the guy?"

"That's right, I forgot you don't work down at Homicide. Captain Nemo, Nemo being short for Nemesis. Courtesy of your niece. The nickname caught on, just inside the department, so you'll kindly keep that to yourself. The last thing we need is a nice new catchy handle for the Dogs of War. This thing is enough of a media circus as it is."

"Don't worry, I won't spread it. I saw the hordes downstairs. Bastards. But it was him?"

"You tell me. Victim, Mrs. Ling Ma, twenty years old and seven months pregnant. She got here three months ago, alone. Her husband's in Beijing, waiting to emigrate."

"Swell," Delgado said sourly.

"She was knocked out with a blow to the back of the skull and strangled with that nylon cord you use on those electric lawn edgers. What do people who grow grass call them? Weed-whackers? Nothing new, same old MO." He shook his head. "Four witnesses! Oh yeah, this was Nemo all right."

"Ugh." Leo hunched her shoulders. "Captain Nemo. What a perfect nickname. How is Mara, by the by? Not to mention Mom. Have you seen her?"

"Talked to her last night—I figured she'd be getting worried and you know Mom, when she gets worried, things explode. She's fine, a little nervous, that's all. She told me to keep an eye on you. Mara's fine too. I get scared, Leo. I can't help it."

This, from Cass, was an admission of weakness. Leo glanced at Delgado, who was staring out the window and ostentatiously not eavesdropping, and felt a surge of affection for him. No two ways about it: Jim was a nice guy.

"Lieutenant Chant?"

Three heads turned at this summons from the doorway. The surgeon, short and stocky and unapologetically bald, strolled into the room and calmly shook hands with each of them. His eyes twinkled with good humor, in a nest of laugh lines. He would have looked at home in a rowboat, holding a rod in one hand and a cigar in the other.

"I'm Dr. Silverberg. Mr. Ching should be waking shortly. I understand you want to question him?"

"You bet I do." Cass met the doctor's steady gaze and held it. "Alone if possible, please."

"In case I'm the Maternity Murderer and you should God forbid give away secrets that I already knew?" The surgeon gave a massive chuckle. "You can question him alone after I've examined him, as long as you remember that he's an old man with a weak heart. I don't think there's any chance of a problem there, but it's my job to make sure and I've got to do mine before you do yours. Okay?"

"Okay." Leo realized that Cass had been worrying about having to deal with a pompous doctor, full of protocols and territorial imperative. Instead he'd been handed an intelligent realist. "When do you think he'll wake up?"

"He's waking up now." Silverberg was leaning over the bed, feeling the old man's pulse. "Steady as a metronome. Very satisfying. Mr. Ching?"

The ivory lids fluttered and opened. Joseph Ching looked hazily around the room, trying to focus. His irises were black olives, the pupils silvery from the effects of medication and the deprivations of age. His gaze touched Delgado, who had drawn closer to the others, went to Leo, resting on her with appreciation and some puzzlement, and travelled to Cassy.

Each of the watchers was aware of a shock. These were the eyes of a surgeon, or a shaman: wise, compassionate, remote. They should have looked out of Silverberg's face. They were bottomless, unreadable, and even under the loosening effect of a heavy sedative they gave nothing away.

"You are the doctor." The tarnished black pools had come back to Silverberg. The old man spoke English with the care of one to whom the language is not native; his idioms were precise, and beautifully articulated. "You took care of me. I must thank you."

"I'm Dr. Silverberg, Mr. Ching. And don't thank me, thank yourself. You had a small heart attack, but it hasn't caused any new damage and you should be ready to go home by tomorrow." He was scanning the chart at the foot of the bed, speaking without looking up. "Very little loss of body heat. Excellent, excellent. How are you feeling, Mr. Ching?"

"Well. I feel well." The black olives were back at Cassy. "I am still sleepy a little, that is all that is wrong with me. Have these people come from the police?"

"Lieutenant Chant, Homicide." Cassy came to the bedside and took the old man's hand. "It's a pleasure to meet you, Mr. Ching, a real pleasure. This is Inspector Delgado and Ms. Chant, who will do sketches from your description. Do you feel well enough to tell us what happened?" He caught a look from Silverberg and added hastily, "If the doctor gives you permission, of course."

"Yes." Ching spoke flatly, a simple statement of fact. This was an ideal witness, unemotional, precise. He would tell them what happened and that was all he would tell them. Too many witnesses acted, embroidered, cluttered up the truth of what they'd seen with the infuriating ornamentation of their personal reactions. Not old Ching. As a witness, he was a gift from the gods.

"You have fifteen minutes." Silverberg looked squarely at Cass. "I'll check back in then. If he's all right and not too tired, you'll be able to continue with your questions. If anything happens, just call for the nurse; she's stationed at the end of the hall. I don't think anything will. Oh, and one more thing. I want no members of the media in this room. Understood?"

"Doctor, you read my mind."

Silverberg left the room, pulling the door firmly shut behind him. They heard a brief murmur of voices from the hall. Delgado and Leo drew up chairs.

Ching told his story simply and plainly. Delgado took notes in shorthand. The calm voice related the grisly tale without faltering; he stopped only twice, once to collect his thoughts and once for a drink of water from the carafe by his bed. As he finished speaking, Cassy nodded to Leo. The look said clearly: *Get your stuff out. It's show time.*

"Thank you, Mr. Ching." Cass spoke gently and easily. "We're obliged to you, and you've been more than helpful. When you're feeling better we'll probably want to go over some of these points in more detail. For now, though, if you feel up to it, I'd like you to concentrate your memory. The killer actually brushed past you, pushed you with his hand. You've described his clothing, black cotton trousers, jacket, gloves, shoes. Small to medium height, very thin but wiry and muscled, you can't be sure of his age but he moved like he was in good physical condition. Is that right?"

"Yes. I do not think he was old, if that helps you. His movements, they were of a younger man."

"It sure does." Cassy leaned forward slightly. "Let me ask you this. Did you get a look at his face?"

"Yes." Ching closed his eyes, the beautiful skin looking more fragile than ever. "Only a poor look, because he had pushed me and I was falling down. Also it was not much to see, because he was wearing a hat, a cap, like the kind the longshoremen used to wear during the Second World War. It was pulled down over his head, his face."

Leo's sketch pad sat on her portable drawing board. While Homicide's staff artist used individual pages of a small notebook, Leo preferred a different technique. She would do today what she had done before: an original sketch, repeated with variations and corrections based on Ching's testimony, all on one large page. It had worked well in the past, making identification straightforward.

Ching began talking, taking his time, working for accuracy. Leo blotted everything extraneous out of her mind, her awareness of the press downstairs and the thought of a girl lying in the morgue with a dead child in her belly, and began to draw.

"A round face, or oval, at least in the lower part." Although the old man's eyes were fixed on vacancy, he was talking to Leo, and the others knew it. "He had a tilt to the nose, a little turning up at the tip, but I might make a mistake, because his head was down, his chin pushed against his collarbone. I am unsure about the chin, but I think it may have pointed. I am afraid I saw none of his eyes or cheekbones. Half a face is not helpful. I must apologize."

"You've got nothing to apologize for." Cassy's voice was quiet. "And you're being very helpful. Tell me, Mr. Ching, was this a white man?"

"That, I could not tell you. He was not a dark-skinned man. Possibly he was Chinese, perhaps not. What I saw was a smooth, thick skin, like mine when I was younger. But the color was uneven. It looked, I do not know the proper word, patched. Prickled?"

"Mottled?"

He nodded at Delgado. "Mottled, thank you. Red against the proper color. He was excited, you see, he was breathing heavily. It was very frightening, that he should take such joy in what he had done."

The charcoal pencil moved, making and fixing. A tilted head. Rounded cheeks. Upturned nose. A slight point to the chin. Everything surmounted by a dark cap. Leo's hand stalled and she stared down at what she'd drawn.

Sweet heaven protect me, she thought, *what am I making here? Is this really the face of a multiple murderer taking life under my hand?*

She showed the sketch to Ching, setting it across his chest and holding it so that he would not be forced to sit up. He peered at it, closed his eyes, and opened them again.

"No. Something is not right." One paper-skinned finger touched the curve of the jaw. "Here, a stronger curve. Not so fat, or so much of it. Less, and sharper."

Leo drew the face again, a second version on the paper beside the first. This time she altered the jaw. Again, Ching stared; again, he shook his head.

"Still I think there is something—oh! I see it! I am remembering it now!"

His sudden excitement was magnetic. Oblivious, he kept his eyes on the page.

"The mouth! When I was falling I was looking up, and I saw his mouth. Like this!"

He was sitting up now in his haste to enlighten them, showing with his body what his lips could not articulate. His fingers went to his face, pushing lightly, indenting two long curving brackets around his mouth.

"Like that!" He spoke in triumph. "The bottom lip was thin, the top thicker. And there were lines!"

Leo began the third sketch. The jaw, the chin, the cap, the tilted nose. The mouth, thick and thin. The brackets.

Just short of completion, her hand faltered and slowed.

She stopped drawing.

Into a bewildered silence, Leo stared down at the paper in her lap. Jaw, chin, nose, mouth, brackets.

"Leo?"

She didn't hear Cass, she was unaware of him. Something was struggling, a tactile sense, almost a memory. Jaw, chin, nose, mouth, brackets. Jaw, chin, nose, mouth. *Mouth... .*

The pencil moved again, adding a twist to the lower lip. Ching exclaimed loudly in Chinese, a sound of fear and recognition. His eyes fastened on the drawing; the skin of his face had gone a sickly yellow.

"Dear God in Heaven." They barely heard Leo's whisper, so soft was it. "Oh God, oh no. I can't believe this. This can't be right, it can't."

"Leo? Leo, what's wrong?"

She lifted her eyes from her work. They turned slowly and found her brother.

"This face." She was whispering, her hands trembling. The board slipped, falling on Ching's knees with a thump; the pencil dropped to the floor. No one noticed, not even Ching himself; they were oblivious to everything but the movie playing itself out in Leo's horrified eyes. "This face, the third one, the one I just did."

"What?" Cass was clutching her hands now, infected by her urgency. "Leo, what the hell?"

"I've seen him," she told him, and this time she wasn't whispering. Her voice rang out across the room like a clarion call. "That face? I *know* it. The mouth, the chin, all of it. Jesus, oh Jesus! Cassy, I don't know where or when, but I know it. This face isn't strange, the sketch isn't new. I've drawn this bastard before."

Chapter Four

"No, Cass. You can't help on this one. So give me a break and stop arguing about it, okay? Yes? Can we just please talk about anything else in the world?"

The ride back from the hospital to Harrison Street was contentious. Leaving Valenzuela behind, they had emerged from Joseph Ching's room to find themselves among a mob of microphones and shouted questions, and the argument which was already brewing was brought closer to the surface.

Driving home, it broke like a thunderstorm. The tension was thickened by the driver, who was obviously dying to ask questions but didn't dare, and whose ears got redder and redder as the furious back and forth between brother and sister grew more personal and more profane. At Leo's request, they kept the sirens off. As she pointed out, sirens drew attention. In her neighborhood, it was the kind of attention that might just set her burglar alarms off.

She sat in the backseat with Jim Delgado silent beside her. The original of her sketch was in Cassy's lap in the front passenger seat; a photocopy, taken at the hospital, awaited her attention in her own leather sack.

Cassy's position reflected the official requirements of his job. Somewhere in her possession, Leo had drawings that would help him catch a killer. That, as he informed her with stinging sarcasm, was called evidence. Since she owned innumerable canvasses and sketchbooks, and didn't have a clue as to where to start looking, the police were offering her as many hands as she needed to find it.

Leo's position, stated curtly after a flat refusal of any help from him, was equally simple. The police might look at the canvasses, almost all of which had been previously shown to the public. They could stare at the sketches she had just made; those were police property and she'd given them to Cass at once. But her sketchbooks were private papers. They were her life, all of it, on paper. The only way strangers were going to get a look at them was by showing a warrant. If they did show her a warrant, she would ignore it and go to jail for contempt because her life was none of their damned business. And that was that, no discussion permitted or invited.

"Leo." Cassy slid the bulletproof glass aside and, ignoring the seat-belt law, twisted almost completely around. "Leo, sweet sister, light of my life, honey baby angel. You're making my head explode. Give me a break, yes?"

"Forget it, Cass. Save the snake oil. Would you let a battalion of my friends, people you'd never even seen before, rampage through your underwear drawer? Well, would you?"

"If I thought it would help get my hands on Captain Nemo, I'd let them search the underwear I was *wearing*." He heard the shrill edge to his voice, sucked in air, and tried to speak reasonably.

"Leo, don't do this to me. Just don't. You've got me by the short hairs and you're pulling, and it isn't fair. I know you didn't have to come down and do those pictures today. I know you didn't want to, I know you did me a favor. Now you're gonna rub my nose in it? Force me to get a subpoena on my own sister?"

"Whatever." Her voice was implacable. "You need to violate my privacy with a subpoena, go ahead. I won't say I'll never talk to you again, but I'm making no promises."

"Leo..."

"Goddamnit!" She exploded. "Those books are my private property! Letting strangers see that stuff would be like stripping naked in the lobby at City Hall. It would be like a rape! You've got no right to ask that of me! I'll go through them. When I find it, you can give it to those hyenas and they can print it on page one of every paper in town. But I'm doing the looking, not a bunch of morons in badges who not only don't know me, they know less about art than I do about astrophysics. And that's final, Cass."

"And what if he bags another pregnant woman while you're being so noble and high-minded, huh?" Cassy was purple-tinged with rage. "You got enough room in your conscience for that? You think you could live with that, Michelangelo?"

"Goddamn you, Cassy, you don't play fair! Don't try manipulating me into believing that I'm forcing this creep to go around killing people, because it isn't true and you know it! I should have known Mister Head Cop would stoop to emotional blackmail to get what he—"

"Excuse me." Delgado broke his silence. "Can I ask a question?"

Leo's head snapped sideways. Delgado caught a flash of heat in her eye, and his nerves sang. He forced himself into calm.

Her voice was dangerous. "You taking sides, Jim?"

"Nope." He spoke mildly. "I can't take sides, because I can see where both of you are coming from. But I do have a question, and then maybe a suggestion, depending on the answer. Okay?"

"If it will open up her head and shove some sense into it, fine." Cassy's jaw was working angrily. Leo said nothing, merely watching Delgado with narrowed eyes.

"Question first," he said. "Those sketchbooks. Are those books chronological, Leo? In order, I mean, dated?"

"No." Leo was calming down, but she was still frowning. "Not with any consistency. Some of the individual sketches are, and some of the more recent books. But a lot of those books date from the days when I had no money. Drawing paper can cost a bundle, especially when you're giving your brother every spare dime you make for his college tuition." She shot the spluttering Cass a dirty look. "In those days I'd go back, find the back of a used sheet or just a clean sheet I'd missed, a year, maybe two years earlier. So it's going to be hell trying to find that thing, and I'm going to have to go through the entire personal history of my life to do it. If that answers your question, let's have the suggestion."

"Right." Jim stretched his legs. "Let me make myself clear first. I do get where you're coming from. I wouldn't want strangers pawing through those books if I were you. But what about friends? Or other artists?"

The combatants were quiet as this sunk in. It was a good suggestion, and Leo considered it. Another artist could see that stuff without her feeling that her history had been violated. And a friend, someone she trusted and with no axe to grind, would be even better.

"Okay, you got it." She ignored Cassy's exaggerated, sarcastic exhale of relief, and kept her eye on Delgado. "That was smart, Jim. Sensitive, too. In fact, it was so smart and so sensitive that I begin to have hope for you. Call me when you get another spare hour and you can come over and we'll call some little Italian place willing to deliver."

"Any time, lady." Delgado was grining. "Any time. Harrison Street with burglar alarms and skylights, dead ahead. Will you keep us up on your progress?"

"Sure, if Cass wants me to." The offer was generous under the circumstances, and it had the effect of calming Cass down completely.

The car pulled up and Leo climbed out, Cassy beside her. He held her art supplies while she rummaged for her keys. As she shouldered the door open, he spoke up.

"Sorry, Leo. I shouldn't have flamed you like that. I've got a personal problem with Captain Nemo, but still, I shouldn't have taken it out on you. You were dead right about the blackmail, and even more right about you not being responsible for what he does. I'm really sorry."

"Me, too. That tuition crack was below the belt; after all, I offered that money. If it makes you feel any better, think about this. Your people might not even recognize what I'm looking for. I don't remember what I drew, or when; it could be this guy's face, or full body, or even part of a group study." She looked at him, his exhaustion and frustration echoed in the lines of her face. "We're talking twenty years worth of work here, bro. And I've used hundreds of models in my day."

"Say what?" Cassy blinked at her. "Why the hell didn't you say so twenty minutes ago?"

"I was too mad. Anyway, I'll be submerged in notebooks for the next day or two, but I won't be doing it alone and I promise to call as soon as I find anything. You want interim progress reports, or can it wait?"

"It can wait. You just keep looking."

Mara stepped out of a discount music store on Third Street and rummaged for her cell phone.

Her grandmother's sixtieth birthday was less than a week away. Cass had probably forgotten about it; he had enough on his plate to make this particular lapse excusable. And Leo was notorious for forgetting birthdays, including her own.

Still, Grandma would feel hurt if everyone forgot. So, without disturbing her father, Mara had withdrawn some money from her savings account and taken the matter in hand.

The present, a collection of big band music on CD, might have been designed to make her grandmother happy. Unfortunately, it had cost more than Mara had expected; she had no money left for lunch. She'd been shopping for hours and she was hungry. Getting home would take ages; she had ten dollars folded small in her change purse, but that ten dollars was emergency taxi money, insisted on by her father. Once a week, he demanded that she produce either the ten dollars or a receipt for the cab ride and an explanation as to why she'd needed the cab. If she couldn't produce both, there'd be hell to pay. So she would have to take public transport home, using her Youthpass, and that meant three buses and close to an hour. As if protesting the idea, her stomach rumbled.

She leaned against the building, oblivious to the admiring looks of some teenaged boys in a parked car. Since she was south of Market Street her options were wide open, and heading straight home was the least efficient. Her father worked a scant six blocks away; she could call and maybe have lunch with him. Leo's place was even closer.

The first call, to Homicide, was unproductive; Cass could not be reached. Mara heard excitement seething in Elena's voice. Something had happened that morning, she told Mara carefully, and he would be unavailable for anything short of national emergency for the next few hours. Would Mara like to leave a message?

"Just say I called, I was shopping and I thought we could have lunch together. And would you tell him that I got a birthday present for Grandma? He's probably forgotten about it, and this way he won't worry if he remembers."

"Will do, honey. And you be careful, there's a loony out there. Are you heading home?"

"I don't know yet. I thought I'd try my aunt, she lives right over here. Tell Dad I'll call in later. Thanks, Elena. See you 'bye."

So much for lunch with Dad, Mara thought. Maybe she'd have better luck with Leo. Thinking about it, Mara decided not to call first. Leo had a habit of ignoring her telephone. Sometimes it was better just to show up and not give her the option.

Mara had rung the bell twice and had just decided that her aunt had gone out when the viewer panel slid back, Leo's face peered out at her, and the door swung open.

"Mara! Come on in, babe. What brings you to this neck of the woods?"

Mara thankfully stepped inside. "Birthday shopping for Grandma. She's sixty next week, remember. How are you?"

"Busy, spooked, and confused." Leo pushed the door shut and sketched a vague gesture of welcome. There was dust in her hair and her hands were filthy. "Mom's birthday, that's right. It's almost Halloween. Shit, I forgot again. That would have pissed her off royally, I'd never have heard the end of it. Good thing there's one member of the Chant clan with a memory."

By this time, Mara had taken a good look around the warehouse. Her eyebrows up around her hairline. She loved this place, and hoped that, one day, she'd find one like it for herself. She loved everything about it: its spaciousness, its feeling of being airy and open, the natural light that poured through the glass in the roof, and above all its consistent tidiness.

Today it looked as though a bomb had gone off somewhere between the butcher's block and the bathroom door. There were cardboard boxes scattered across the room; piles of notebooks teetered precariously, about to topple. Canvasses were stacked on the sofa, the floor, even on the kitchen stools. Mara looked at the mess and then at her aunt.

"Lose something?" she inquired politely. "Can I help you find it?"

Leo, who had been following her niece's eyes around the room, tilted her head. The suggestion, which had been casually made, seemed to catch her attention.

"Maybe you can." Leo sounded completely distracted. "Hell, I'm a moron. Maybe I should have thought of you in the first place, you're perfect. No, wait, your father would have kittens if I told you anything about it—but he's the one who said someone I trusted ought to help—oh, goddamn it!"

Mara dropped her jacket and bag on the floor beside her. "Leo," she said gently. "you're losing your mind. You're babbling. You don't do the babble thing well, really. So stop it and tell me what's going on, and then I'll help you with finding whatever it is."

Leo squinted up at her. Mara, at five foot five, was average height; she was, in fact, Jim Delgado's height. Compared to Leo, though, she was a willowy goddess.

"You're a weird, weird child, you know that? Nobody your age has any business being so calm and so logical. Yep, you're just the person I need." She took a breath, nodded decisively, and turned away. "Come over here. I need to show you something."

The photocopy lay in solitary splendor on Leo's bed. Mara bent and took it up. She was silent for a while, studying it, concentrating, committing it to memory. After a minute she turned to her aunt.

"Nice work. Very delicate, very clear, even if it's only bits and pieces. That's one ugly model, though. Who is it?"

"I believe you call him Captain Nemo."

Mara's throat closed. The chill was momentary, a mere flash of instinctive alarm which brushed her and then dissipated. Then she set the picture on the bed and sat down, crossing her knees and resting her weight on the palms of her hands.

"You know," she said judiciously, "I think you'd better tell me what's going on."

Leo promptly gave her the whole story, beginning with Cassy's frantic call. Mara listened without interrupting. She watched Leo's face; several times she nodded in agreement, and once or twice she shivered.

"...so that's the situation," Leo ended. "If you're not an artist you probably won't understand it or believe me, but you'll have to take my word for it. Sometime during the past twenty years I've drawn this face, all of it, not just bits and pieces as you phrased it. I don't remember how or when, but I did. I know it sounds preposterous—"

"No, it doesn't." Mara reached for the picture and gave it a hard stare. "It wouldn't be an easy face to forget, especially the mouth. That twist at the corners, that's very individual. So are those brackets—they make the face mean and restless. But unless the rest of him was as striking as that, why would you remember him? No, I do understand."

Leo stared at her. "My God, I think you really do. Look, Mara, will you help me with this? Your dad's half out of his mind with worry."

"Of course I will. I know Dad's worried. But he shouldn't have made that crack about Nemo getting another neck and it being your fault. That's hard to forgive. Did he really expect you to turn your stuff over to a bunch of bull-necked guys whose idea of art is probably the *Sports Illustrated* swimsuit issue?" She gave her peculiar, elegant snort. "My father. Hell, I thought he had some brains."

"He does have brains. Just not as many as you. Mara, you are the best, aces, a queen and a scholar. I didn't want to show anyone this stuff, but I don't mind showing it to you. When we're done I'll take you out and buy you dinner."

Mara grinned. "I'll let you, too. Mexican, maybe? Speaking of food, have you got anything I can eat now? I spent all my money on Grandma's birthday present and I had no breakfast and I haven't had lunch and my stomach is making weird moaning noises. That's why I landed on your doorstep in the first place."

Twenty minutes later, stuffed full of cheese and sliced tomatoes and leftover Krispy Kremes, they settled down to the hunt.

They began with the canvasses. At Leo's suggestion, they split the pile between them, checking each one and setting it aside. Every twenty canvasses would bring a small rest break, used by Leo to return the canvasses to their proper storage places and by Mara to stretch her legs.

Occasionally, when the canvasses had been undisturbed for long periods, they washed the dust from their hands. Mara, studying and checking, saw that a small group of the canvasses bore the marks of much handling. Idly, she shoved the information to the back of her mind.

They found nothing. Leo had warned her niece that, in her own mind, she thought the paintings would prove to be barren territory. The familiarity that had caught her this morning had been triggered by the feel of the pencil, and she had no feeling for ever having put color on that twisted mouth, that curving jaw. But they had to be checked and, since the notebooks far outnumbered them, it made sense to start with the smaller stack. Mara had agreed.

The paintings took an hour. When the last one had been returned to its closet, Mara stretched, washed her hands and left another message for her father. When she returned to her place on the floor, Leo was considering her with a puzzled look on her face.

"You know," she said slowly, "I've always had trouble reading you. We all do, you know that, Cass and Grandma and me. You probably also know I've never really been able to see you as a kid, not since you were in diapers. I know you're as much your own woman as I am, you're very much a female Chant in that way, but I'm still wondering about something."

Mara arched her back, her cheekbones catching color from the skylight above her head. Her tilted eyes looked enormous, her skinwas the color of iced mocha, her neck as elegant as a swan's. Leo thought, without envy, that her niece was staggeringly beautiful. Why had she never drawn or painted her? Mara caught the considering, appraising look, and gave her slow smile. "Wondering about what?"

"You've got to pose for me someday." Leo leaned back on one hand and regarded her niece. "Okay. You have just gone through enough paintings to stock a small museum. You're not insensitive to art; hell, I got you that Magritte book for your birthday last year because you asked for it, and you were barely twelve when you stood in line for five hours to get into the Impressionist exhibition. But you haven't said one word about what you've been looking at. Not a good word, not a bad word, nothing. Somehow I don't think it's tact. Tact isn't a Chant family strong point."

"Thank you so much," Mara told her ironically.

Leo ignored this. "So I'm puzzled. You don't have to explain if you don't want to; I'm not leaning on you. I'm just curious, that's all."

"There's no big mystery. I just don't happen to be an art critic."

The faint emphasis on the final word was not lost on Leo. Leo looked at her for a moment, and got to her feet.

"I thought so." She rummaged through the cabinets under the kitchen unit. "He who can't do, criticizes; she who can do, paints. What's your preferred medium, oils?"

"At the moment, pastels." There was nothing to be gleaned from Mara's voice, no hint either of relief at sharing a secret or of resentment at Leo's acuity. For all the emotion in her voice, she might have been reporting the weather. "Not the chalks, the pencils. They're easy to transport, they work on almost any surface, and they blend like angels. Also, they're cheap, only a buck a pencil. I've only got seven colors right now. I don't have a lot of money, and I can't ask Dad, not for that, anyway."

"Because he doesn't know?"

"That's right." Anyone else on earth might have shown anxiety, might have begged Leo to keep it secret or demanded a promise. "It's got nothing to do with him. Nothing to do with anyone, really. It's...just my way of living."

The odd phrase was neither justification nor excuse; Mara was merely explaining. It occurred to Leo that had there been any doubt of Mara being a worthy descendent of the Chant women, the girl had just dispelled that; she would have kept quiet about her talent until doomsday if she hadn't been asked. A thought, as new to her as it was startling, moved through Leo's mind: *pot, meet kettle. You ever planning to tell anyone about your little intra-painting wanders if they don't ask...?*

Leo straightened up with a narrow wooden box in one hand. She tossed it to Mara.

"Here," she said. "Two dozen colors. You're right, they're terrific *and* portable. I used them for a while, but these days I work big, and for size you need paint; pencils take forever on a three-by-four canvas. Do you need paper, too? I know how much it costs, believe me."

"Not at the moment, thank you. Shouldn't we be getting down to those notebooks?"

"Let's have some coffee before we tackle them. And if you need supplies, ask me, not your father. I know what it's like not to have the tools. Mara, can I ask you a personal question?"

The girl smiled faintly. "Yes, I'll show you some of my work. That's what you were going to ask, wasn't it?"

"Actually, no. I wouldn't ask another artist to show me their stuff; the artist offers or doesn't, but I don't ask. I was going to ask you how long you've been working."

"Since I was eight. You left some conte crayons at Grandma's, and I, um, well, appropriated them. When Dad and I moved out, I took them with me. I hope you don't mind. I've still got a couple of the stubs if you want them back."

"Drink your coffee." Leo was smiling. "Whether you know it or not, this makes you a little easier for me to understand. Sorry if that upsets you."

"Not if it doesn't upset you. Why should it? Push over some of those notebooks, will you?"

Four hours and seventy notebooks later, Mara spoke.

"Leo?"

Leo took one look at Mara's face and dropped the sketchbook she'd been holding. Shoulder to shoulder, they stared at two adjacent pages of sketches done in charcoal.

"Got you." Leo's voice was savage, oddly gentle. "Here you are, you son of a bitch."

Mara tore her eyes from the pencilled monster and looked at Leo. "This is it? These...these cartoons?"

"Uh-huh." Leo, making no attempt to retrieve the sketchbook, touched the surface with the tip of a dusty finger. "Pointy chin, brackets around the mouth—where in hell is that photocopy?"

"Here." Mara dropped it between them. Her eyes moved from the old sketches to the ones Leo had done that morning. There was a furrow between her brows. "Leo, I think we've got a problem."

"Actually, I think it's your father who's going to have a problem." Leo and Mara stared at each other. "Damn. Pass me the phone, will you? I have the feeling, what with one thing and another, that Cass isn't going to be pleased."

"What in hell do you mean, I may not be able to use them after all?"

Cass, alone at his desk, asked this question in a high-pitched wail. A gruelling afternoon had begun with finding an interpreter and taking the statements of the three truckers. It had ended with a horrible discussion with the Chief Medical Examiner, whose gruesome sense of humor was heightened by the accusatory bite in which he presented his autopsy report. Cass had also suffered through a furious lecture by the district attorney and a painful conversation with His Honor the Mayor, who was getting shrill.

As an added irritant, thanks to half the task force being down with the flu, he'd had to handle the press himself. Even the small consolation of handing them the bombshell of a tentative description was tainted by their demands for a hard print. He'd stalled them, told them to stay on red alert and be ready to run a sketch. He wasn't about to tell them that the sketch had to be found first.

And now here was Leo, saying not only that the damned things might not be usable, but that Mara—*his child*—had seen them before he did. It was too much for his temper.

"You promised! You told me that when you found it I could pass it to the media! You even pulled my baby in to help you, without asking my permission! And now you say I can't have them! Of all the flaky, inconsiderate—"

"Jesus, Cass, will you pipe down?" Leo said irritably. "You're jumping the gun. First of all, I didn't pull Mara in. She showed up while I was looking, and since you told me to use someone I trusted, that's just what I did. And I'm not saying you can't have the sketches, I'm just saying they might not be as useful as we hoped. How about you close your eyes and take a deep breath and let me tell you what I'm talking about before you start calling me names?"

Cassy blew air between clenched teeth, mentally counted to ten, and started over. "Right, okay, fine. Sorry. It's been a bad day and you sounded like making it worse. Let's try this from the beginning. Why might they not be useful?"

"Because they're not really studies, they're more like caricatures. This model must have scared the hell out of me. Or maybe I was in a bad mood when I drew him. You know," she said thoughtfully, "I'm surprised I don't remember more about him, since I reacted to him so strongly. They're heads, by the way, not figures. No hair either—more like skulls. They aren't dated, so I don't know when I did them and yes, don't bother asking, I'll try to remember, but don't hold your breath."

"Caricatures?" Cassy had a headache, a dull pulsing agony over his right eye, and he desperately wanted a cigarette. Damn this no-smoking stuff and the horse it rode in on. "You mean like *cartoons*?"

"No, I mean caricatures. The features are drawn realistically, but everything's exaggerated. It's like I saw this guy's face as the embodiment of viciousness and nastiness and drew him that way." Leo sighed; she'd had a long day, too. "I can't explain it, Cass. You're going to have to see them."

"I'm going to see them. In fact, I'm going to see them in about twenty minutes. I've had about twelve hours sleep in the last five days and half the department is in bed with vitamin C and orange juice and, now that I think about it, I don't feel too good myself. I'm going to close down for the night, get in the car, drive over there, and look at those things. Then we're all going out for a good dinner. When we're done eating, I'm going to drop you off and take my daughter home. Then I'm going to crawl into bed and sleep until someone offers me a damned good reason to wake up. Understood?" He paused, casting a glance around the office. "You'd better say yes, because if I don't get the hell out of this room pretty soon there's going to be film at eleven and it won't be of Captain Nemo, either."

"Come on over. We'll be waiting."

Cassy hung up, grabbed his jacket, and left the office. He'd gone beyond tiredness, reaching a level of rarified exhaustion that was new to him. Closing the office door, summoning the elevator, nodding to the officer on night duty in the lobby, were done without mental awareness. His body seemed to be moving under some basic compulsion of its own. That had to be it, he thought vaguely, the only explanation.

One thing was for sure, his brain wasn't doing anything worth mentioning. Maybe he ought to leave the car where it was; this tired, he probably wasn't safe behind the wheel and he would have both Leo and Mara in the car with him...

The night air revived him like a shot of adrenalin. It was a beautiful night, cold and clear; apparently, the fog was giving them time off. There were tattered bits of high cloud, blowing east across the bay. For a few minutes he stood and breathed it in, letting it kiss him awake. Then, lighting the much-desired cigarette, he went for his car.

Fifteen minutes later, he looked up from the sketchbook. The two women watched him, one intent, the other impassive.

"Damn!"

Mara merely nodded. Leo, who had found her second wind, shook her head energetically.

"Maybe not. I've been thinking about it. Can you wait until tomorrow for it? Can the press wait?"

"I can. Whether the Dogs of War can wait is their problem. And, frankly Scarlett...What's on your mind, Leo?"

"These things"—she flicked at the sketchbook—"are not going to be much use. I think we're agreed on that."

Cass thought of the probable public reaction to the snarling Samurai face, the lines of concentrated evil sneering from a cartoon on the front pages of newspapers and off local television screens. He shuddered. "We sure are. These things get printed and we'll have a citywide panic on our hands. Folks are scared enough as it is; the way you drew this guy, they'll be rioting in the streets. These pictures are advertisements for a nightmare. Hell, he looks like the original bogeyman. You said you had an idea?"

"The ones I drew this morning aren't caricatures. If I work from both, I don't see why I couldn't do a third set, maybe capture the features without the Lord of Death effect."

"A composite? Will that work?" Cass squinted at the three pictures. "The eyes. In one you've got them round and bulging and here, this one, they're mean little slashes in the guy's face..."

"I can work around it. Anyway, Joseph Ching didn't see the eyes. I have no way to know what they were really like. Hell, maybe playing with them will jog my memory. "

"Do it." Cassy didn't pause to consider further. Leo sounded very sure of herself. "Call me at home tomorrow, the minute you're done. I'll send a messenger over, or come get it myself."

"Okay." Leo went for her jacket. "You consider that would be, what was the phrase, an offer of a damned good reason to wake up?"

"You bet I do. The minute you're done?"

"The minute I'm satisfied," Leo corrected. She threw Mara her jacket, and the girl caught it with a graceful swipe of one arm. "And now can we please go eat?"

Chapter Five

Charcoal pencils, paper, coffee. The tools of a job, of a promise to keep. Leo rubbed her bleary eyes and wondered why she wasn't producing.

It was after one, and she was hunched over her drafting table. They had lingered over dinner; some tacit chemistry had kept Nemo out of the conversation. Normally, a Mexican dinner and two beers would have sent her crawling into bed. Tonight they had merely sated her appetite; she was as wide awake, as alert, as she had been twelve hours earlier.

She simply couldn't concentrate. She had done all the usual things, taken a hot bath, read a magazine, stretched out to relax. She had prepared herself to do something she knew would be upsetting. She was ready, or so she thought.

But her mind kept wandering, her hands refused to cooperate, and the vital sketches that she had promised Cass for the following day had yet to be done.

So, at half past one, she sipped her coffee and gave her mind to the problem of fleshing out a phantom. As she waited for the water to boil, she tried to focus. Something was keeping her from doing what she had to do. What was it?

It was simple enough. The distraction was Mara.

Okay, Leo thought. I don't want to draw Nemo, I don't want to meld that nightmare face into something that will stare at me from every paper in California by Monday morning. I want to draw something beautiful, and that means Mara.

She explored it further. It didn't make sense. Mara had been there, the perfect subject, for fourteen years. Yet Leo had never even considered drawing her. Now she was the only thing Leo did want to draw. Why?

The answer was obvious. Until tonight, the girl had been a beautiful unknown; now she was not. Drawing her would have produced a lovely anatomy study, form without substance. The girl was her own flesh, someone Leo ought to know. But she hadn't known her. The failure to understand her niece would have been like trying to do a self-portrait and painting a stranger in her eye's mirror instead. The idea was unnerving; no wonder she'd shied away from it...

Leo came out of her reverie with a start of surprise. Her coffee had finished dripping, and was cooling in the mug. She checked the clock and swore; exorcising the demon that had been monopolizing her had taken half an hour. She took the mug, went back to her drafting table and, with renewed energy, tackled the problem of capturing Captain Nemo on paper in a way that wouldn't cause a public panic.

Since the realistic work of Saturday afternoon was fresh in her mind, the lower part of the face posed no difficulty. The tilted nose, curving jaw, and highly idiosyncratic twist to the mouth, were completed quickly and accurately.

She studied the caricatures, those visual records of a maddening gap in her memory, and thought ruefully that they represented full moments in her life. It was infuriating and ridiculous not to be able to pin them down. Since there were no other faces on these pages, Nemo must have been the only model, or at least the most stand-out of the day. So why couldn't she remember him? Why hadn't she asked for his name, asked him for another sitting, done some full body sessions?

Maybe she had.

Leo's pencil faltered at this dismaying thought. They'd stopped looking when this lot was found. It was possible that she actually had done more work on him. There was a pile of books they hadn't even glanced at. They'd been stupid, criminally careless, to leave it that way. If there were other, realistic studies, this nightmare blending job could be avoided by a sketch that already existed.

But she'd promised Cass something by morning. What if she spent the night looking instead of drawing, and found nothing? The precious hours would be wasted and she'd have nothing on paper. No, she couldn't risk it. Get something done first and later, when the pressure was off, she could go through those damned books at her own leisure and see.

She flipped the pages to the first caricature and laid it out beside her new drawing. Captain Nemo, rounded eyes bulging in circles of gleeful malice, stared up at her, mocking her, daring her to name him.

Joseph Ching had thought he might be Chinese, and there was certainly something Asian in the cast of mouth and jaw. Or was he Hispanic? The cheekbones were strong in a way that made that possible. She had drawn him with rounded eyes in one sketch, slitted in a second, animal eyes in the third. Which was real, which was right?

The memory was so close that she felt the bite of frustrated tears behind her eyes. It was tantalizing. There was something at the edge of remembrance, not a physical setting but a feeling, a mood...

Leo set the pencil down and met the eyes of her charcoal monster.

Okay, baby. Come out, come out, wherever you are. It's there, I can feel it. A mood, a physical thing. Now that I think about it, this isn't so different from walking into a painting. Good evening, ladies and gents. Grab the cord and walk in. Come on, Leo. Concentrate, cough it up, remember.

For a swift, bright moment, she had it. The setting was there, all of it; the physical geography of where she'd been, the platform, the wheezing mutter of breath from an asthmatic art student working a few feet away. It had been a classroom or a studio, with a group of students, the model, easels and palettes and cups of water and turpentine.

And a really bad mood. She'd just had a fight with her lover—which lover, who had that been, what age, what era?—and she'd been furious, despising herself and all men, sullen and sore and fighting a headache. She hadn't bothered to open her paint box, the asthmatic was using oils and the smell was making Leo sick, no wonder the moron had asthma, using that stuff without ventilation, and Leo had reached for her pencils and glanced up at the model and then away and—

Thump. Bang.

The sound came from directly above her head. Leo jumped, her arms jerking involuntarily, sending pencils and paper to the floor. For a moment she knew how Joseph Ching must have felt, this morning on Washington Street; her heart was beyond her control, clutching up in a spasm of pain, cutting off the blood supply to her brain.

Whoever was up there was right at the edge of the skylight; another two steps and the night would be full of wailing sirens. Her hands moved wildly, waving toward the roof as if to push away whatever held watch, so short a distance above her head.

A thought came, lucid and amused: *This is not a good time for a burglar.* Beneath that, a spear of superstitious terror: *Maybe it isn't a burglar. Maybe he knew you were remembering. You said it wasn't so different from walking into a painting. So maybe he jumped out of your memory and off the paper and now he knows you, he knows where you are, he's tracked you down and he's going to...*

Thump. Hiss.

The angry spitting, the throaty, menacing howl of a tomcat on the hunt, cut through her fear and dragged her back to normalcy. The howl crested, sank, became a growl. An answering snarl, evil and deep, from the enemy. Then the thud of the chase, away into the night.

Leo stood where she was, eyes closed, hands limp. She knew she was swaying, that she was going to be sick or fall down or both, and promptly let herself collapse onto the floor, ducking her head between her drawn-up knees.

She stayed that way, head down, until her heart stopped lurching and her breathing steadied. *Good one,* she thought distantly. *Absolutely brilliant. Scared into cardiac arrest by cats on the roof. Woman, you are not the stuff of which dragon-slayers are made. Now get your sorry ass off the floor and into that chair and draw the damned picture.*

By five in the morning, Leo had three good sketches. She called Cass and woke him up, told him to hurry up because she was exhausted, and waited for him. When he had come and gone, Leo crawled into bed. Her eyes were swollen with exhaustion, her body incapable of any movement beyond what was required to nestle beneath the blankets.

She was asleep almost before her head hit the pillow. Her last conscious thought was hazy and comforting; as nice as the bed felt, it would have felt even nicer if Jim Delgado had been in it with her.

At about the moment when Leo Chant fell asleep, Captain Nemo lay staring at a darkened ceiling through cold eyes.

The monster was smiling.

Pictures, invisible but vivid, appeared for the chimera's enjoyment. Nemo needed no equipment; the pictures were projected by recall, by a monster who lay in happy calm, ugly, twisted lips deepening the bracketing curves of flesh, watching the memories as a child might watch a cartoon.

They were not so much movies as a succession of individual stills, horrors in freeze-frame; they came in precise clicks and brought the supine projectionist a chilly satisfaction, an artist's appreciation of work well done.

A woman, moving slowly. Nemo watched carefully, noting small details, the reddish tint to the western sky, the roughness of the pavement, graffiti scrawled on the backdrop of a building wall. The bottomless frosty eyes fell on the woman's hands. She had beautiful hands, slender and tapering, perfect even while the rest of her body swelled and deformed under the weight of the child inside.

What had her name been? The chimera cared nothing for the victim's names, had not known them until the papers gave them out. In the killing jar of Nemo's mind, the women were remembered for their spiritual perfume, their movement, their personae as new members of a demon afterlife.

The picture froze, held, and shifted. More details. Long, straight brown-red hair, a piquant little face. She wore designer maternity jeans, an oversized cotton sweater, a leather jacket that was surely too heavy for an August night.

Nemo frowned, watching the ceiling. Incongruities like that spoiled the picture, distracting and annoying. And the woman had risked a severe cold, perhaps endangered the child. As if controlled by a human hand, the picture clicked and died, replaced by another in the sequence. Another hand, gloved in black cotton, holding something smooth and heavy. An iron pipe. It froze in an arc above the victim's head.

In and of itself, this aspect of the shot gave Nemo no special delight; the chimera's attention was on the woman's shoulders, stiff in the realization of danger. She had heard something behind her, paused to gather the rags of her agility, prepared to turn.

Click. Pop. The picture faded and was replaced once more. Nemo was aware of a certain regret at its passing; the woman's fear had been very pleasing.

But it was all right, this new scene even was better. The blow had fallen and the prey was falling too, collapsing and crumpling, her eyes rolling back up into her head, her face a study in contorted muscles. The beautiful hands clutched at vacancy, hopelessly trying to protect the vulnerable belly...

Click, click, click.

The pictures came in rapid succession now, a starkly potent sequence of dancing death. They were powerful images, wonderful, sensual. Nemo began to pant with the mounting onrush of pleasure.

Black-gloved hands touching the empty, vacant face on the ground.

Those same hands turning the heavy body, not without effort, until the head aligned properly and the sightless bruised lids pointed where Nemo had planned.

Reaching into a pocket in the black cotton jacket, emerging with a loop of clear nylon line.

Quick clever hands in their black gloves, yes, making the difficult slip-knot in the slick nylon, clever hands, yes oh yes, moving the killing cord around the slender throat yes yes pulling it yes the face was turning blue and the tongue was protruding she was dying, dying in slow motion, beautiful death, yes, she was more beautiful in death than in life yes and even in unconsciousness she had struggled and the child had struggled too and the struggles were perfect yes oh beautiful and the eyelids bulged and the beautiful fingers spasmed and convulsed yes yes oh *yes*...

The victim was gone, the spirit flown. But there were others, more of them, many, many more of them. And it was still dark in this nightmare theatre. Just so long as it was dark, the pictures and the pleasure would come on command.

Spent and happy, the chimera lay relaxed, watching the ceiling until dawn came to put an end to delight.

At five o'clock on Sunday morning, a third player in this game was also awake.

Jim Delgado had been deeply asleep. An active man, he needed seven hours a night; during the past ten days, he'd averaged four. His integral energy was becoming ragged, degenerating from strength into nervous weakness. His own weak spot had got the better of him, something that only happened when he was really exhausted; one of the guards in the headquarters lobby had made a comment about him looking short on sleep, and he'd nearly taken the guy's head off. He'd mumbled an apology, and fled. In this state he was good for nothing but mistakes, and he knew it.

He'd arrived home at just past seven on Saturday night with the fixed intention of sleeping until something woke him up. He'd heated some soup, made himself a sandwich and warmed some milk. There were no messages, a fact which caused him an obscure disappointment. Only when he admitted to himself that he'd been hoping Leo would call did the feeling back away. Well, it made sense; they'd been having a damned good time until Captain Nemo and the real world had intervened.

He rolled into bed. It was barely nine; with any luck, he'd be able to sleep until noon. As he drifted off, he offered up a small, inchoate prayer that the phone would remain silent. Please, he thought, whoever is listening out there. Please don't let anyone get killed tonight.

But no one would get killed tonight. No pregnant woman in her right mind wandered around San Francisco after dark these days. And even Nemo would hardly go for two in one day... .

If the gods were willing to cooperate, his body wasn't. Perhaps it was accustomed to seven hours and refused to adjust; perhaps he was less tired than he'd thought. Whatever the cause, he woke to darkness just after four.

Delgado came back to awareness without the interim stages. He had trained himself to sleep like a cat; waking was simultaneous with the subconscious command to do so. There was no loginess, no confusion, none of that sense of being drugged that so many people go through. No matter what the circumstances, Delgado literally snapped to attention. The moment his eyes opened, his mind cleared.

On this dark Sunday morning, he had woken from a dream, the only one he could recall from the hours of rest. In recent weeks, his sleep had been uneasy, fragmented images of dead faces and shouting headlines. This one had been different. Leo had been in it, just Leo. And himself.

Even as the chimera was doing in another part of the city, Delgado stared at the ceiling and projected what he'd been seeing. After a few minutes of mental replay, he had a thought: It was a good thing no one else could see this, or they'd have him up on a pornography charge and Cass would shoot him.

He lay and relived his dream.

Himself, stripped bare from the waist up. He lay on his stomach on some hard wooden surface which, as the picture grew clearer, resolved into the long free-standing kitchen unit in Leo's studio. She stood beside him, dressed in red, her hands covered in something warm and slick and wet. She was rubbing him, massaging him, the strong painter's fingers working with a slow, deep thoroughness that was unbearably exciting. Shoulders, neck, the muscles that ran down his spine, sometimes light, sometimes deep.

She was silent throughout, but he could hear her soft, regular breathing. He could feel her there, feel her with his whole body. He was enormously aware of her.

In his dream, her hands pushed at him. The pressure was light but imperative, the message clear. Obediently, he rolled over. She stood beside him, a dominant presence whose power was utterly female. He gave in to her, closing his eyes in deference to her strength, trusting her to do whatever she chose.

The most astounding thing about the dream was the certainty that it was right. It was all right, everything was all right. He could trust Leo. Wherever this massage was leading, and its course was apparent from his own mounting excitement, he could trust her.

She massaged him, the oily hands manipulating the base of his neck, the line of his jaw, pectorals as taut as wire. It was amazing that a dream could be so real. Lying in his bed and watching the ceiling, Jim knew that, if the phone should ring, the act of standing to pick it up would be beyond him. Even real sex wasn't as intense as this slow-burning fuse...

The picture wound on toward its inevitable resolution. Leo began at his temples and worked her way down. She had reached his waist and she was undoing the buckle of his belt, by Christ he could *hear* the zipper as it slid down and her hands were on him, fingertips as light as butterflies against his groin and he could stand this no longer, no, not one second longer, he would reach up and pull her down and get his mouth and his hands and his weight on her and...

Far beyond the point where most men would have carried it through, Delgado realized what he was doing, where this was leading. He stopped cold.

The pictures faded and were gone from his mind's eye.

It took a long time for his body to subside, but in the end he mastered it. When he could move without physical discomfort, he got out of bed and wobbled to the bathroom. The icy pre-dawn air brushed him like a breath from the grave. He turned the thermostat up to seventy and crawled beneath the covers to wait until the place warmed up. Out in the bay, foghorns sounded intermittently.

His hands placed deliberately outside the blankets to head off temptation, he thought about Leo, about the dream, about the fact that she had been present on the periphery of his thoughts since the first day they'd met.

The bottom line was that, in some way, he understood her. Also, he silently admitted, he wanted her. He wanted her very much. He was surprised by his own comprehension.

It wasn't just sex, although that was certainly a factor; there was more here than physical want. There was something waiting between them, not so much a likeness already acknowledged but a recognition of kind, a sympathy, that could develop a life all its own. He couldn't remember ever feeling quite this way. And he was going to have to do something about it.

Was he falling in love? Delgado mistrusted the feeling, the overblown rhapsody most people used as a cage. Love was confusing, upsetting. Like most of his sex, he rarely dealt with love. Respect, affection, were so much cleaner.

The flat was warming up around him, the electric air had softened. He felt it against his chest, a gentle brush of air. It was calming, relaxing, almost as good as a massage by a painter with talented, talented hands...

Jim Delgado got his extra few hours after all. In the safety of his bed he slept, smiling and without dreams. Shortly after noon, he was roused by the telephone.

At the first ring he was out of bed and moving, swearing under his breath as he went. He hadn't meant to leave the damned heat on. The temperature was uncomfortable; even completely naked, he was sweating. He reached the phone on the third ring and was adjusting the thermostat before the caller was able to answer his first words.

"Delgado speaking."

"Jim? It's Leo."

He nearly dropped the phone. For a few seconds he gaped at nothing, wrestling with disbelief. The witching hour had been and gone. He had been thinking about her as intensely as possible. Had she picked up on it somehow? Read his mind?

"Jim? Are you there?" She sounded nervous, hesitant. It occurred to him that he'd never heard that in her voice before. "Hello?"

"Leo, hi, good morning, I'm sorry, I just woke up." He made it back to his bed and sat down hard. No, it was too much. It just wasn't fair. Her voice on the phone was pure electricity; he'd been able to fool his brain into thinking the dream had faded out, but his body wasn't buying it.

He got his voice to behave, or so he thought. "How you doing? Is everything okay?"

Apparently he'd thought wrong. "I'm fine, but I'm not too sure about you. You sound strange. Did I wake you? Should I hang up and you can call me back later?"

"No!" He bit his lip, furious with himself. What in hell was the matter with him? He sounded like a virginal schoolboy talking to a prom queen. Hell, in another minute he'd be squeaking in falsetto. Get a grip, he told himself. You did puberty a long time ago. "No, that's fine. You're the best wake-up call I've had in months. What's going on?"

"Oh, nothing much." He listened to the uncertainty in her tone, and wondered at it. If he sounded like a teenager, she sounded even younger. "Um...look, are you, well, on duty today? Or busy? I mean, you got any plans?"

"I'm on call, not on duty." A forgotten period of time was coming back to him with this conversation, the advance-and-retreat coyness of adolescence. Leo sounded unsure of herself; true to form, Delgado discovered that the more self-confidence she lost, the more he found. He was beginning to feel like an adult male again. "Outside of that, nothing at all. Why? Would this happen to be a reference to that suggestion of Italian take-out you made me yesterday?"

There, that sounded better; light, affectionate, even a bit teasing. Leo went for it like a trout chasing a fly.

"It sure is, but there's something else—oh, hell. To tell you the truth, Jim, I was thinking about you this morning. I was up until five doing those makes for Cass—did anyone tell you that Mara and I found the sketches?

The originals, I mean?"

"Hell, did you? You're a fast worker, lady."

There was something in her voice that made him wonder if she was blushing. "I've been known to speed to my doom, yes. Anyway, Cassy came and got them hours ago. I'm not doing anything today, and we were having such a good time yesterday, so I thought, well..."

"Your thought processes are excellent. I'd love to come over." Back in the saddle, he thought exultantly, I'm back in the saddle again. Through the flush of power he felt, he understood that this hesitancy and shyness were hard for Leo. Surely she deserved a little honesty from him. "Tell you the truth, I was hoping you'd call."

"Glad to hear it." She sounded a bit more like herself. "So when can you get here?"

"After a strong, hot cup of coffee. And I need a shower, I'm a little...sweaty." Sweaty was right; the phone was slipping around in his hand.

"Sounds dangerous. Okay, take a shower and have some coffee and I'll see you when you get here."

Delgado went through his morning ritual whistling like a skylark. He got to Harrison Street an hour later, having stopped at a local deli for a bottle of red wine and a pound of smoked salmon. He was feeling good, the nerve-storm had ebbed. He was a grown man, calling on a grown woman he admired. She had asked him to come. There was no reason for butterflies in the stomach; there was nothing to worry about.

His first look at Leo brought his self-confidence crashing down around his heels.

He'd become used to seeing her in bulky sweaters that emphasized her tininess. In fact, he couldn't recall that he'd ever seen her in anything else. Today she was wearing something on top that was red and stretchy, and a pair of ragged cut-off shorts.

Delgado nearly dropped the bag. He knew his jaw had gone slack. Why hadn't he ever noticed the way she was built? She had a perfect torso and beautiful collar-bones, and her not quite five feet of height seemed primarily composed of exquisitely muscled indigo legs. Through the red haze obscuring his brain, Delgado remembered something Cass had mentioned. Leo had studied ballet and still kept it up when she had the time...

"Don't stare, it's rude." Unexpectedly, she stretched on tiptoe and kissed his cheek, the merest brush of lips against skin. It might as well have been branding iron, so immediate was Delgado's physical reaction.

"Come on in." She stepped back and waved him inside. He thought for a moment that he wouldn't make it, that his legs wouldn't work. Nerve-storm? Hell, this was closer to panic. She'd been wearing red in that damned dream. *Had* she read his mind? Was the energy between them stronger than he'd recognized, or had she simply recognized it before him?

He was sitting on a kitchen stool and putting the deli bag on the long wooden kitchen unit before he realized he'd moved from the front step. Leo, across the counter, reached for the bag and emptied it.

"Sangiovese! My favorite wine. Jim, you are psychic or something. And lox! Angel, an absolute angel. Did you have breakfast? Are you hungry?"

"No. I mean yes. I mean I haven't eaten and I'm hungry." It was a lie. He wasn't hungry, not for food; the inside of his mouth was as dry as his hands were wet. The dream was back in all its power, the brutal merciless tactile sense of want. He could smell her, a soft peppery smell, a faint touch of something clean and fresh. Laundry soap? A natural perfume? Her ultra-short hair had been pomaded with something that smelled like violets, light, vagrant, nonintrusive.

He forced his hands to relax, willing them to lay open on the pale wood. They wanted, quite desperately, to reach out and grab her. Leo spoke gaily, vividly, yet with that same odd nervousness.

"I'm hungry, too. Let's pig out together. I've even got bagels and cream cheese."

He ate two bagels without tasting anything.

Leo was edgy. She would open her mouth, let the first words fall and die, take a bite of the food, swallow convulsively. She seemed to be swallowing more than the food could account for, and she was having trouble meeting his eyes. He watched his hands for all he was worth, avoided looking at her, knowing that his self-control depended on detachment.

Then, out of nowhere, she pushed her plate aside.

"Jim. God, this is stupid, this is nuts. I feel like, maybe, twelve years old. Why is it so difficult, damn it? Jim, listen to me. Just listen. Okay?"

Delgado looked up involuntarily, and knew that his eyes had given him away. With a certain delicacy, she looked away from his face and stared down at his hands. They seemed to fascinate her.

"I told you I worked until five," she said slowly. "I was played out, exhausted, drained. You know how you get real thoughts, honest thoughts, when you're tired like that?"

"When all the defenses are down? Oh, yes."

"Then you'll understand what happened to me this morning." She met his eyes, a bright clear gaze that impaled him. "I'm being straight with you, Jim. This is straight. You follow?"

"Yeah. But you don't owe me a damned thing, Leo. If you'd rather not tell me... ."

"It doesn't matter what I'd rather. I have to tell you." She visibly steeled herself; he saw her do it. "I crawled into bed and it felt wonderful, mattress and blankets and the way the pillow curved right up to meet my head, you know? I was almost asleep. And then I had this thought, a real live honest laser beam of a thought. I don't know where it came from, or how long it was hiding in my head, but I meant it."

"I had a thought or two this morning myself." It was coming, that thing he had known was there. However hard this was for Leo, she was dead right; for whatever was to come, she had to tell him. And why should she have to bear the brunt? "I'll tell you mine, but you go first."

Her eyes were alight. "Like I said, it was just this. That as good as the bed felt, it would feel even better with you in it."

"Just that?"

"Just that."

Delgado stood up. The stool, pushed by his weight, tipped over and clattered to the floor. He didn't hear it.

"It's enough," he said, and reached out across the wood and the dirty plates and cupped her face with his hands, hands that were no longer controlled or forcibly relaxed. His words rang across the studio. "It's plenty."

"A deal's a deal," she reminded him. Her body arched toward him across the wood, but somehow she was keeping her mouth from him. "You promised you'd tell me your thoughts from this morning. Let's hear it. If it's true confessions time, take your shot. You owe me one."

He told her, leaving nothing out. Words were not his strength, but this time he might have been reading poetry. The firestorm was in control now and it rampaged through his words, burning the dream scenario into the air around them, consuming its subject. He saw it reflected in her eyes; they seemed to be full of smoke. His hands moved down, touching neck and shoulders and gorgeous curving breasts.

Their eyes were locked now; neither could have broken the gaze. By the time he ran out of words, he was holding her waist. And still they were not together; the pale wood lay between them, not an obstacle but an unspoken invitation.

She pulled herself lightly out of his grip. "A massage, huh? On my butcher's block counter?" Her voice was moving up and down, fluttering.

"That's what I said. You wore red. And here you are, wearing red. Hell of a coincidence." His fingertips rested on the counter itself. Speech was easier now; it was amazing how simple things got, once you opened up a little. "Heavy body oils were involved. Which is weird, because I'm allergic to most of them."

"Wait there. Stay." She went quickly across the room, the muscles of her back stretched tight under the red lycra, and disappeared into the bathroom. For a moment she was out of his view. Then she was back, and she was holding a small plastic bottle in one hand.

"Do me a favor," she said shakily and it was the dream, he could trust her, they were sharing some kind of power he'd never come across, "and for heaven's sake tell me you're not allergic to baby oil."

"I'm not allergic to baby oil." He swept the kitchen unit clear with a single brush of the hand. Plates, glasses, forks, everything went flying. There was a wild crashing of crockery, not nearly as loud as the roaring in his head. She came around to meet him.

He had hold of her now, she melded against him and her lips moved along his throat. For a moment he was dimly aware of panic. After all, when did reality ever measure up to fantasy? Suppose it went wrong, suppose it wasn't any good...

"Kiss me," she said, and bit his shoulder. "Don't stand there like you're scared of me. Just kiss me."

He kissed her, once, twice, and stopped. He had to say something. He had to make some kind of noise.

"I'm sorry about the dishes," he managed. His hands were all over the place and she was unbuttoning his shirt and right this moment he didn't care about anything else in the world. "I'll buy you some new dishes."

"Screw the dishes."

"Your brother will kill me."

"Screw my brother."

"We ought to put the fish away, it'll spoil."

"Stop talking. Sing, yell, whatever, but just don't bother me with details. You're still wearing your shirt. Take it off, take mine off. Hurry. And where's that damned baby oil?"

Chapter Six

Delgado, drowsing contentedly, heard Leo swing her feet to the floor. He opened his eyes to watch her.

She stood and stretched, a hand resting on the small of her back. Most women, he thought lazily, would have grabbed a bathrobe with a man in the room. Leo seemed unconscious of her nakedness; if she was vulnerable anywhere, he couldn't spot it. He'd never known a woman so secure with herself.

"Hey," he said. Except for the hand rubbing on her back, she wasn't moving. He saw her wince, and pulled himself up on one elbow. "Leo? You okay?"

"Bruise." She grimaced down at him over her shoulder. "Butcher's block. Typically male. Next time I'll pick the fantasy. Something with a lot of big, soft cushions."

"Sorry. I'm not usually the hairy-brute type. It's your fault, too; you percolated my testosterone count." He caught the amusement in her eyes and laughed. Her throaty chuckle sounded as a counterpoint.

"Believe it or not," she said, "I'm not usually nearly this spontaneous. I never even asked to see your last blood test. In this day and age, no less!"

"Clean. I give blood once a month, and they check you every time. Anyway, I believe in protection, since I never had any pull toward parenthood. Forgot about it this time, though." He hunched his shoulders. "What a miserable question, you know? It never even occurred to me."

She sat down beside him. Her skin gleamed; she looked like a miniature carving of an African warrior goddess. "I know, it's a real passion-killer. Too bad it has to be asked. How you feeling, son?"

"If I was worth your time, I should be feeling about half as good as you are. What time is it?"

She glanced at the clock. "Almost four. Why, you got a hot date or something?"

"Nope. I was just hoping you weren't going to kick me out yet." He touched her hand. "Are you?"

"Not at the moment. What were you thinking about, when you first woke up? Something was puzzling you, wasn't it?"

He blinked at her. "How the hell did you know that? You had your back to me."

"Not sure. I could feel it, a little wave or something. You want to answer my question? There's no law says you have to."

"Sure, I'll answer it." For a moment Delgado felt trapped. Was that connecting line stronger than he'd thought? Oh, hell, she was beautiful, brilliant, and sexy. Why shouldn't she be psychic, too? "I was thinking that most women aren't too happy about walking around naked in front of a guy. And I wondered why."

"Training," she said, and tucked pulled up both legs into lotus. He was already attuned enough to her comfort level to feel no disturbance. "Pressure. Think about it. Magazines, movies, TV. Women have to live up to an ideal that doesn't exist. They're trained to hate their bodies. I read about this gorgeous actress who bursts into tears when she looks in the mirror. And she *is* the ideal."

"Huh." Jim thought it over. "That stinks."

"Big time," she agreed. "Lucky for me I'm a realist. I mean, short, black. Hell, I'm not stupid. I knew right off I wasn't ever going to look like the statuesque blonde on the magazine cover, so I didn't worry about it too much."

"You're the dish of the day, but I still say it stinks. On behalf of my sex, please accept my apology."

"You spend too much time apologizing when you haven't got a damned thing to be sorry for." Her eyes were steady, and a bit fierce. "I'm serious, Jim. You've apologized for the dishes, for the bruises, for the sins of the Y-chromosome. Enough already. Let's talk about something else. Do you still think Cass is going to kill you?"

"Honey, for all I care he can cut out my liver and sauté it in lemon juice. And speaking of lemon juice..."

"An Italian restaurant that delivers, I know." She reached for her bathrobe, caught his eye and winked. "I don't hate myself, sir, really I don't. It's just chilly in here. Please don't apologize again."

"Stop *apologizing*," he said mockingly. "Actually, I was thinking of cooking us dinner."

She gaped at him. "You mean you *cook*?"

"I'm Italian. Of course I cook. My grandmother taught me how to make lasagna al forno when I was six." He swung his legs over the edge and stretched luxuriously, aware that she was watching the muscles in his chest ripple, and absurdly proud of it. She seemed to be bringing out all kinds of petty ego trips he'd never realized he was susceptible to. "You know, I thought I'd be stiff as a board, and instead I feel like a rubber band. How do you feel about *vitello con funghi*?"

"Depends. What is it?"

He grinned. "Veal with mushrooms."

"Then I feel like I'd eat it, that's how I feel." She shook her head. "Man, he cooks, too. I think maybe I'll tie you up and keep you in the kitchen for life. If the food's good enough, you can have evenings off for sex."

"Thank you so much," he told her politely.

"Don't mention it. It's just a little courtesy I like to extend to my domestic slaves." She watched him stand and stepped back. "Hold still for a minute. God, what a killer body—compact and delicious. Would you be upset if I asked you to sit for me?"

Her tone was light, almost bantering. Yet, suddenly, he understood why Leo had known he was puzzled without even looking at him. It was there in him, too, that wave, that awareness. She was serious. She would judge him by his answer, by the color of his response. He knew it, and she knew he knew. Were they psychic, or was it just the natural result of intimacy? And did it matter?

"That could be tricky," he said slowly. "Not posing, I'll pose and my masculine ego will be flattered, but the timing. I can't vouch for my time these days, Leo. Not until we've got Nemo in a cell."

"Ugh." She shuddered. "You know, I hadn't thought about him today, not once. I'm surprised Cass hasn't called about those sketches. I did a few different versions, composites really. He said he'd go over them and get them out to the media. Maybe he's taking the day off."

"I doubt it." He dropped an arm across her shoulders. This was the first time he'd felt glad to be short. They were as well-matched standing as they were lying down. "Easy way to check. We've got to go out to get dinner supplies. If the papers have them, they'll be in the late edition."

"Doesn't that depend on what time the papers get the stuff? I mean, since it's Sunday?"

"Right, I forgot. My brains must be scrambled." He found his mind tensing, moving back toward the outside world, and knew a sudden, violent resistance. It wasn't right; it wasn't fair. This magical day was his, theirs, nobody else's business. He wasn't at work, and he wasn't hunting... .

"You're thinking about him, aren't you?" Leo was watching him. "You just went tense as hell."

"Only for a second." He shook himself. "Ah, screw Nemo. I say we forget about him unless someone calls and orders us to remember. Let's go buy stuff and I'll cook it and we'll eat it. If we talk about work, it can be your work. Okay?"

"Sounds good to me. You want the shower first?"

Cass was not taking the day off, merely the latter part of it. He sat with his mother and daughter, making small talk, eating at the kitchen table where he had done his homework thirty years before. Leo's sketches would appear on the late news, and on the front page of Monday's papers. He knew that although he had done what he could for the day, the phone might yet ring. He willed it to stay silent.

One corner of his mind was overheated. It was a small heat, more a rash than a forest fire. The mental irritation had begun on the previous evening, standing in Leo's studio. Something about those sketches bothered the hell out of him, and he couldn't pin down what it was.

That was the rash, caused by picking at this sore place in his mind. Whether he was too tired to think, or because he was trying too hard, the fact remained that he ought to understand something about those pictures. Whatever it was, he wasn't getting it. It wasn't coming across.

None of this showed on the surface; Cass was a master at separating work and family. By the time they sat down to dinner, the family unit had discussed a wide range of topics that included almost everything except the Maternity Murders. Cass got to spend so little time with Mara that even this interlude in the middle of a hurricane was gladly welcomed. He knew how stupid it was to feel guilty about it. Mara was such a private person that having anyone around too much would have driven her nuts; anyway, the time they did spend together was quality time. Yet he did feel guilty. Hell, his mother saw more of Mara than her own father did...

"Daddy? Are you expected back anytime soon?"

He blinked. How long had he been sunk, oblivious, in his private reverie? Mara watched him, her face unreadable as usual. His mother Rhea, a tiny, non-stop talker with her daughter's powerhouse energy, looked from one to the other in silence. The sudden tension in the air was palpable.

"Sorry, honey," he said easily. "Just an attack of brain-lock. Happens when you don't get enough sleep."

"Well, unlock your brain and pass that child the mashed potatoes. She's asked you twice now." If Rhea saw past the glib explanation—and she was too acute to be taken in where her children were concerned—she was unwilling to press him. "I told you before, you work too hard. Seems to me your last break was three years ago. After Christmas, you ought to think about getting yourself out of that dusty old office and on to a beach someplace. Mexico, maybe."

For the life of him, he couldn't help grinning. She knew he couldn't go anywhere until they had Nemo sewn up. That "after Christmas" was a tactful declaration of her confidence in him; Christmas was less than two months off.

Mara had caught it. She offered Rhea one of her exquisite, earthshaking smiles.

"That's a nice idea," she said calmly. "If he takes a vacation New Year's week, during the school break, he can take me with him. Hawaii, the Bahamas, maybe Mexico like you said. I could live with that."

"I bet you could," Rhea snorted. She looked at Mara's beautiful body and luminous skin. "You want to work on your tan, maybe? Show off a bikini? I said for your father to rest, not stand around playing bodyguard. He takes you along, he'll spend all day and night chasing the boys away."

"No, he won't. Boys don't chase me." Mara was as unruffled as lake water. "I'm too beautiful. Boys don't like beautiful. They like pretty, but they're scared to death of beautiful."

She offered this adult insight placidly. The others were silenced.

It was true, Cass thought grimly. It wasn't only boys; grown men felt the same. Maybe it was because prettiness was trivial while beauty demanded to be taken seriously. Beauty was scary; men knew instinctively that it was a dangerous snare. Hell, he'd fallen into that trap himself, with Mara's mother... .

Mara helped herself to a small mouthful of potatoes, swallowed, and patted her lips delicately with her napkin. That done, she continued with her devastating explanation. "Most boys think that if I'm beautiful, it must mean I'm somehow superior to them. I am, as a matter of fact, but that's because my brain works and their brains don't. They'd like me better if I had a few pimples or crooked teeth or something. That way, they could be domineering or have a weapon or something."

"It's all right, honey." Rhea spoke with surprising gentleness. "Don't worry about it."

Mara looked surprised. "Do I sound worried? Why would I want attention from idiots? It doesn't matter that beauty is really just a natural accident. They aren't smart enough to see that. They don't see me as a girl, they see me as some kind of picture, a masterpiece, Da Vinci or Monet, you know? They're awed, not attracted. So they don't chase me, they're too busy trying to figure out how to control me. May I please have some more juice?"

Rhea pushed the orange juice across the table. She caught her son's eye and saw her own feelings reflected there. Mara was neither bragging about her own physical perfection, nor regretting the lack of schoolboy attention. She was merely stating a fact as she perceived it, and the tragedy of it was that her perception was correct.

Cass felt as though he'd been hit in the head with a brick. He'd grown up in a culture where beauty was a woman's pass to whatever she wanted. His daughter was beautiful; therefore, she would always have it easy.

Subconsciously, Cass had fostered that belief. She'd never lacked love, and if she came from a broken home he'd made sure she didn't live in a dysfunctional family. He gave her all he could, simply from a desire to enrich her life and to make her acquisition of simple pleasures automatic.

He had labored for his pleasures, his triumphs; his child would get them by right.

Now his adored, lovely daughter was calmly telling him that, for everything he had been raised to believe a woman really wanted, her beauty was not an asset but a handicap. Boys were afraid of her because her looks somehow rendered her incomprehensible to them. And she didn't seem to mind.

A cold thought surfaced in his mind. What did men do to what they couldn't understand, or couldn't control? Every cop knew the answer to that one. They destroyed it. The history books and police records bore witness to that truth.

Mara herself had mentioned Da Vinci and Monet. Before either Cass or Leo were born, some nut had attacked Michelangelo's *Pieta* with a hammer, damaging the statue. Cass remembered it clearly because Leo, reading about it long after the fact, had gone temporarily nuts herself, weeping with inarticulate rage. Rhea had held her, seeming to understand what the disfigurement of such perfection had meant, both to the artist and the girl. Cass himself had understood nothing, not then.

He understood now. Mara was as superb as any painting or statue. She was a perfect target for a destroyer. And in the end there was nothing Cass could do about it, except make sure that his beloved child kept her eyes open and a weapon handy and used her brains. Fortunately for both her safety and his peace of mind, her brains were formidable.

A wave of resentment washed over him. It wasn't fair that he should have to be so frightened; it wasn't fair that Nemo and Mara, occupying the same place in his mind, should make him so weak. And it wasn't fair that this killer should dominate his thoughts on an evening he'd managed to spend with his daughter.

So he changed the subject, drawing the others into a discussion of a controversial author's latest book. And after dinner, when they settled down on the sofa, he suggested watching a movie and selected a comedy.

For just one evening, he thought as he queued up the DVD and caught the cheerful expectancy on Mara's face, just one evening in this cold miserable season, I am going to not think about this killer and his footprints, his victims, or his ugly face. I'm entitled to forget about him, even if it's just for one evening. Just one.

Delgado had left, and Leo was unable to sleep. Her memory moved back and forth between the events of the day, touching on one tiny detail after another, weaving a tapestry. She thought of how she had watched Delgado slicing onions and garlic and mushrooms; his thin, nervous hands were as deft as her own, and she had mentally sketched those hands. She thought about the smell of his skin, light and teasing and somehow salty. She thought about his reaction to the few samples he had seen of her work, and how he had responded to them, with intelligence and without pretension.

The memories were good, they were fine. But they kept spiralling around, and Leo was getting annoyed. Her usual reaction to sex was classically male: drowsiness, torpor. Something, the nap or the unaccustomed smell of food lingering in the air, kept her hovering between sleep and consciousness in a state of mounting irritation.

Eventually she climbed grudgingly out of bed, aggravated by the situation. She had to get some rest; those illustrations were due at the *Inside Look* offices at half past ten. If this kept up, she'd sleep right through the alarm and Susan Ortiz would have kittens.

Leo pulled on her robe and turned the studio lights on. Luckily for her, she had an avenue for relaxation open to her, and it worked every time.

Tonight there was no hunting through old work; she knew which painting she wanted. She had rediscovered it during the search with Mara, and shown it to Delgado earlier. It was fresh in her mind.

It was a landscape, serene and sunlit. She had painted it from memory after a trip to France a few years back. She had visited the chateau country and parked the rented car in a cul de sac. On one side of the road ran the Loire river; off to the other side were thousands of acres of forest, beautiful wooded country, the dark green of the foliage dappled with living light under a crystalline sky.

She hadn't brought a camera and she hadn't needed one. Her painter's eye recorded the scene she had found that day, and held it until she could lay hands to canvas and color.

She set the painting on the easel and studied it. While usually analytical about her own work, she was aware of a flush of pleasure. This one was beautiful. And she had done it for herself; it had never been for sale.

She sat straight in the hard-backed chair, and stared into her painting.

Tall trees capped with green darkness. A small glade, rolling from steeper ground into a pool of sunlit grass. The trunks, painted as a mass, attained idiosyncrasy; here was a massive bole with a pucker in the bark, there a knothole in the gnarled wood.

She stared at the painting.

Something small and pale in the lower boughs of a crooked tree. A bird's nest, perhaps, a tiny perfect home where something sang and slept and reared its young.

Birdsong, humming insects, moving water. Warmth on the bare skin of her arms. Somewhere beyond vision was her little car, left by the side of the road. Somewhere was the highway, lorries or whatever the French called their eighteen-wheelers rumbling up hills that curved and rolled until they met the horizon, leading perhaps into some unknown dreamscape as magical as this hidden corner of the woods.

Her body was still. She had left it behind her; only her hands, holding to the lifeline of her waking self, were real. Birds, tiny moths, their wings humming as they moved from flower to flower, a patch of wild rhubarb in a distant part of the forest...

The air was warmer here; it was France in September. Leo could taste it, sense it in her lungs. It had a different quality from what she breathed at home. Her ankles were warm and cool at the same time, with a coolness that must be moisture. A fine mist had crept along this grass during the night, moving lazily where tree met earth, coming down the slope to this little gully. There it had lost momentum, pooling here, saturating the grass. No wonder the sun's heat had no power to turn this grass yellow. No wonder it grew so green.

Her ears picked up the harsh caw of a crow. It sounded loud, louder than she had ever heard in a painting. It came from directly above her head, startling her. For a second she wavered, nearly losing the battle to remain; there was something demanding, almost too real, about this vocal intrusion.

The cry came again from farther away, and she was calm once more. It had been in the trees above her head. Now it flew, searching the land, riding the thermal currents in its quest for food, water, things that glinted and shone.

There was water here. Leo could hear it, a faraway musical chatter of life against rocks. A stream, some tiny joyous slash in the grassy hills. Or was it the river she was hearing, the Loire, flowing toward the sea? She could feel it, visualizing the ancient stone bridges and the gaily painted boats that plied their trade along its banks.

The picture faded, and her attention shifted to a new awareness of the glade itself. It was strewn with twigs, and piles of stones. Again Leo knew a momentary wavering, for the stones lay at oddly regular intervals around the edge of the place. They were heaped neatly into small, unsteady pyramids. Surely nature had not set these cones of rock in so precise a pattern...

Again Leo won the battle for control. Something new had caught her eye; a row of tiny footprints, one set larger than the others. She smiled, feeling her facial muscles stretch. Not only birds lived in these woods; a vixen had come this way, leading her young. Had something frightened them into the protection of their own lair? No, she thought, no. If the family had been in flight, the rows would not have been so clean. They would have run, getting in each other's way, crossing the prints.

She felt a prickle of uneasiness, her shoulder blades tingling and twitching. It was almost as if someone watched her, as if she had abruptly become aware of hostile eyes fastened on the vulnerable spot at the back of her neck.

But that was impossible. This is my place, she thought. I made this. I'm alone here, except for what I put here. There can be nothing else, to intrude or to hurt.

The crow called, close at hand. There was a trampling in the underbrush, an indrawn breath. The crow must have seen something on the ground, and swooped down to take it.

But no crow would come down at that speed. The trees were not only a barrier but a potential death trap. It could break a wing; it could break its neck.

Another cry, almost directly behind her. A different cry, higher, shriller. It sounded human.

And suddenly Leo knew that this was different, this was new, something was happening here that had never happened to her before. Her instinct had been right all along.

She was not alone. The eyes on her back were real.

The crow screamed, and was answered. From somewhere in the darkness of the great forest, a human voice screamed out in an extremity of terror.

The glade wavered, flickering in and out. Leo was aware of pain, a physical cramp that took her and held her there, unable to move. What was happening here? What atrocity had been committed to desecrate this natural cathedral?

I can't let go. I've got to see, I've got to find out what's happening here, this is different, this has never happened, it's not supposed to happen, someone is being hurt and I won't let it happen I won't I can't I...

For a frozen instant, she had control of the scene. The lifeline held in her grip, she marshalled all her power.

Silence. No crow, no scream, nothing but the hush of distant water and the movement of butterflies on the wing.

Directly behind her, a man laughed.

It was a baritone chuckle, rich and deep and horrifying, echoing in a diminishing spiral. It was answered by a tiny whimper, pleading for mercy, for some kind of reassurance that this was not happening, for an end to pain.

One of the stone pyramids shivered and collapsed. In a parody of slow motion, the uppermost stone cascaded down the pile. It landed in the grass with an almost inaudible thump.

The chuckle, sound without soul, came again.

Then it was gone, and Leo lay on the studio floor, sobbing harshly, wracked with pain. She knew what had happened. Her brain and spirit had collided at gale force, wrenching her back through the tunnel of reality and causing this sickness.

Slowly, the pain subsided. Leo gritted her teeth and breathed in jerky, irregular gasps. She looked at her hands, clenching and relaxing; she looked at the legs of her chair, at the baseboards of the room. She listened to her own breathing. At no time did she look at the painting that had promised serenity, and brought horror instead.

What finally brought her back was the faint, lingering smell of Italian food. It was a reminder of Jim Delgado's presence, a ghost of reality. He had cooked that food and they had both eaten it. There were no shadows in the kitchen, no deep chuckles, no whimpers of agony. It was safe, and real, and comforting. There were no devils.

Sick, sweating, Leo climbed into bed. The painting, which she had never titled, remained on the easel; she had not been able to bring herself to touch it. Later, in the blessed sane light of day, she would wake up and drink coffee. She would take a shower, washing with real water whose source she could see and identify. She would put clothes on, real clothes, and climb onto a real bus and deliver her illustrations to Susan Ortiz.

And when she had come completely back to her own self, she would sit down in front of that damned picture, which had been born of a lovely memory and was now ruined forever, and she would figure out just what had happened tonight.

Her last thought, before falling into a nightmare-ridden stupor, was that at least the painting finally had a name.

She would call it *Beyond This Point Are Monsters.*

Chapter Seven

If those most nearly concerned with identifying Captain Nemo withdrew deliberately from Monday's media circus, the rest of San Francisco was eager to participate.

Leo's sketches screamed off the front pages. Having drawn them in a state of exhaustion, Leo had not spared them a glance before passing them to her brother. If she'd been questioned, she could not have accurately described them. She wasn't even sure they'd been up to her usual standard.

As it turned out, her opinion was irrelevant. The work had its own life, its own effect. And the first papers of the week sported front pages with banner headlines and a face that might have sprung from the darkest vaults of the human fear bank.

The city papers gave all three sketches equal billing; the morning edition, eschewing sensationalism, offered black and white evil under a factual header. The East Bay daily enlarged the scariest of the three to half-page majesty; the other two, only slightly smaller, flanked it like demonic bodyguards. The headline, in huge type, was guaranteed to cause nightmares. The South Bay papers, fifty miles away, had been more circumspect. Still, front-page news sells papers, and even the rumored crash of one of Silicon Valley's most powerful corporations was relegated to page three.

Each paper reported Joseph Ching's brush with darkness. All tacitly ignored its "old news" status; local television, after all, had shown little else since Saturday morning. The local print media, knowing its job, had two goals in mind: inform the public and sell papers. Their second objective was successful beyond their wildest dreams; by noon on Monday, the newsstands were empty. If the information was tainted by the horror-movie presentation used to convey it, the editors were not overly concerned.

So a three-faced chimera walked out of the realm of shuddering tension and onto the breakfast tables of the city of San Francisco. By the time the city's children had been sent off to school and breakfast eaten, conversations were springing up all over the Bay Area.

Not surprisingly, women reacted more strongly than their male counterparts. The dream monster stared up at young women sipping coffee, at grandmothers thankful to be past the age of child-bearing, at well-dressed professional women briefly distracted from the stock market quotes and their husbands' enthusiastic recapping of Sunday's football game. A million readers reacted with atavistic similarity; while perhaps secretly ashamed of the sensational excitement beneath their civilized concern, each knew the momentary blankness that comes from a cold touch against a warm place.

The bulk of the population was concerned only in a random fashion. Others were more nearly involved.

Elena Gonzales read the paper over a cup of coffee at a South of Market cafe. She had a morning ritual during the working week; she left her apartment at a time guaranteed to deposit her at her favorite cafe twenty minutes before she was due at her desk. Here she relaxed, drinking two cups of strong coffee and reading whichever articles in the paper caught her eye. Elena understood that a big city's homicide department was a more stressful working environment than most jobs could ever be. Those twenty minutes pushed the pressure back, keeping it at bay, relaxing her for the human horror stories guaranteed to descend upon her in the later hours.

She had not seen the sketches, but she knew about them. Valenzuela, that sensitive bullish man with the cathedral-bell voice, had been on the desk when Cassy brought them in on Sunday morning. He'd phoned her at home to give her an update. She was not unprepared.

But she was unfamiliar with Leo's work, and the raw power of the demon startled her; startled her so much, in fact, that she skipped her second cup of coffee and walked around the block to calm herself down and clear her mind.

Valenzuela reacted differently. With Cassy, he'd been the first to see them. That first look had produced a muttered prayer in Spanish. As he obeyed Cassy's orders, following the necessary routine for reproducing the sketches and getting them to the media, his mind was busy with the drugged, broken face of Theresa Gabriel's husband. That face haunted him all through Sunday, following him like an echo throughout the day.

When he opened his Monday paper—delivered to his house just south of San Francisco, in Daly City—he thought of Elena's comment about men and the desirability of letting their emotions show. In his mind's eye, he saw the widower, all feeling sedated past expression. Then he pushed his breakfast away, put his head down on his arms, and broke into great tearing sobs, a harsh angry weeping that hurt his chest and shattered the peace of his bright kitchen.

Jim Delgado had woken with a happy, relaxed sense that he had found something rare and valuable. The feeling of well-being stayed with him, even when he saw the paper. His mind wanted no part of Nemo or anything else to do with the real world; it wanted to linger on the previous day. But he was a realist, and a good cop, and he forced his attention back to where he knew it belonged. Along with his newfound sense of peace, he also pushed away some considerations that would not have occurred to Leo. He'd have to look them straight on eventually, those unpleasant possibilities: Cassy's reaction, the thought that should the affair ripen and become known, there might be those who would accuse him of dating his superior officer's sister in search of preferential treatment, the fact that an interracial affair might provoke some ugliness. Jim shoved this all away, and focused his mind back firmly on Nemo. Everything else would have to wait for another day.

Cassy's reaction was brief. He'd seen the originals, after all, which held the discontent that Leo had felt at the moment in time she had drawn them. The new ones were scary, and made him jump. Yet Cass knew his sister, understood better than anyone else how her spirit worked. The newsprint was a dark, incomplete map of a killer's face; they could not hope to recreate the virginal, fathomless blackness that had moved her in the first place. For Cass, who could associate them with Leo, the pictures were no shock.

A thin figure in dark clothes had gone out before sunrise. A coin was deposited in a vending machine, a corded, muscled hand pulled the cover up and pulled a copy of the paper free. The machine had been loaded only minutes earlier; the figure had stood across the street and actually watched the paper truck pull away. The ink was not quite dry when Nemo rolled up the morning paper and walked back to a small apartment. There was no expression to be read on the monster's face; it was smooth and calm, completely unrevealing.

Mara Chant regarded the paper with a purely analytical interest; like her father, she had seen the originals. She studied Leo's newer efforts, approved of the flow of line and use of shadow, and filed them away at the back of her mind. Sharing juice and toast with her father, there was nothing to provoke a stronger reaction. She shrugged on her jacket, picked up her books, and headed for school without exchanging a word with Cass on the subject of Leo's triptych of murder. That this detachment was a lost cause became apparent before she set foot through the school's front gates.

At about the time Mara was getting bored denying any knowledge of her aunt's sketches to her fellow students, Leo left Susan Ortiz's office at *Inside Look* and realized she was afraid to go home.

Leo, like most people with high metabolic rates, required a lot of sleep. She preferred eight hours a night, and could get by with six. Since Saturday she'd managed nine hours total and her body was distant, remote, separated from her mind. The first symptom of exhaustion, clumsiness, had set in. Nothing scared Leo worse than clumsiness. Artists are not supposed to be clumsy.

She'd delivered the illustrations, answered questions about them, and exchanged the normal social pleasantries. These things had been done without thought or memory; her sleep-deprived brain performed and then faded out entirely. She didn't remember a word Susan had said, or what she'd said herself; she didn't remember handing Susan an invoice and accepting a check in return. Leo was running on automatic. She desperately wanted sleep. And she was afraid to go home.

It was because of that damned painting, she thought as she emerged into a busy Fisherman's Wharf street. It was because of *Beyond This Point Are Monsters*. The painting was unfinished business. How was she supposed to sleep with that goddamned painting in the studio? Even if she turned it to face the wall it would still be there, dormant, dark, waiting for her like a spider enticing a fly...

A wave of vertigo made her stop and lean her head against the building wall. She wanted to cry.

Don't be a moron, her rational mind said calmly. *You try dealing with that one in the state you're in, you'll never do it. You'll break into a million pieces. Face it, honey, you need sleep. You don't have to go home. Call a friend, borrow their couch for a couple of hours and for heaven's sake get some rest.*

Leo straightened her back and made up her mind. She knew several people who lived nearby. One of them could surely offer a temporary bed, without demanding an explanation. Briefly renewed, Leo hoisted her portfolio and headed for a bus stop, settling herself on the sheltered seats.

Ten minutes later the strength had deserted her, and she was on the verge of tears. Five calls had produced five recorded messages on five answering machines. She'd tried everyone she knew within a ten-minute bus ride, and no one was home. Now what?

Unexpectedly, a voice spoke into her ear. "Homicide, Delgado speaking."

Leo was too disoriented to respond. When had she dialled Cassy's number? And had she asked for Delgado, spoken without even knowing it?

"Homicide, hello? Can I help you?"

"Jim?"

"Leo, hey." He sounded pleased. "How you doing? Elena's at lunch and so is your brother, which is why I picked up his line. What's going on?"

Leo felt relieved. She must have hit the selection for Cassy's work number without even knowing it, but at least she hadn't held a conversation she couldn't remember. Nobody that tired was safe out alone. She gathered her wits.

"I'm at Fisherman's Wharf, I'm dead on my feet and I can't go home right now. I wanted to borrow Cassy's key and take a cab out to his place for a nap. Goddamnit, he's never there when I need him. Where does he get his energy from, anyway? This is his murder case and I'm the one losing sleep." She heard the petulance grinding in her voice and bit down on it. "Sorry. I'm just wasted. When's he coming back, Jim?"

"Not for a couple of hours. I'd offer you the office couch, but you wouldn't get two minutes worth of shut-eye. Thanks to those drawings of yours, the phones are ringing off the hook and the place is a zoo." Here was another proof of his sensitivity; if he wondered why she couldn't go home, he didn't ask. "Tell you what. Come over here and borrow my key. I'm working late tonight, so you can have the place to yourself. If you get hungry, raid my fridge. When you're ready to leave, call me. You can drop the key off here, or I'll stop off at your place and pick it up. Will that work?"

She could fell tears of weakness and gratitude pricking at the back of her lids. *Stupid,* she thought, *stupid damned little idiot. What am I crying about, anyway? I never cry. I must be more tired than I thought.* "Thanks, Jim. You're a life-saver. I'll be there as soon as I can find a cab."

Fifteen minutes later, she made her way through the Hall of Justice metal detector and up to the fourth floor.

If she'd been more awake, Leo would have noticed the looks she was getting. Everyone in Homicide knew that she was responsible for the Nemo sketches, and the Nemo sketches, in six hours, had become the talk of the town.

Elena, who had returned from lunch since Leo's call, gave her a respectful stare and a visible shudder. Sergeant Bruce Friedman, staff artist, knew good work when he saw it. He was just back from sick leave and he was burning to discuss those pictures. When Leo walked in he thought that heaven had offered him a perfect opportunity. Then he saw the blind weariness and sagging lines of her face, and decided that another day would be better.

Delgado, seeing Leo's exhaustion, felt a protective surge which Leo herself would certainly resent, and hid it. He was aware that an extra reason for prudence was useful. He'd been worried that her presence there, his reaction to her, might set the office tongues in furious motion. But their conversation was brief and to the point; it offered nothing for even the most avid gossip to work with.

"Here's the address, I wrote it down." He handed her a slip of paper and two loose keys, detached from a ring. "The bigger key does the building door, and the smaller one works the deadbolt on my flat. I don't think I'll be done here before eight, so just call over here when you're done and we'll make arrangements about picking these up. Oh, by the way, it's the second-floor flat. Okay?"

"Fine, perfect. I'll call." She managed a tiny smile, produced only for him and beautifully intimate. "Thanks very much, Inspector Delgado. This is really kind of you."

"My pleasure, Ms. Chant." Startled by the formality of his tone, she glanced at him. The tiny wink he gave her was reassuring. "Would you like to sit down for a while? Elena just made coffee, and I'll get a cab over here. This time of day, it'll take about ten minutes."

In griping about her brother's boundless energy, Leo had done him an injustice. While she'd been coping with Susan Ortiz, Cass had been working at the edge of overdrive. Long before she called, he was as weary as his sister.

Monday mornings were always busy. Since most violent crime seems to happen on weekends, the first day of the new week always brought a heavy load of mopping up in its wake. Cassy had mopped dutifully, going through reports that ranged from a liquor store shooting to the grisly killing of a known crack dealer suspected of welshing on a shipment.

After half an hour of eroding concentration, Cassy dumped the entire pile in the lap of a dismayed junior inspector and returned his brain and energy to the Maternity Murders. After all, he thought, that was what they were paying him for.

Now that he had his mind back on the case that he considered his real priority, Cass could concentrate. He checked the forensic and pathology reports on Mrs. Ling Ma, and got depressed; these were mere repetitions of six earlier reports. One blow at the base of the skull—forensics still would not commit as to the weapon used, except to say that it was wrapped in soft fabric. The single blow had knocked her out; Nemo knew just where to hit for maximum efficiency. The same nylon cord, which came in spools and could be found in the garage of anyone who owned an electric grass-whip tool. The same hard twist around the throat, cutting off the same breath, turning the new victim's skin the same mottled blue, bringing the same death.

Always the same; only the victim's personal statistics, now snuffed out, ever changed. It made for dreary reading. Cassy moved on to a psychiatrist's evaluation.

This kind of report was less dreary than irritating; when you are mired by responsibility in grim reality, you don't need pompous fiction offered by so-called experts. And it was fiction, Cassy thought glumly. How could it be anything else? Until they caught the bastard, the ghost of Freud himself could do nothing more than speculate.

It is reasonable to extrapolate from the pattern of repetition that this killer has at some time in his life been exposed to a negative experience involving pregnancy or childbirth...

Cassy didn't want speculation, however knowledgeable. He could do that himself. Hell, did these people think they were telling him something new? Seven dead pregnant women was a pretty good indicator that the killer didn't like pregnant women. The shrinks were just wrapping up an obvious guess in fancy jargon. Cass was willing to bet that most of these shrinks, if questioned where they couldn't be quoted, would say that every human child born of woman had suffered a negative experience involving pregnancy or childbirth. Birth itself was traumatic; wasn't that one of their favorite songs? The arrogant dumb-asses couldn't even manage consistency.

It wasn't that he didn't respect the head-doctors or their opinions; he was one of the few cops to consult them voluntarily after an arrest was made. But until it was made, the opinions would conflict. It was the unfortunate nature of an inexact science.

...impossible to speculate at this point whether the experience was direct or indirect...

"Brilliant, Sigmund. Absolutely brilliant."

"Excuse me, Lieutenant?"

Cass glanced up at Elena, realized he'd spoken aloud, and shook his head at her. Ah, screw this, he thought. He dropped the psychiatrist's report and moved on to harder fact.

Joseph Ching had been released from the hospital this morning, sent home quietly and without fanfare. He was, with his knowledge and consent, being watched by two members of the uniformed branch. The surveillance was routine, since Cassy didn't believe that Ching was in any danger from Nemo. But he genuinely respected the old man, and Ching was the only witness to see Nemo close up. If Nemo tried something, Cassy was going to make damned sure that it didn't come off. That they might take Nemo in the process was a secondary consideration, albeit a real one. It was a credit to Cass that he hoped Nemo would stay away; a second shock, and one of such magnitude, would probably put Ching out for good.

Behind the routine, the unhealthy fascination of Leo's sketches moved through Homicide like a dark thread. Although no one mentioned it, it was there in the sidelong looks, the whispered exchanges just beyond his hearing, in the heavy crucifix hanging around Valenzuela's neck. Only Delgado was unaffected. Cassy blessed him for it. It was nice to know that one of his inspectors, at least, could keep his head.

Just before lunch, it occurred to Cassy that Delgado was not merely unaffected by the pictures; he seemed completely uninterested in them. Cassy, grabbing his raincoat, decided that there was something new in Jim's easy, relaxed strength. In Cassy's experience, the only thing that gave a man that kind of release was some really good sex. He grinned to himself and headed for the door, stopping at Delgado's desk.

"You have a good day yesterday?"

The question, the merest casual throwaway, produced an unexpected result. Delgado stiffened, turned a dusky red, and looked up at Cassy through lowered lids.

"Yeah. Yeah, not bad. How about you?"

Cassy tilted his head, one eyebrow shooting up. Jim didn't sound like Jim, he sounded wary. And what the hell, in that simple question, had put Delgado's bristles up?

"Pretty good. I spent some time with my mom and kid. Eating dinner and watching the Marx Brothers, you know? Nice change of pace. You get some sleep?"

For all his caution, his belief that this would be the worst possible time to complicate to Cassy's impressive list of hassles, Delgado could not help the sensual, tender smile that curved his lips. He saw Cassy's eyes suddenly narrow, and cursed himself silently. Elena might say men hid their emotions too well. He sure was making a botch of hiding his.

"Some sleep. Actually, it was a nice, restful day. I'm feeling a whole lot better."

His voice was casual, and gave nothing away. But Cassy was no idiot. He knew quite well that Delgado had a thing for Leo; and here he was, smiling, relaxed, the entire set of his posture a giveaway. There was awareness and a certain hard speculation in the look Cassy gave his inspector.

"Good." His voice was very dry. "Glad to hear it. I'm going to get myself something to eat. Anybody calls, I'm out, I'm gone, you'll see me when you see me."

When Cassy had left, Delgado let his breath out. One way or another, he thought, he was going to have to deal with this situation. There was no way to avoid it. He hadn't liked that hard-edged look Cass had given him. He only hoped the upcoming confrontation with Cassy would not cost him anything he really valued. Like Leo, he thought grimly. Or his job.

In Jim Delgado's flat, Leo Chant woke from a deep untroubled sleep.

There was no disorientation; she lay in bed and revelled in a sense of well-being. This was just what she'd needed to get herself together. Leo rested, feeling how cooperative her muscles and bones were after the sorely-needed sleep

She turned on the bedside lamp and checked Jim's alarm clock. Seven o'clock. Would she be awake all night? She debated the question and decided that she didn't give a damn. Stretching, she went to explore the kitchen. Jim had told her to help herself, and she was ravenous. This was the first sign of appetite she'd felt all day.

To Leo, who hated cooking, the refrigerator was a fairyland. There was a roast chicken, cheese, assorted deli meats, leftovers in the form of a carefully wrapped pan of homemade lasagna. There was milk, and white wine, and grapefruit juice; there were even fresh coffee beans, to supply the espresso machine on the counter beside the stove. And, of course, there were eggs and butter. Leo, starving and happy, decided that Jim Delgado was not a man under her definition of the word.

The flat itself was a revelation. The place was clean and well-kept, but it was neither a museum nor an antiseptic hospital ward. It was a direct reflection of the man who lived here; generous, comfortable, and easy to be around.

She took a chicken leg, some cheese and a glass of wine. The meal kicked her back to full consciousness before it was halfway eaten. After washing her dishes and leaving them in the drainer—obscurely, she decided that drying and putting them away would be excessive—Leo reached for the phone.

"Homicide, Lieutenant Chant speaking."

"Cass? Hi, it's me. Listen, is Jim Delgado there?"

"Delgado? Yes, he's here, or he will be after he winds up his dinner break. Why? You want him?"

Every alarm bell in Leo's head began to clang. Cassy's voice was so chilly, there might have been ice in the phone wires. Remembering Jim's worry about her brother's reaction, she got cautious. A lifetime of handling Cassy shaped her caution; she went for a balanced mixture of surprise and sarcasm. After all, in over thirty years, that tone of voice had never yet failed to put Cass in his place.

"Well, when I came in looking for you today and you weren't there, he was kind enough to give me his keys and his address and let me sack out on his couch for a nap." She produced this amendment to the truth without compunction; if Cass had an attitude, it was better not to even mention the word bed. Leo had never been willing to sacrifice the world for a quiet life, but this wasn't a good time for head-on combat. "Since I assume he'd like to come home and use his own flat, and since you were out stuffing your face when I needed you this afternoon, I thought I'd stop off there and give him his keys back. By the way, little brother, tomorrow is Tuesday, assuming you're willing to give God your written permission for the calendar change."

There, she thought. A nice little speech, designed to make him feel guilty and sting his sense of injustice at the same time. That ought to distract him.

It didn't.

"He didn't say anything about you coming by. Why not?"

"Damned if I know." Her surprise was real. "No earthly reason not to mention it. I was up all night working, and I had to deliver some sketches by ten. Problem was, I couldn't go home for a while and I was wasted. I wanted to borrow your keys, but you were out. I was going to crash on the couch in your office, but the phones were ringing and people were running in and out. Delgado was very nice about it. Cass, what's your problem?"

"The problem is that the whole department knows that Jim's got a thing for you and today he was walking around here like he'd found the Holy Grail. That's the problem."

"Maybe he did find the Holy Grail." Leo was dangerously reasonable.

"Have you asked him?"

"No, but I thought..."

"I don't give a flying damn what you thought." Who in hell did her brother think he was, the Grand Inquisitor? "Get this straight, junior. I'll say this one time, so listen up. If I want a priest or a daddy, I'll hire one. I don't take this kind of crap from anyone, especially when I've changed their diapers for them. You try this Torquemada crap on me, I'll knock you on your ass so hard you won't know what hit you. You copy that, little brother?"

"Don't you be giving me attitude, honey." Cass had a temper of his own. "Your problem is, you're man-happy. And if you think I need you wrapping yourself around one of my inspectors in the middle of this Nemo mess, you can just—"

"I'll give attitude if I feel like it and if you don't like it you know what you can do about it." Leo was in a towering rage. "Listen to Professor Happy Relationships giving me advice! Seems to me the one serious relationship you ever had was nothing to write home about."

For a moment, she thought she'd pushed too far. Cass was being a pain, but she didn't want to fight with him. Damn the family temper, anyway. Only Mara was free of it. Maybe that was why she never got into messes like this...

"Leo?"

She gripped the phone, hard. "Now what?"

"Sorry. You're right, it's none of my business. It's just that I can't afford Jim Delgado's attention to be anywhere but on Nemo right now—"

"—and you can't help worrying about me," she finished for him. "I know. Batten down the hatches and make sure the women and children are under them. Cass, let me ask you something. Have you ever actually *looked* at the women and children in this family? Do we really strike you as needing the masterful protection of your strong masculine arm?"

There was a pause as Cass considered his indomitable mother, his incomprehensible daughter, and his fireball sister. His roar of laughter nearly made Leo drop the phone.

"*Touché,*" Cass managed when he'd regained control of his voice. "Maybe I need glasses. Okay, forget it. It was nice of Jim to lend you his keys and you want to get them back to him, and that's the end of it. Jim lives out near the university, doesn't he? That area's pretty dead at night and the fog's in.

You pack up his keys and put your shoes on and I'll send a cab down there. Does he have an intercom?"

"I don't know. I've never been here before." That he was worrying about her, breaking the promise he'd made two minutes earlier, Leo let pass without comment. All things considered, this fear was legitimate. "Let me check—yeah. Here it is. Anyway, you can see the front of the building from the kitchen window."

"I'll send a cab. Don't go down until he rings."

"Yes, master. And by the way, don't forget that note for God," Leo said cheerfully, and hung up.

Chapter Eight

During evening hours, long after the normal working day was over, the Hall of Justice had a forlorn feel. While the uniformed police remained on guard to keep out troublemakers, their numbers seemed excessive, and they themselves had the uneasy effect of toy soldiers. With the daytime bustle of office staff reduced to a trickle, the lobby had the air of an abandoned military encampment.

Leo, waiting for the elevator, decided that painting the scene would require a special touch. One wrong move, in setting or artistic approach, would produce an unsatisfactory and inaccurate effect of pathos. It was definitely tricky. Maybe that was why never got around to painting it.

In contrast, Homicide had the air of a conference site awaiting the janitor's cleanup. Elena's unoccupied desk bore a lipstick-stained coffee mug and an untidy litter of papers; the back of her chair was adorned by a lightweight jacket. The wastepaper baskets were filled to overflowing.

Cass must have been on the lookout, for he came out to meet her. Through the glass office wall, Leo saw Delgado in conversation with another inspector, a woman named Anne Rubens. Leo, who had met her before, sometimes wondered why anyone so elegant would choose so gritty a career. She looked more like a socialite than a cop.

Whatever they were discussing obviously interested Delgado; Leo saw concentration in the set of his shoulders, the tilt of his head. Rubens, a leggy blonde with beautiful cheekbones, tapped her desk with one finger, apparently making a point. Delgado threw his head back and laughed, exposing strong muscles in his throat. Leo saw his lips moving in reply.

Leo was aware of a stabbing jolt that might have been jealousy. It was followed immediately by shocked astonishment and a fierce inner repudiation. She refused to be jealous. Jealousy was self-destructive juvenile crap, suitable only for those who wanted to control other people. She wasn't like that; she didn't own Jim and she didn't want to own Jim. Just because...

"Hello there, earth to Leo, come in please."

Leo jerked her head and realized that any chance of hoodwinking her brother was gone for good. She'd stood there for a good two minutes, staring at Delgado. Presumably Cass had been talking the entire time, and she hadn't heard a word. So much for convincing him that there was nothing going on. Damn.

She looked up at her brother, grimacing, her face crinkling up into the mask of a puff-cheeked gargoyle. It was a familiar expression, one that Rhea Chant referred to as "Leo's damn-I-got-busted look." The general effect was to make her look about twelve years old.

Cass began to laugh. A deep chuckle, disturbing at first in its echoes of last night's adventure, became a bellow of joy. Despite her realization that he was reacting to his sister's discomfiture, Leo found herself laughing in response. It was impossible not to; Cass didn't laugh often, but when he did it was irresistible. The fact that the amusement was at her expense didn't matter.

Delgado glanced up, excused himself with more haste than civility, and headed for the Chants. Rubens, well aware of Jim's infatuation with Leo and of the hot rumor that he'd spent Sunday scratching that particular itch, grinned with unholy amusement. She'd heard about Leo's borrowing of Jim's keys; a couple of the older and more conservative squad members had been making noises under their breath. There was also a scuttlebut that Cass was being kept in the dark. From the look of it, that was no longer true. Rubens had seen Leo's face. She'd also seen Cassy's.

Like the rest of the department, she'd expected fireworks when Cassy found out; unlike Jim, she had no illusions about Leo's ability to hold her own against her brother. In her opinion, Leo could hold her own against Attila the Hun with an army at his back. The confrontation, whatever the outcome, was likely to prove interesting.

Delgado, stiff with foreboding, reached the outer office in time to see Leo taking a swing at her brother's shoulder. The punch, light and playful, connected nicely. Cass didn't even try to duck, but parried with a poke to his sister's stomach. They were both breathless with laughter.

"What I want to know," Leo was saying, "is if I get six points or only three. You're the jock, you tell me. Was that a touchdown or a field goal?"

"Neither. You get points if you score. I scored, you didn't. Ha! Touchdown! Homicide six, artist nil—*oof!*"

Leo, catching him unawares, had poked him back. She was smiling maniacally. "The game's now officially tied—and don't you even look like saying that the game's officially up. Hi, Jim. I just dropped by to give you back your keys and tell you that I owe you a chicken leg. How you doing?"

"Fine." Delgado looked from brother to sister, relieved but wary. Cass didn't look mad. In fact, he was grinning like an idiot. Catching the same expression on Leo's face, Delgado thought that he'd never seen the family resemblance so pronounced. Fully aware of Anne Rubens watching from the other office, he decided to go carefully. After all, you could never be sure about Cassy's temper.

"Is something funny?"

"Only if your sense of humor is at the preschool level," Leo said sweetly, and promptly ducked. "Ha, you missed. Better stick to basketball. Of course, at your height, you're not exactly Shaquille O'Neill."

Cass, a bare two inches over the department's minimum height requirement, shook his head at her. "My sister," he told Delgado cheerfully, "has got a tongue like a bee's ass. Makes snake venom look like oatmeal. Be warned."

This masterly speech, conveying not only awareness of the situation but tacit acceptance, was reassuring. Delgado, seeing approval in Leo's face, responded in kind.

"Not a killer bee, I hope."

"Not a South American killer bee, anyway." Anne Rubens strolled over. "We've got Elena, and one's enough for any office. Hello, Leo. I caught the Wylie show. Wonderful stuff. Did anyone buy *Contralto in Flight*?"

Leo, surprised, turned her attention to Anne. "The lady with her mouth open? Yep. A member of the San Jose Opera bought it, on the second day. Why, were you interested?"

"Utterly. I fell in love with it. Pastels, wasn't it? The problem was, my car insurance was due..."

"...and the lady with the tonsils didn't come cheap. Sorry." Leo didn't sound particularly sorry. "If you want one like it, I take commissions. A smaller version wouldn't be the same, I don't do clones, but it would sure cost less."

"Definitely possible. I'll call you about it after I see how much Christmas is going to cost me. Good night, all." Anne nodded regally, and wandered out.

Now that no one was laughing, the silence was awkward. Leo rummaged in her bag and produced two keys.

"Thanks, Jim, this really saved my life. Now I can go home and cope with the world."

"Any time." Delgado, one eye on Cass, dropped the keys into his pocket. "Glad I was able to help out."

"Leo," Cass asked suddenly, "Can I ask you something?"

Both Leo and Delgado stiffened. Leo, battle-ready and wary, nodded at him.

"You've got a perfectly good home of your own. So why couldn't you go home to sleep?"

Leo cursed silently. Would she never break Cass of this idea, that he had some right to interfere in her life? Why couldn't he take a lesson in discretion from his inspectors? It wasn't his business.

As she opened her mouth, the phone rang. Cass, still watching Leo, answered it.

"Homicide, Chant speaking." They saw his face change. "Hello, Mr. Ching. No, of course you aren't bothering me. Is everything all right? Can I help you with something?"

Delgado and Leo, side by side, heard the soft faint chatter of Joseph Ching's voice through the phone. They exchanged looks, Leo's frustrated and Delgado's unreadable. It was impossible to make out individual words.

"No. No, anything you can remember would be useful. Excuse me? Yes, suggestions would be welcome. We want to catch the killer, not grab the glory. Um, Mr. Ching, wait a moment, I'll need to take this down. Let me get a pen."

Something's happening, Delgado thought, and shot a taut look at Leo. *Something's going to break. Cass only looks like that when the knot starts coming apart. Here it comes. Something's up.*

But there was bewilderment, not enlightenment, on Cassy's face. He glanced up, saw the expectancy on Delgado's face and the yearning curiosity on Leo's, and punched the speaker button on the phone.

"All right, Mr. Ching. I'm ready now. What was it you remembered, and what's this suggestion of yours?"

Joseph Ching's beautiful voice filled the dusty office.

"It was the woman, the woman he had killed. He moved her, just a little bit, but he moved her. I wondered why. He was seen, he knew this. He had no time, for time was his enemy. Surely he should have finished his crime and run away as quickly as he could go. Yet he moved the body so that this poor woman's head pointed in a particular direction. So you see..."

The words trailed off. The Homicide office was dead silent. Cass expelled air through his nostrils and spoke calmly, reasonably.

"Which particular direction, Mr. Ching?"

"South," Joseph Ching's voice told them. "That is what I remembered. And I saw also, I do not know this word, a streak, a patch, on the ground. As if the body had been in one place and had been moved. When he stood, the woman had been moved from where she fell. And I thought I should ask a question of you, if it is not a secret, you know, confidential or classified."

"Of course, Mr. Ching. Ask me anything you want."

"Very well. Were those other poor women also moved, to face differently from where they had first fallen down?"

Cass met Delgado's eyes, an unspoken command in them. But it was unnecessary. Delgado was already at the filing cabinet, rummaging through a drawer and emerging with a thick folder. Leo, frozen, held her breath.

"One of my inspectors is checking on that right now, Mr. Ching," Cass said clearly. "It may take a few minutes. I'll call you back, if that's all right."

"Of course." Ching repeated his number. "I think you will find that it is as I suspect."

"Now let me ask you something, Mr. Ching. Suppose we do find that some of the victims have been moved so that their heads pointed south. What would that tell us? What possible point could there be? And how will it help us?"

"Well," Joseph Ching said, "I thought he might be Chinese, this man, but we were in Chinatown, and I might have been misled by expecting that to be true. But this—I do not know any western people who would practice *feng shui* to such a degree as this, or so wrongly. This kind of geomancy, this perversion of it—I cannot imagine this being done outside the Asian community. It takes knowledge, to take such a risk."

"*Feng shui*? But..." Cassy's voice trailed off. He didn't know enough about it to argue. His knowledge didn't go beyond a vague awareness of some architectural New Age conceit that led rich yuppies into spending a lot of money to point their beds in the right direction. He needed information, and he needed it now.

"I will wait for your call." Ching had been speaking all along, Cassy realized, and hoped he hadn't missed anything. "If your reports are within reach, it will not take long."

"Oh god, god," Leo whispered, but the words were lost in the buzz of the dial tone as Ching hung up. Cass punched the phone off, turned his back, and jumped to Delgado's aid.

It took only a few minutes to confirm that five of seven victims had been moved after death. The left profiles of all seven victims had been aligned to face the sunset. The two who had been left to lay where they fell had fallen with their heads pointed south.

<hr />

Dark trees, a sunlit glade, the air of France. The painting was just the same. Nothing had changed.

Leo stared at it. *Beyond This Point Are Monsters*. This was the scene that had echoed a moment of timeless serenity, capturing in paint her own memory of peace under a distant sky. Yet something had happened here. Something had left an evil imprint so resonant, a scar so deep, that it had permeated her palette without her knowledge. Where, in this placid miracle of color and shape, did the heart of darkness live?

Leo was aware of the situation's irony. Hell, she'd spent the day sleeping in Delgado's bed because she was afraid to come home and sleep in her own. Exhaustion had sapped her courage; she'd been unwilling to return to this haunted painting, to discover why her beautiful fruit held poison. Now she was eager, challenged, unafraid. And why?

Because you don't want to think about Nemo, that's why. You don't want to deal with this geomancy thing. It was bad enough when he was just a dangerous fruitcake, and now you know there's a twisted logic to what he's doing, it's even worse. The painted monster is less scary than the one in the real world right now. How nuts do you have to be to kill people and align them with demons?

Wondering about it was pointless. She knew nothing about *feng shui*, except that the word *shui* meant water; she knew that because a beautiful Chinese model she had once worked with had borne that name, and had translated it for the studio. Leo considered that, even if she had known more, it wasn't her business. She couldn't justify using Cassy's problem as an excuse for not dealing with her own. And this was her own problem, no way around it.

Beyond This Point Are Monsters.

She stared at it, thinking that this was a new thing, a different thing, a first time. She'd never before had any reason to fear walking into anything she'd ever done. Now she was going to have to push herself, and hard. She took a deep breath, held it for a count of five, released it.

Beyond This Point Are Monsters.

Dark tree boles, stylized bark, knotholes; the color, thickened with oleopasto, gave the rough bumps a textured immediacy. Glimpses of a sky awash with merciless light. A glade on a gentle slope, running down to the privacy of shadowed forest.

She stared, waiting, beginning to be angry. Her foot itched, her skin felt hot and dry. Her eyes hurt with the effort to penetrate, to do what she had done effortlessly a hundred times before. She felt the tension in her muscles and knew she was expending a tremendous force. Something in the painting was blocking her, barring her entry, denying her. She tried furiously to relax her mind.

A crow, circling overhead. Small pyramids of stone, arranged in patterns of sacrifice. A deep, vicious chuckle, ultimate and dreadful in its happiness, its joy, its delight in whatever twisted agony it was causing...

Stop it, Leo. You're spooking yourself. This won't do. So just stop now.

She gave it one last try, putting every ounce of her formidable mental strength into the effort. Even as she sweated and yearned, she knew that whatever her first visit had unleashed within this forest glade was now stronger than she was. It had taken her memory and perverted it, body and soul. Spirit and sense reached for the life-colored cord and found only vacancy.

The painting was no longer hers, no longer the world she had remembered and made. It had passed into the control of the beast she had captured there. And the beast, her painted prisoner, had locked her out.

All right, you bastard. If this is the way you want it.

She got up slowly, her jaw clenched. Backing away, her eyes on the canvas, she fumbled in the knife rack on the butcher's block. Her fingers closed on a carving knife. The handle was smooth and chilly; the blade glinted wickedly.

Here it comes, bastard. Right here. Right now.

She approached the easel. With her left hand, she made certain that the adjustable lock on the easel's back support bar held the stretchers of the canvas firmly in place, unable to fall without taking the easel with it. Her right arm felt weightless, alive, detached from the rest of her body.

She raised the knife above her head and brought it slashing down. It connected, met resistance, triumphed. She heard the faint echoing drumbeat as the tautly stretched canvas shuddered with the impact.

Then it gave way.

The first stroke tore through the picture's upper edge, glancing off the stretchers and leaving a deep white gouge in the wood. The knife had ripped through sky and forest canopy, in a diagonal tear five inches long.

The light from the ceiling spots bathed Leo's face, highlighting the sweat on her cheekbones. If she had been able to see her own face, it might have prompted the ultimate self-portrait. She looked wild and beautiful, possessed, a primitive death mask brought to life.

Eat cold steel motherfucker, going baby going going gone...

The knife rose again, descended again. This time it sheared through two trees and the upper grass of the glade.

Steal my world, no way, ain't gonna happen uh-uh baby, let me introduce you to death you bastard you miserable no-good...

This time, she was answered.

Something, a sexless inhuman voice, screamed out. It formed no words, only a roaring inarticulate gurgle of hate and rage. Leo flinched, but she lifted her arm for another stroke. Was the voice in her mind, or had it come from the mutilated painting? She didn't know. She hoped it had come from the painting. She hoped that, if the cutting edge of that blade had touched the beast, the next stroke would cause it pain beyond imagining, slow death, disintegration.

Her third stroke was reasoned. Where would the chuckling monster stand? Where had the eyes watched from? Surely on flat ground; surely no one, however crazy, would opt for the chancy footing of a hillside.

She aimed for the heart of the glade, the center of the circle made by those invisible stone pyramids. Knife met canvas, and bit deep. She made her grip two-handed, adding strength and control; the weapon twisted, cutting a jagged abyss through the sunlit grass. The easel rocked with the force of her anger.

Come on, baby, dodge this one. Just try, you bastard, you crazy mother, you sadistic miserable...

The roar came again, high and shrill, a full-bodied scream with no indication, no clue at all, as to its source. It held pain, anger, defeat.

Leo's mouth stretched into a nightmare grin of triumph. Something ugly and dangerous, something with no business being there, was getting a taste of its own medicine. She felt like a brand of flaming justice. Her mind was full of violent burning light.

A fourth blow, a fifth. The tip of the knife caught a loose piece of canvas, lost it, sent it like a feather through the air.

The canvas shredded into nothingness.

The strength and power left Leo as suddenly as they had come, leaving her weak and empty. Her arms hung limply at her sides. The knife had slipped from her fingers. She stared at the easel.

The glade, the sky, the trees, were all gone. The wooden skeleton of the easel now framed only her comfortable studio, bizarrely adorned with flapping canvas strips. Of *Beyond This Point Are Monsters*, only silence remained. The studio floor was awash in tiny chips of paint, and the dangling strips looked like shredded bandages, loosely wrapped around a wounded soldier in a surrealistic war.

She bent and retrieved the knife. Slowly and carefully, she replaced it in its proper slot. Her eye caught a touch of color on the blade's edge; a mix of black and pthalo green, all that remained of a slaughtered tree trunk.

Pictures moved through Leo's mind. She saw herself years earlier, of her reaction to the damage done to the *Pieta*, and tried to understand why destroying a much-loved piece of her own work should cause her only satisfaction. She thought about Jim Delgado's body, of how a corner of her brain had detached far enough from physical passion to memorize the ripple of shoulder muscles. She thought of Joseph Ching, frail and aged, lying in a hospital bed. She remembered her frustration at not being able to identify the beast she had drawn long ago. Lastly, she thought of her own supernormal ability, of how she could paint what she wanted and then walk inside to explore it.

Something, a germ of an idea, had taken root; perhaps it had been there all along, waiting for the nutrient of suggestion. Now it sprouted, full-blown and complete. When Leo saw it and recognized where it led, she turned cold.

No. No way in hell. She couldn't do it.

Of course you can. The voice of reason spoke clearly. *You can't walk into those Nemo drawings because there's nothing to walk into. They're faces, just faces. But you could paint a scene, a nice harmless backdrop, and then paint Nemo into it. You could walk into that. Why not?*

"Because I can't." So strong, so persuasive, was the interior voice, that Leo spoke aloud in response. "Because I won't. This is stupid, this is a ridiculous idea. I just walked into a piece of work I *knew* was harmless. Look what happened. I can't deliberately walk into something where I know a killer is waiting."

Isn't that what you just did? All that happened was that you got the crap scared out of you. You weren't harmed, no big bad bogeyman came after you...

"That's not the point!" Her breath was harsh in her throat, her chest hurt. The invisible presence that was her courage and self-confidence was almost tangible in the quiet room, and she argued with herself for all she was worth. "I wasn't hurt because I got out fast enough! How do I know I won't walk in, get bopped over the head, choked with a nylon cord, snuffed out?"

Coward. You stupid worthless little coward.

"Damn it." Leo spoke dully, her eyes on the floor that was littered with flakes of dried paint. She was losing the battle with herself, and she knew it.

Damn this conscience of hers. Someday she was going to dump it, get rid of it. She might not be as nice a person after it was gone, but she'd sure as hell be more comfortable. *"Damn* it."

She gave it one last try. "How do I even know this crap will work? Huh? How do I know that?"

You don't know. But ask yourself this: Do you have any right not to try?

Chapter Nine

"I want to know why neither of you bothered to mention that Nemo might be using this *feng shui* stuff."

Cassy's voice was past the safe edge of anger; there was rage bubbling underneath. Inspectors Hsia and Takamita exchanged glances. While Takamita looked slightly amused, Hsia had outrage in his eye.

Cassy's anger was as undeserved as the question itself. The way they saw it, the lieutenant had called his two Asian inspectors on the carpet to indulge in a fit of racism. Neither of them expected this kind of behavior from their superior officer, and neither of them liked it.

"I'm waiting for an answer, gentlemen!"

The words were barked. Takamita cleared his throat, and replied with deceptive mildness.

"Well, Lieutenant, I can't answer for Rick. Speaking for myself, I didn't mention it because it never occurred to me."

Cassy's face was a study in mixed emotions. "What do you mean, it never occurred to you?"

"I mean that this *feng shui* thing is Chinese. Anyway, that's what Rick tells me. I wouldn't know. My name's Takamita, Lieutenant. I'm Japanese, not Chinese." He added, with stinging gentleness, "I know we all look alike, but we don't happen to come from the same culture. Sashimi and chow mein are *not* the same thing. I'm no more likely to have Chinese culture pop into my head than you are. You're black. Is voodoo the first thing you think of if something looks weird?"

Cassy, blinking, opened his mouth to reply. He was forestalled.

"And before you can ask me, maybe you'd better let me tell you." Rick Hsia's anger was less perfectly controlled than Takamita's. "All I know about that stuff is what anybody else might know, that's it's all about moving objects to attain the best balance in a place. Hell, pretty much all I really know was in some documentary about it, on one of the PBS networks. What the hell does that have to do with moving dead bodies around? And how the hell should I know that crap? I'm a fourth generation American, I was born in New York. My family have been bankers since the turn of the century. Bankers don't usually dance around in embroidered robes, waving a *luopan* over their heads and measuring for demons on Lexington Avenue like some kind of sorcerer. For that matter, neither does anyone else I know. Sorry to disappoint you."

The sarcasm was brutal. Fortunately, Cassy's innate sense of fairness asserted itself, and he grinned.

"Sorry, guys. I didn't mean to sound like the Ku Klux Klan. But for Christ's sake, help me out here, will you? I need to find someone who knows about the finer points of *feng shui* because what I know about it is diddly-squat, or maybe just what Rick said: moving things, not people. I thought it had to do with which way to point bookshelves and where to stick your back door, if you wanted your stuff to have good luck, or something. I sure as hell never heard anything about arranging dead people being any part of it. Here, sit down, both of you. Rick, you said you saw a documentary. What do you remember about it? And what's a *luopan*?"

Hsia and Takamita, sensible men, accepted both the seats and the apology. Takamita, now only an interested spectator, relaxed. Hsia glanced at him, then turned back to Cass, who had pulled out a notebook and pen.

"A *luopan* is the compass those guys use. The only reason that it stuck in my head was because one of my cousins, a Baptist minister, is named Lo Pan."

"Compass," Cass was writing furiously. "So it's actually about measuring directions? North, south, east and west?"

"I'm pretty sure there's more to it than that, and I don't think measuring is the main thing, at least not measuring numbers. I think, don't quote me, that it has to do with measuring aspects, directions, stuff like that. Measuring the best placements for whatever you need. Like I said, boss, I don't know crap about this stuff. Really."

"Man oh man," Cassy said plaintively. "I need help here. Rick, was there anything else in that documentary? I feel like a moron, way out of my depth."

"Well, let me think." Hsia searched his memory. "I know they won't even build a toilet in Hong Kong without consulting a geomancer first, and I'm pretty sure the wealthier Chinese immigrants in North America use them, too. It's used as an accessory to architecture, everything from office buildings to temples to schools. Even private homes."

"What about cemeteries?" Takamita asked quietly. "The way I see it, that's the main issue here."

There was a moment of silence. Then Hsia nodded. "Yes, cemeteries, too. They mentioned an island off the coast of Hong Kong, about how geomancers looked all over for the right place for a graveyard. They chose this island because it had something called good cosmic—shit, what was it? Right, good cosmic breath, and for Christ's sake don't ask me what cosmic breath is, because I don't have a clue. The point is, the mourners were willing to take boats to visit their dead relatives, rather than risk having their afterlives screwed up by bad luck. That's all I remember." He added apologetically, "The show wasn't specifically about *feng shui*. It was about Hong Kong culture in general."

"Every little bit helps. Just one more question." Cass sighed. "Who would I talk to about setting up an appointment with a sorcerer?"

"The Chinese Merchants Association," Hsia said at once. "They'll know if anyone does. Leave it to me." He could not restrain a correction. "And if I were you, I'd call him a geomancer, not a sorcerer. Whoever he is, he'll probably be pretty touchy on the subject."

When the two inspectors had gone, Cass leaned back in his chair and closed his eyes. His neck hurt, his shoulders were knotted, and his back felt like he hadn't stretched in years. Every muscle in his body was a guitar string tuned up one note too high for safety. What he needed was a good massage... .

"What you need," said Jim Delgado's voice from somewhere above Cassy's head, "is a good massage."

Cass opened his eyes. "You been reading my mail, pal? I was just thinking along those lines myself."

Delgado dropped into the chair vacated by Rick Hsia. He looked, unfairly, as if he'd slept ten uninterrupted hours. He was bright-eyed, energetic, and alert. Cass, who was trying to put his mixed feelings about Jim and Leo out of his mind, regarded him sourly.

"And we're both right, I do need a massage. On the other hand, you look like you just climbed off the table."

Or the butcher's block, Delgado thought, and his face twitched with a suppressed grin. Cassy's look got more sour than ever, and Delgado hastened to distract him.

"I stopped off at the gym on Ninth Street and worked out for half an hour. It helped burn off some stuff, and I don't mean calories. So what did Rick and David have to say about this *feng shui* thing? Anything useful?"

Cassy, glad to leave the uncertain ground of other people's relationships, promptly filled him in. Delgado listened, nodded, and choked down laughter at Cassy's request for an appointment with a sorcerer. When Cassy was through, Delgado nodded decisively.

"Sounds like the right move to me, boss. After all, if Nemo believes he's some kind of magician, we need to know what's going on in his head. It may not help us catch him, but it sure will help after we do."

"With the prosecution, you mean? God, I hope you're right. I hope there is a prosecution. I hope we do catch him. I *hope.*"

Cassy's voice was so flat, so dragged with hopelessness, that Delgado regarded him with dismay. While he hadn't been to mass in twenty years, Delgado had been raised a Catholic. He knew that this black despair, this belief that things were so hopeless that even God couldn't help out, was considered one of the big sins. There were other trouble signs as well; Cassy's hands, usually restless with non-stop motion, lay like dead things on his desk.

Not good, Delgado thought. Definitely not good. When the guy in charge succumbs to emotional defeatism, they were headed for trouble. If the media got their claws on it, the insinuations could get brutal. Someone was going to have to snap Cass out of it, and fast. He spoke bracingly.

"Of course we'll catch him! Why the hell shouldn't we?"

"Because they never caught Jack the Ripper." Cassy began to enumerate reasons in a dull, rhythmic monotone. "Because there's no sign at all that these women ever met this guy. Because a lone wolf with a screw loose is the toughest kind to catch. And because I have a nasty feeling that the only way we're going to get this son of a bitch is by pure dumb luck. Unless he makes a nursery school level mistake and starts leaving fingerprints all over the place, I don't think that all the investigation, all the technology, all the hard work in the world is going to nail him."

The voice held flashes of despairing anger. Delgado was glad to hear it; as far as he was concerned, it was a real improvement over what had preceded it.

"Cheer up, Cass. He may do just that. Besides, aren't you forgetting something?"

Cassy stared at him. "Such as?"

"Such as Joseph Ching."

Cassy's eyes came up, met Delgado's, and focused. "Joseph Ching? What about him?"

"Think it out. The Ling Ma killing? Done in broad daylight, with a pack of witnesses a half-block away. The Gabriel killing, he left a heel-print. He's getting a little more careless every time. I'm starting to wonder if he isn't daring us to catch him."

Cassy gave a wry grin. "You sound like you've been memorizing the psych reports."

"Hell, I haven't even read the latest psych reports. I don't have to. I haven't been a homicide cop for ten years without being able to tell when one of these babies reaches the I-am-God-you-can't-touch-me stage."

Cassy's eyes were alight. "You think so?"

"Damned straight I do. At the rate he's going, he'll probably hire a director and a full production crew when he decides to collect his next neck."

"You know," Chris Winter told his wife, "It would help if you'd put the camera down and give me some directions."

Chris and Meg Winter, of London, England, were on holiday. They had saved for this trip, argued over the itinerary, and agreed not to panic at driving on what they considered to be the wrong side of the road. They had checked into their Lombard Street motel on Monday afternoon. The eleven-hour flight had left them both disoriented and weary. Meg, who suffered from asthma, was particularly uncomfortable.

A good night's sleep, undisturbed even by reading the details of the latest Maternity Murder, restored them both. On Tuesday morning, they picked up their rental car, and were spending their first full day exploring San Francisco. They drove randomly at first, with no specific destination in mind, following the flow of traffic and the dictates of street signs, heading generally west.

Now, unexpectedly, Chris found himself driving up steep hills. The car passed huge mansions, stately trees, private gates. A brief flash of familiar orange towers and a sudden breathtaking expanse of blue-grey water was enough for him.

"Meg? Hello? Where are we, please?"

Meg, a disheveled map in her lap, lowered the expensive digital camcorder and regarded him. "According to the map, this area's called Sea Cliff. And very nice, too. Shall we stop?"

With a sigh of relief, Chris pulled the car over to the curb. "That's better," he said. "I can't believe anyone willingly drives in this town. How on earth do they cope with stop signs at the top of vertical streets? In fact, how does anyone build houses at angles like these?"

"I don't know. But I certainly couldn't do these hills walking, not with my asthma." Meg peered out the window, craning her neck at the street sign. "El Camino Del Mar. The street of the sea, and very well named, too. From the looks of things, I'd say we've fetched up in banker's heaven. Oh, Chris, isn't this beautiful?"

She was right; it was beautiful. The Golden Gate Bridge gleamed in the weak autumn sunlight, the ocean shone like gunmetal. While the smell of Old Money was annoying, Chris admitted that the natural grandeur of this wealthy enclave was lovely indeed.

As sometimes happens in happy marriages, Meg caught at his unspoken thought. "The houses absolutely reek of Ye Olde Money, don't they? It's like those advertisements in the Victorian newspapers: Gentleman's Residence, with Quality Fittings and Fixtures. Still, it would have been criminal to put a slum in the middle of this view."

"They wouldn't," Chris replied absently. "Simply never happen, love. Those with the biggest bank accounts got first crack at the scenery. Besides, no one deliberately sets out to build a slum, the Greater London Council notwithstanding. They just happen. What's the massive pile of greenery just ahead, love? Is it Golden Gate Park?"

"No." Meg had already checked the map. "It's something called the Golden Gate National Recreation Area. There seem to be all sorts of things in there, trails and picnic areas and whatnot. Want to explore?"

"If you think your asthma's up to it."

They went on foot. The air was clean, the views were wonderful, and the feeling in this part of town relaxed. Meg stretched out on the grass, languid and sleepy; Chris aimed the camcorder randomly. When the first wisps of fog drifted through the trees, Meg sat up and looked at her watch. It was after four; in another half-hour, darkness would fall.

Heads together, they studied the map. There was no reason to brave the hills and the rush hour traffic; the road through the Presidio would leave them within three minutes of their motel. There would also be more of those astonishing views of the ocean and the bridge.

Lincoln Way, running through the Presidio, is not for the timid. Though in good repair and offering reasonable visibility, the road is narrow, with a single lane in either direction. If you are caught behind a slow vehicle during peak traffic hours, you have two choices. You can sit behind it, or you can pull into one of the scenic rest-stop areas and enjoy the sights while waiting for traffic to ease up.

After three minutes behind a slow-moving diesel van, Meg was struggling for breath. Chris flipped his turn signal, waited for a break in traffic and mentally told the local ordinances regarding left turns to go to hell. With a punch of the gears and a violent wrench of the wheel, he cut across the oncoming southbound traffic with inches to spare and pulled into a designated area on the shoulder of the road. An outraged blare of horns followed their progress.

"*Voila*," he said virtuously. "We have achieved parking in the City by the Bay and lived to tell the tale. You can open your eyes now, love."

"Ha." Meg let her breath out, tensing as she felt her throat catch and protest, and reached for her inhaler. "I'm getting out of the car. I think I pulled every muscle in my body, just from clenching my teeth and trying not to choke to death on that exhaust. Now this is what I'd call a view. It's like being in some unexplored part of the world, isn't it?"

She was right. Despite the whir of traffic, the scree below was wild and devoid of people. An hour earlier, the hillside had swarmed with visitors. With darkness coming on and the fog moving inexorably inland, the effect was savage. The open places were ringed with trees and bound by water.

Chris went to the car, retrieved the camcorder, and grinned at his wife.

"Last of the light and last of the tape," he said. "We might as well make use of it. After all, you don't often get an effect like this in the middle of a major city!"

He lifted the viewfinder to eye level and focused the camera.

Moving water, sea birds flying low, the sparkle of lights as the evening traffic pushed into Marin County across the Golden Gate Bridge. Across the bay, ghostly in the thickening mist, the towering bulk of the Marin headlands. The hillside, the hiking trails that led down to the beaches below. The trees, green with the oncoming winter, here dense, there sparse. To the west, the sky was a vivid, bloodied color, heralding a spectacular sunset. A lone pelican caught an updraft and went straight up, then disappeared towards the horizon.

The camera moved from water to birds to bridge, noting them, recording them, imprinting them forever as a visual stimulant. It came down the hillside, swept the beach, moved up again. It rested on the trees less than fifty feet away, flickered, jerked back again.

"Chris?" Meg whispering. He had stiffened and sucked in his breath. "Chris? What?"

"I don't believe it." The camera was locked, the indicator light blinking, telling him that the light was failing. "God in heaven. It isn't possible, it can't be..."

"*Chris!*"

Two figures, just inside the perimeter of trees. A thin shape, compact and purposeful in motion, bending over. At its feet was a second figure. Chris, momentarily shocked out of the capacity for action, saw a pair of hiking boots. One foot twitched. Although it was impossible at that distance, Chris thought he heard a tiny whimpering moan.

Chris's fingers tightened around the camcorder. Without thought, one finger slid up until the tip rested on the zoom control. Suddenly the distance was gone, the figures leaping into prominence and a dreadful closeness.

The first figure held something in one hand, something thick and obviously heavy, apparently wrapped in fabric. It was slipped into one pocket, and the hand that had wielded it came out again. At this distance, it seemed to be empty. Yet the hand was clenched, obviously holding something.

The memory of printed words came into Chris's mind with a dreadful accuracy. He and Meg had read them together, sitting on the motel bed, staring at sketches of a monster: *The killer first stuns his victims from behind and then strangles them with what has been identified as transparent nylon cord.*

The camera held steady. It recorded the killer's hands, moving in a parody of mime, stretching something invisible, getting the tension right, preparing to use it. *What has been identified as transparent nylon cord...*

The hands jerked, once. The figure bent over.

Chris Winter came out of his trance. Shouting wildly, he shoved the camcorder at Meg. He was in excellent physical shape, and vaulted onto the steep scree without a second breath. Yelling, he slithered down the hill, straight at Captain Nemo and his eighth victim. The noise he made was followed by the crash of feet through the greenery as Nemo, understanding the situation, ran like a deer for safety and deep cover.

On the scenic overlook, Meg Winter ran to the side of the road. She, too, was shouting and pointing. After three or four endless minutes, a middle-aged man driving a Volvo made the hard turn into the space beside the Winters' rented car. By the time he had extricated himself from his car, the killer was gone.

Just inside the first trees, Chris Winter knelt beside a pregnant woman in hiking boots. She lay on her back, her belly protruding, her auburn hair damp. The lid of one brown eye was partially open, revealing a glazed, unseeing stare. There was no cord around her neck. It was clear and unmarked.

Trembling, his sides aching from the sprint down the hill, he reached out a finger and touched the side of her neck.

It was warm. A tiny pulse jumped erratically under his hand.

His shout reached the watchers on the road above.

"She's alive! She's still alive! For god's sake, somebody call the police and get a bloody ambulance!"

"This is Professor Walter Lum. Professor Lum is a certified architect and a practitioner of *feng shui.*"

Rick Hsia performed the introduction with the air of a conjurer pulling a rabbit out of a hat. His satisfaction was justified. Hsia had learned one thing about *feng shui* today; experts in the field were heavily in demand and most of them were booked solid, months in advance.

"Thanks for coming, Professor Lum. Have a seat."

Cass was confounded. Whatever he had envisioned a geomancer to be, Walter Lum did not fit the picture. Instead of the embroidered robes conjured up by Rick Hsia's annoyance that morning, the slim little man settling himself elegantly in the battered chair sported a three-piece business suit from the hand of a master tailor. The phantom shades of burning incense were replaced by a faint whiff of expensive aftershave. And the leather attaché case in Lum's lap, while larger than normal, was an attaché case nevertheless.

"You find me not what you expected?" The question held nothing but gentle amusement.

Cassy was surprised into an honest answer. "Sorry, I guess I do. When I asked Rick Hsia about *feng shui* this morning, he made a crack about embroidered robes and sorcerers. I guess the picture stuck in my head. Can we offer you some coffee, Professor Lum?"

"Thank you. May I ask what this is about, Lieutenant Chant? Are you considering having some building done?"

"No. Before we talk, Professor Lum, I'd like to specify that this conversation must be kept strictly confidential. Nothing to anyone about it, anyone at all. If word gets out to the press, all hell could break loose. Agreed?"

"Naturally." Lum smiled urbanely. His eyes, fixed on Cassy's face, were intelligent and aware. "All my clients are assured of that. Let's not beat around the bush, Lieutenant. This is Homicide, you're the man in charge, and you urgently need services not connected with building. Am I right in assuming that this has something to do with the Maternity Murders?"

"Yes, you are." Cassy took a deep breath. "I'll put my cards on the table, Professor Lum. It's like this. If you've seen the news, you already know there was a witness to the Ling Ma killing, an elderly Chinese man named Joseph Ching."

"Yes, I knew that."

"Last night he remembered a small detail; the killer had moved the victim so that her head was pointing south. The way Ching figured it, that must have been done for a good reason, or at least a reason important to the killer. There were witnesses and it was daylight and the killer didn't have much time. Ching suggested *feng shui*. When we went back and checked the other killings, we found that they'd all been moved to point south. Now, I don't know a lot about it; I mean, you can buy kits for this stuff at Pottery Barn, but I always thought it was about object, geography, furniture. Obviously, I was wrong."

"And that's why you requested my services. I see." He adjusted his chair slightly to make room for Hsia. "What exactly do you want to know from me?"

"First of all," Cass replied, "I'd like to know just what *feng shui* actually is. Rick, will you take notes?"

An hour later, both officers were reeling under the weight of new information. Lum answered every question put to him, and offered corollary information, with the calm precision of a schoolteacher.

He gave them the basic purpose and philosophy of *feng shui* in uncomplicated terminology. Cass had expected abstracts; Lum instead produced science and good, solid reasons. He was a fluent, interesting talker. Even the ancient concept, Lao Tze's belief that the space contained within the physical boundaries of a structure is more real than the structure itself, made sense.

When they asked for specifics, Lum got into his stride. He told them about *chi*, or cosmic breath, and explained how it is measured and its importance in selecting a site. He listed and explained the factors—location, foundation, surroundings, water source and orientation—that govern such sites. He detailed the use of *feng shui* in the construction of cemeteries, patiently repeating the smallest details. And, when they had absorbed all they could, he listened to case history and examined murder scene photos.

"Mr. Ching was right," he said soberly. "This is a perverted attempt at geomancy. It is basic to *feng shui* that the dead should be buried on a south-facing slope, with the dragon's crest for protection."

"The dragon's crest?"

"The profile of the burial site itself. It is vital in *feng shui*, a protection symbol for living and dead both. The presence of the dragon in all these pictures is apparent. That is why I am sure about your killer and his interest in geomancy." He tapped the pile of photos with a forefinger. "You know that the heads of these poor women were turned south. Now look at the terrain. All hilly, undulating, some with the profiles of buildings and some courtesy of Mother Nature. There is no doubt in my mind; the locations are deliberately chosen."

Hsia's brow was wrinkled. "But, Mr. Lum, you said the dead were supposed to be buried *facing* south. If the killer turned their heads to the south, then aren't they actually facing north? Isn't it backwards?"

"It is indeed." Lum nodded, an adult pleased at a bright child's awareness. "That is why I said the attempt was perverted. Your killer is trying to consign his victims to an eternity without rest. And since he can't manipulate the terrain or burial sites, he has chosen to manipulate the dead themselves."

Cassy found himself cold; this, after all, qualified as true malevolence, a killer controlling his victims even after death. "Would you say that this guy is an expert? I mean, a real expert? Or do you think he's just some whacked-out amateur playing with magic?"

"Oh, certainly not an expert. I think he plays with it in the way many western people play at astrology without knowing even how to read an ephemeris. I can give you my opinion, that he is probably Asian. The probability of a Caucasian being fascinated to such a degree is very small indeed, to my mind."

Cassy suddenly remembered his curiosity of this morning. "Rick here mentioned an instrument, a *luopan*. Can you tell me something about it?"

"I can do better than that." Lum opened the leather attaché case and pulled out a velvet-wrapped object about the size of a dinner plate. "This was my grandfather's; now it is mine. We have been geomancers and architects in my family for five generations. It is bronze, a hundred years old. The black and red are lacquer, the metal surrounding the dial is pure gold; the color represents celestial glory, a very favorable aspect. I happen to think it very beautiful."

"So do I." Holding the disc carefully with both hands, Cassy felt an odd sense of reverence. While some of the feeling came from the *luopan's* great age, he was aware that this decorated piece of metal was, in the true sense of the word, a power tool. Those qualified to use it measured for power, for spirit, for darkness and light of the natural world. Gently, lightly, he handed the compass to Hsia. As he sat back, the phone rang.

"Homicide, Chant speaking."

The voice on the other end was tight with excitement. "This is Sergeant White of the Military Police. I'm down at the Presidio. I think you ought to get your people out here pronto, and send someone over to St. Mary's Hospital. We've got a tourist couple from England, and they've got a tape of the Maternity Murders guy and an eyewitness account."

"*What?*" Cassy bellowed.

In the next room, three inspectors and Elena all jerked their heads. Hsia, who had been examining the *luopan*, nearly dropped it. Lum, his black eyes fixed on Cassy, sat very still. Cassy himself was unconscious of everything but Sergeant White's voice, racing breathlessly down the wire.

"Wait for it, sir, that's not the best part. When this tourist, his name is Winter, realized what was happening, he chased the killer down the hill, just off the Presidio. And he got there just in time."

"Are you saying—"

"She's alive, sir. Unconscious from the whack on the head and the paramedics tell me there may be a problem with shock-induced early labor, but she's alive."

Chapter Ten

Another nameless painting. Another ghost.

It sat on Leo's easel, seemingly harmless enough. At first glance, it was nothing more than a simple acrylic landscape with trees, so devoid of details as to be almost featureless. It was also dry, a fact which robbed Leo of any excuse to not finish it. The self-imposed necessity to complete it had given her uneasy dreams the night before.

She didn't want to finish it. She hadn't cried for fifteen years, but every time she thought about climbing into a canvas with a murderer, she felt the hot, tight sensation in her throat that meant tears waiting to fall.

The sketchbook that held her original work on Nemo lay on the floor beside the easel. Four times Leo had gathered all her courage. Four times she had taken the book in one hand and made to open it. And four times she had set it back down unopened, because her throat had closed up. She knew that if she looked at those pictures, she would cry. She hated this feeling, hated and resented it. Crying stripped her self-control away; tears were easy, and cheap, and unworthy of her. Right now, Leo hated Nemo more for exposing her weakness and making her face it, than she did for seven deaths.

Leo realized she needed outside support, a dose of courage from another source. Of course, the support would have to be given without the donor's knowledge; no one knew of her particular ability, and no one was going to. Still, secrecy was possible. It all depended on who she called.

She decided on Jim Delgado. Yes, she thought, Jim would be perfect. He amused her, stimulated her; besides, he asked no questions, even yesterday when he rightfully could have. And what the hell, if some good sex didn't key her up, nothing would.

Leo called Homicide, and was lucky enough to get him. The conversation was short, cheerful, and laced with a nice erotic undertone. The tone changed abruptly when Delgado told her that, if God was willing and the creek didn't rise, he'd be over shortly after six. With some amazement, Leo heard herself asking if they could go to his place instead. She was so surprised at herself that she didn't register how puzzled he sounded. In truth, he was very puzzled, not so much at her request but at the diffidence he'd sensed in her. Diffidence was not an attribute he associated with Leo Chant.

She hadn't realized that she didn't want anyone in the studio until her experiment was over until Jim's assumption that he was coming over. His impression of diffidence had been correct; Leo rarely asked favors, and she wasn't used to relinquishing control of a situation. She put the phone down, realizing how close to the bone her discomfort had gone; her hands were damp, leaving a patch on the phone. *Jesus,* she thought, *this is nuts. Just how spooked am I, anyway? Jim must have thought I was losing it.*

But he'd accepted it, neither probing nor prying. Yet more points in the "yes" column for Jim Delgado.

Now that escape was arranged, Leo was able to consider what lay ahead. She glanced at the unfinished painting. It was an unusual style for her, a hybrid of impressionism and surrealism. While the colors were true, the forms were nonspecific blocks of darkness, elementary suggestions of hills that cast no shadows. Try as she would to see why she had avoided realism, she couldn't find the justification.

A mechanical decision, that acrylic paint would dry too quickly to make its use feasible, was reached, accepted, and mentally filed away. It would have to be oils; ink would never stick to the acrylic. And just why had she backed off from any suggestion of realism in the background, anyway?

A surge of impatience shook her. What was the point of going over it now, when eyes and brain and feelings were all locked up? More hedging; another waste of time and energy.

She turned the painting backwards and went to get her mail. Riffling through it quickly, she kept two bills and a notice of an upcoming show at a downtown gallery, and tossed the rest of the pile into the recycling bin.

She checked the clock. She had plenty of time to soak in the tub, do a little necessary housecleaning, and decide what to wear tonight.

At five o'clock, as she was hunting through drawers in search of a misplaced scarf, the phone rang.

"Leo? Jim. The date's off." He was taut with concentration. "Nemo tried it again, over at the Presidio. This may be an all-nighter. Looks like the damned creek rose after all. I'm sorry."

"Don't be an idiot." Her heart was suddenly making noises somewhere inside her. "What do you mean, he *tried* it again? Didn't he succeed?"

"Not this time." Savage satisfaction echoed down the line. "The bastard was interrupted. Some English guy and his wife, tourists, saw the whole thing, and they chased Nemo away before he could wrap his cord around her neck. She's over at St. Mary's, still unconscious and maybe going into premature labor, but alive. The Presidio cops are bringing the tourists who filmed it down here, for Cassy to talk to."

"Filmed it? Jesus, Jim! You mean they got Nemo on a camcorder?"

"That's it. This could break the case wide open. And if this Morisco woman makes it, she's going to be—"

"Who did you say?"

"Morisco. Her name is Carla Morisco." There was a subtle change in Delgado's voice; it took on the intent note of a man on the job. "Do you recognize the name, Leo?"

"I know her." Leo's voice shook. "She's a painter, kind of a friend of mine. We did a show together at the Kepple Gallery, about ten months ago. I was thinking about her the other day, thinking that I hadn't seen her for a while and wondering what she'd been up to. I didn't even know she was pregnant. Jim, I don't know how to deal with this. This is too strange. Should I...can I see her?"

"Not yet." He spoke gently. "We're not sure she's going to make it. Nemo gave her a conk on the head, hairline fracture and concussion. He must be one strong bastard, not too surprising—crazy and strong go together sometimes. It looks like they're going to have to do a c-section, and the baby probably won't pull through. If she makes it, I'll try to arrange for you to see her. For now, all you can do is sit tight and let us all do our jobs. Cass will want to ask you about her, probably not tonight, but you never know. So stay home or let us know where we can reach you. Okay, honey?"

"Okay."

"Excellent woman." He hesitated, so briefly that the pause was scarcely noticeable. "You know something? I have this crackpot little idea that I might just be in love with you. Gotta go, 'bye."

The phone went dead.

Leo replaced the receiver. Thoughts, impressions, and memories jostled together in her mind. Delgado's last words, while not ignored, were forcibly pushed back; there were other things demanding the full capacity of her feelings.

Foremost was the fact itself, that a woman she knew had been targeted. She'd been hit over the head. If this tourist couple hadn't been there, she would have been choked to death with a nylon cord. Her body would have been found, wet from the fog, cold, with all the life stolen from it. No more paintings, no more lovers or sorrows, no more giggling with friends over spiced cider at the local cafe. Nothing. Just—dead.

Carla Morisco would have been no more than a shell, an object, a thing. Its head would have been turned to the south. *It.* No longer she; it. A woman Leo knew.

The sudden glow of the overhead lights startled her; she had switched them on without thinking. She was certainly thinking now. Rage was forming in her stomach, sour and nourishing. She turned the landscape to face the room, laid out her palette and opened the sketchbook. Nemo stared up at her, evil and twisted.

"You bastard," she told the drawing softly. "You crazy bastard. Bad move, real bad move. You just messed with a friend of mine. It's show time, crazy man. I'm gonna paint you in, and then I'm gonna take you out."

<hr>

Cassy's feelings were not so clear.

He sat at his desk at the Hall of Justice, facing Chris and Meg Winter. Delgado, in a chair at one side of the desk, was a soothing presence.

No one could mistake this for anything but a critical moment in a critical situation. If the naked tension crackling in the air was not enough, the innocuous DVD on his desk, made from the download of the digital images on the Winters' camcorder, was a silent reminder.

And Cassy, the man in charge, could not sort out his own reactions. He should have been pleased, perhaps jubilant. After all, he'd been handed a survivor, given a crucial piece of evidence, and one that could break the case wide open. Until Delgado had reported on his conversation with Leo, he had felt nothing but exhilaration.

The discovery that Carla Morisco was a friend of Leo's changed the situation. Why he should feel that this fact slanted everything to a dreadful closeness, bringing it right to the Chant family doorstep, was a mystery. Yet he couldn't get away from it; he felt invaded, soiled, powerless. It was as if Carla Morisco had been attacked on his property.

He'd talk to Leo, of course, get her down here and find out if she knew who the baby's father might be. But that information was unlikely to have an impact on the case itself; if Morisco was simply one of the series, the baby's father was out of it as a suspect. And right now, Cass had other things on his plate.

Homicide, which at this hour should have been staffed by two inspectors, was as crowded as an airport lounge. Hsia was still there, talking with Takamita; Elena remained at her desk because, she had explained to Cassy, something else might come up. Shansky and Soufriere, the two inspectors whose normal duty fell that evening, had arrived and were feverishly catching up on details. Anne Rubens had breezed in, told Cassy that she thought an extra presence might be a good idea, and got busy. And of course Delgado was still there, his mind completely on the job.

"Is that poor woman all right, Lieutenant?"

Meg Winter was still very pale, but she had improved drastically during the past two hours. When the first city police had arrived, she had been gasping for breath and unable to speak without choking and crying. Her husband was a different story; Chris had grimly stood guard over Carla Morisco, draping his jacket over her, taking her pulse. He reminded Cassy of a cat guarding an injured kitten, refusing to let anyone near it until he was assured that they were qualified and entitled to do so.

They answered every question put to them, explaining Meg's asthma, their decision to pull over, their jet lag, their feelings about the scenery. Chris even remembered to tell Delgado that the camcorder was a European model, which meant that the digital data would need to be put through a PAL-compatible format converter before the crucial tape could be made for viewing on American equipment.

Cassy knew he'd been lucky with witnesses in this case, first with Joseph Ching, now with this couple. They were smart, plausible, sensible. They could be asked almost anything, and any jury in the world would believe them. But, seeing the anger in Chris Winter's eyes and hearing his wife's still-ragged breaths, Cassy walked lightly just the same.

The news that Carla Morisco was going to pull through came from St. Mary's Hospital shortly before seven. Meg burst into tears of relief, while Chris visibly relaxed in every muscle. The Homicide detail, who had been treating their star witnesses with kid gloves while trying to hide their own anxiety, relaxed too.

Meg's question came after an update from the hospital. Carla Morisco's life signs were stable, the contractions had ceased, and the monitors showed the baby's heartbeat going strong and true. They would continue to give Lieutenant Chant hourly reports, but they expected no complications. Short of a bolt from the blue, Carla Morisco would pull through, and her baby with her.

Cassy relayed this to Meg Winter. "Apparently she's doing even better than we hoped for, Mrs. Winter. As far as they can tell, even the baby is okay." He smiled. "And we know just who we have to thank for it, believe you me. You two are superstars. Not too many people would have—"

"Rubbish." Chris spoke crisply. "I'm sorry, but that's simply not true. Most people would have, because they couldn't help it. That's not heroism, it's instinct. I'm afraid we don't deserve this high praise, as nice as it is. You might as well congratulate a hay fever patient for sneezing."

He was so clearly not fishing for a compliment that Delgado laughed. "Maybe so, Mr. Winter. But you two are going to be the toast of the town while you're here." He exchanged a look with Cassy. "Speaking of which..."

"We'll have to come back, when you arrest him?" This came from Meg. "Of course. But I'm afraid I won't be very useful. I only saw him at a distance, you know. Chris was the one holding the camcorder."

"And I don't know how useful I'll be," Chris added. "I got more of an impression than a solid look. Still, a few things did strike me. If you think that would help..."

"Anything you can give us would help, Mr. Winter."

"Well, I can tell you this. He wasn't a big bloke."

A glance passed between Cassy and Delgado. That tallied not only with Joseph Ching's opinion, but with the footprint found near Theresa Gabriel. It had been a small size for a man. Of course, now that they were fairly sure of Nemo's ancestry, it made sense; Asian men are often compactly built.

"And he wasn't an older man, either." Chris had caught that glance. "I doubt he was much past thirty."

"Really?" Cass thought that Chris Winter had sounded very sure. "Why do you say that?"

"It was his reflexes. The way he jerked his shoulders, the way his head turned, the way he ran. An older person slows down a bit, don't they? The human body won't do at forty what it did at thirty, at least not as smoothly."

"Hell, my body won't do what it did last week." Cassy saw a faint smile on Meg Winter's face. "You don't have to convince me, Mr. Winter. I'm already convinced."

"Even though I only saw his back?"

"No," Cassy said slowly. "Because you only saw his back. You can disguise a human face with makeup or with a mask, even with a hat, if you pull the brim down. That's how Hollywood gets rich. But the human back is almost impossible to disguise. It's as individual as a fingerprint."

"He's right, Chris." Meg nodded. "Once or twice I've seen men with your coloring coming toward me and thought they were you until they got close. But I could pick your back and shoulders out of any crowd. It must be something about muscles and motion."

"Right." Chris was thoughtful. "I suppose the only way to hide it would be to disguise one's walk. And this murdering lunatic certainly wasn't doing that. He was too busy running for his life."

"Tell me something," Delgado said suddenly. "I'm curious. What would you have done if you caught him?"

"No clue, Inspector." Winter had obviously given this question some thought. "I've never been in a situation like this, so I have no reference point. I'm a complete coward, and I don't suppose yelling at him to stop would have been very useful." His jaw tightened. "I'll tell you one thing, though. I should never have let him get away. I'll never forgive myself for that."

"Don't feel bad, Mr. Winter," Cassy told him gently. "You did just fine.

Now, if we can go over the sequence of events again?"

It was after ten when the Winters were sent back to their motel. Cassy stretched until his joints cracked, yawned, and let his eyes settle on Delgado.

"Jim," he said tiredly, "this DVD here. Is this the transferred copy? Is it ready to roll?"

"It's the transfer. Takamita had it done two hours ago. Five extra copies, too, for the local stations. Do you want them sent out for broadcast?"

"Not until we've seen it ourselves. Have we got the original data? What did you do with their camera?"

"Impounded as evidence," Jim said, and just managed not to blurt out the surprised "naturally" that wanted to follow. He added carefully, "Just following the standard procedure, Lieutenant. I don't think the Winters minded. You gave them a loaner. Oh, by the way, I almost forgot. Your mother called a few hours ago. She said to tell you that Mara's over at her house, and will spend the night there."

"Good." Cassy reached out and touched the case. "Looks like we need a DVD player."

"It's next door, in the inspector's room. Elena called for one, and they brought the TV up from the press room. It's next to Elena's desk. You want me to hook it all up?"

"Yeah. Ask Elena if she's got some popcorn. The department's going to watch ourselves a movie."

As night wore on towards morning, the monster took shape on Leo's easel.

If the background had been slapped on thoughtlessly, the mask of the beast was handled very differently. From Leo's earliest years, she had worked at whatever tempo felt right at the moment. A massive painting with many themes might be completed in a week if the function so demanded; a miniature might take twice as long, for the same reason. Mostly she tended to work quickly, letting the painting dictate the pitch. On those occasions when she slowed down, it was because a single detail had cried out to her, demanding her attention; the glaze on a model's hair, the bloom on a peach.

She had never before worked as slowly as this, certainly never for this reason. Every curve, every line, every pore of Nemo's face was a cold-blooded exercise of realism and precision. There was no creativity in this work, and Leo knew it. She was not painting to achieve the idealization of her own inspiration, but the virtual representation of a chimera. It was something living, something reeking of death, that must be confronted and killed. If a chimera was a mythical thing, a formless fear, then this chimera broke the rules. Leo understood this. On a hidden level of creativity, she knew that she would have to break a few rules of her own in order to meet this monster face to face.

So she worked through the night, slowly but steadily, and the face solidified inch by frightening inch.

There were snags, of course. Sometimes her hand wanted to hurry, to change, to put something of the artist into the work in progress. At those times Leo stopped, stepping away and turning her back, gulping down water and waiting until the creative fret had burned itself out. Sometimes she stepped back and took up her sketchbook, forcing herself to coldly compare the old with the new. This was difficult, for she had never been purely a copyist; her talent and vision were too strong to allow her the graphic impartiality of a photographer's eye.

The night wore on, and the hard self-control never wavered. She forgot her own fatigue, reaching a level of exhaustion in which hand moved almost independently of eye and mind. The precision she was struggling so hard to achieve had become automatic.

Toward morning, the dense fog outdoors became a chilly drizzle. Making coffee, stretching her stiff limbs, Leo heard birdsong and glanced at the clock. It was after six.

"Another night gone," she told the empty room. "Another all-night power party with the paint gods. Jesus. Leo Chant, creature of the night. Too much more of this and I'm going to turn into a vampire. Pass the B-positive."

The bird called again, sounding dispirited and forlorn. Its damp, miserable chirping was drowned out by the whistle of the kettle. Leo poured water, inhaling the fragrant steam of the coffee, thinking of sleep and paint and the face of the unknown.

Had she been more awake, she might have agonized over the decision: to sleep or to hunt? In this rarified state of weariness, it seemed no choice at all. She had worked through the night under the compulsion of a primitive rage. To turn her back on it now, to reach for the trappings of daylight and normalcy, would be to deny what she had just done. Exhaustion had not drained her of anger or the sense of power she felt; it had merely focused it, made it easier to handle, a tool to her purpose.

She drank her coffee slowly, not procrastinating, merely savoring the rich acidic taste of it. She finished the cup and made another. When the second cup was empty, she went to the bathroom and came back to her easel.

Without reluctance, she fastened her eyes on Nemo's twisting lips. They were a peculiar color, she thought, bloodless and pale. She did not touch it; oil, unlike acrylic, stays wet a long time.

She settled in the chair, her eyes on the painting. Her mind was moving, twisting, holding her in place. With a sudden jolt under her diaphragm, she wondered whether this would do any good at all. Suppose she did make it in; suppose Nemo was there. What could she do? Killing a picture wasn't killing a killer. She might keep last night's promise to the chimera, painting it only to destroy it, but to what end? Was the whole concept just voodoo symbolism, self-satisfaction? Or was it possible to actually achieve an execution in flesh by executing the fetish?

Of course it's possible. I did it before, in Beyond This Point Are Monsters. I heard the bastard screaming his sick-assed perverted head off when I slashed the painting. What I did once, I can do again.

That the death of the painted beast might not affect the living beast didn't matter; the thought was comforting, reassuring. It removed some of the pressure from her conscious mind. She let her awareness slip, relaxing, knowing that concentration on a distracting factor would keep her in the real world. Another thought, amusing, edged that real world even farther away.

Transference as art. Ain't that a major-league boot in the ass? All these years I've been practicing voodoo and never realized...

Hills, trees, blocked-in color. A bland, harmless sky. Soft puffy clouds, scudding in the landscape's unseen breeze. In the foreground a devil, obsessed with a magic no one else believed in. The skin was a smooth miraculous map, showing no blemish, hiding an infinity of them. The eyes were slitted and black, almond-shaped, long and deep and...

Leo drifted, let go, easing painlessly out of her body. The life-cord solidified under her mind's questing fingers. She touched it, reassured, and held it. The painting beckoned, flirting with its maker.

Light as a bird's wing, she moved toward it. Her spirit was composed of a thousand iridescent muscles, each working with supernatural precision; a mental knee bending, a mental neck stretching. The essence of Leo Chant climbed into the painting like a homeowner who has misplaced her keys climbing through an open window.

The painting came up and closed around her with a rush of claustrophobia. She mastered it, taking control of herself and of the situation. She had made this place, with its undefined skyline of hills. It was her place, her child, her world of the moment. There was nothing to fear.

It took only a moment of this immeasurable time to comprehend her own ease, her total lack of danger. There was, indeed, nothing at all to fear; this place was empty, uninhabited. No birds sang in these painted trees, no grass grew on the hillsides, no streams absorbed the morning sun. The only life was her own. She had failed.

Nemo was not here, had never been here. Leo was alone in a dead place, alone with some uninspired shapes and a rainbow of dried paint.

Disappointment took her like a cramp in her stomach, bitter and intolerable. For a moment, the primal rage that had spurred her to try coursed through her emotional circuitry. *Come on, you son of a bitch,* she thought savagely, *come and get me. I dare you. I know you're out there somewhere. And I want you dead.*

She concentrated her feelings, offering herself as a magnet, asserting her will. The effort was pointless; if the monster had been there, she would have known. There was no disturbance, no response. The emptiness was absolute. Yet she waited, giving it time, her spirit probing the nameless place while her fingers held tightly to the life-cord.

Nothing came, nothing moved. This world was barren.

She came back to corporeal reality without effort, her body waiting and quiescent in its chair. The cord flickered into a shower of light, faded and died. She was Leo Chant, back inside herself, staring with wet cheeks at a voodoo fetish which hadn't worked after all.

The dislocation which always resulted from these forays was absent this time; there was not even the usual numbness from sitting too long in one place. Leo got to her feet and approached the painting. Her eyes, burning with lack of sleep, were fixed on Nemo. The creature stared back at her, mad and passionless and somehow smug.

Blew it blew it blew it all to hell and gone.

"Now what?" Leo's whisper met the surface of the paint and dissipated. There had been no force to the question, no strength behind it, not even the urgency of despair. She was played out, spent, wandering in the middle of nowhere. "Now what the hell do I do?"

Blew it screwed it up blew it yeah right.

Nemo's eyes watched her, offering no answers. Leo thought that she'd never been so limp, so devoid of purpose, in all her life. She felt like a balloon with the air let out of it. *I need some help,* she thought bleakly. *I need inspiration. And I sure won't get it standing here.*

After a moment of indecision, she turned her back on the easel and wandered to where her jacket hung. She was so drained of energy that it took all the strength left in her body merely to open and close her front door. Even the blast of cool morning air against her face could not shock her back to awareness.

From the monster on the easel, painted as are all good portraits to face its maker, Nemo's long dark eyes seemed to follow her as she went.

Chapter Eleven

Too close too close too close...

The chimera sat upright in a hard-backed chair, this fierce tiny litany monotonously looping as a silent litany. The chair was the only one in the apartment, and came with the rent. Nemo inhabited a furnished studio, faceless and without personality, a *tabula rasa*. Every city offers such places, small blank caverns waiting for a temporary occupant to come and impress himself, however briefly, on the walls and floors.

Nemo had not done so. Only a master of psychic reality or an expert in forensics could have told who, or what, had taken up this plain dull space: dead skin cells, strands of hair, the microscopic detritus of humanity.

Too close too close too close...

The chimera was a creature of instinct. Tonight, however, something had pierced the malformation of its remaining human senses and was making itself known. It demanded the chimera's attention. While normal feeling had long since burned itself away, surprise was still an option. Diverted, vaguely interested, the chimera figuratively raised its head and examined this phenomenon.

What had happened tonight, after all? A failure, the first of its kind. A physical interruption by one of the faceless, the herd, the Walking Alive. The chimera blinked.

The word itself, failure, was explored with a chilly surprise. It *was* a failure; any way the situation was approached, it represented incompletion. If the chosen woman, the chosen child, had lived, that was failure. There would be two less now in that blackly magical land of eternal sleeplessness, two who had escaped the alchemist's noose. Besides, the woman had dared to defy her own destiny, and moreover had succeeded, and the child with her. Surely, a failure.

And even if one or both had died, that was still failure. Ever since the pounding feet and the shouting on the hillside, Nemo had been trying to remember which way the woman had fallen. But memory was elusive, refusing to be pinned down. All Nemo could remember was the fact, the gray-shot reality, of interruption and incompletion. It added up to one thing only: Dead or alive, this woman was failure, and the pattern had been disrupted.

Too close too close...

Twice, now. It had happened twice, the eyes of the Others, the Walking Alive, finding a sorcery in action and seeing it, seeking to interrupt. Something was badly wrong there. Nemo believed with perfect conviction that the act, the performance of that sorcery, was invisible to those who did not believe and thus could not do. The seeing was the power source, wasn't it? And the doing was the power itself?

But the Walking Alive had seen, and it was twice now. The old man in the misty morning, he had seen, and so had those others in the heavy shoes, who carried food in crates. And again today, the owner of those pounding feet, that shouting incoherent voice.

There was no fear of capture in Nemo, and no anger. Nor did the monster desire revenge; there was merely a mental shrug, terrifying in its indication of omnipotence. If they had interfered, sought to taint the ritual of necromancy, they would be punished. It was not Nemo's concern to punish them. Their punishment would merely happen. This, too, the chimera believed.

Too close too close...

Nemo sat the hours of darkness away, eyes wide, the words running in a power loop behind its eyes. There was nothing else there, nothing to distract it; its concentration was total, both visceral and cerebral.

Perhaps this was why, when someone in another place sought to control it with a sorcery of a different kind, the monster knew it. For this was the root, the genesis, of Nemo's dark kingdom; this beast was not without power.

The knowledge that someone was attempting a magic of their own came suddenly, solidly, in a form beyond logic or argument. It was nearly daylight when Nemo blinked once, violently, and jerked against the wooden support of the chair. Its eyes widened with interest; if the attempts of the Others to snare a god of the night with rationalism bored it, sorcery could still capture its deranged attention. The chimera, after all, was also a necromancer.

So it looked into space, trying to see. The feelings came in a barrage, confused, multiple, impossible to ignore. Some of those feelings were surprisingly powerful. The strongest and most defined was hatred, a concentrated loathing aimed straight at it. For a moment, the chimera flinched away. Then the cold core of its ego and power regained control and pushed the hatred away.

Finally, just as the chimera thought the barrage had ended, there was something else: a pull, a tug, psychic fingers trying to yank Nemo into its domain in an attempt so determined that Nemo could actually see the vague outline of the magician at the other end. Female, angry, a burning psychic interior.

For a moment it hung on a thread, the nameless Other commanding, Nemo resisting. In a microsecond of real time Nemo felt the command, the control, the power on the other side. Then it was over, as the Other conceded the round.

It would not stop here, and Nemo knew it. There was a cold determination behind the Other's shadow, a concentration and focus, and a will as strong as Nemo's own.

For many hours after, Nemo sat motionless, sending out psychic antennae, trying to locate and identify, to put a name to the offender. The chimera had recognized the Other as someone once before encountered, someone with power, someone formidable. The adversary's essence, its physical reality, was definitely familiar. Here was a sorcerer, eager for battle. And whoever the sorcerer was, she would be back.

Too close too close not close enough...

The morning was firmly established as a new day when Nemo stirred from the hard-backed chair. The situation had been considered, and a decision reached.

Whatever power the Other was using, it was inferior to Nemo's own. There was no threat to Nemo there, only another potential shadow puppet in the chimera's playpen.

This Other, with her staggering impudence, would learn that Nemo was not to be controlled. She would learn it the hard way. When she returned for another try, Nemo would be ready and waiting.

Cass had spent the night at his desk in the Hall of Justice, trying to capture an elusive ghost in the shredded nets of his memory.

The DVD was still in the player. Since the Homicide squad had watched it the previous night, Cass had been deep in a private screening of his own. He had run the pertinent section many times, at normal speed and in slow motion. He had played it frame by frame, freezing it, trying to focus on the fleeting, tantalizing shape among the trees. He had wracked his brains, pushing his memory until his mind refused to function.

All this work, this tortuous concentration, sprang from one simple fact: Leo had been right. She had seen Nemo before, and Cass had seen him, too. And he couldn't for the life of him remember where.

The puzzlement, the frustration of recognition, had begun with the group viewing. With his subordinates, he had stared through Chris Winter's eyes at the Marin headlands, the churning waters moving beneath the Golden Gate, the scrubby ground cover of plants that bristled across the hills. He had seen the trees, slightly denuded of their usual greenery by the rigors of the season. He had watched the dreadful activities below, the feet protruding from between those trunks, the thin back of a shadow in black.

The squad had jumped as the zoom lens clicked into gear, pulling the nightmare too close; they had all shared Chris Winter's horror, sucking in their breath as the viewfinder recorded the dizzying shift in perspective as Chris had shoved the camcorder into his wife's hands and tumbled, shouting, down the scree.

When the tape was through, the group was so stunned that no one noticed Elena turning the lights on. Delgado, recovering first, glanced around at the appalled faces and reflected that, whatever capacities time may blunt, the human capacity for amazement was infinite. Every person in the room was a professional who dealt with murder every working day, and every person, Delgado thought grimly, looked as though they'd been hit over the head with a baseball bat. No matter how spontaneous the digital age had made the everyday world, the sight of a hunter bending over human prey was still rare enough to shock.

The silence stretched out too long, threatening to become unnerving. Delgado cleared his throat. "Well," he said quietly, "there he is, folks, the Maternity Murderer, appearing live in your living rooms, fresh from a previous engagement in Chinatown, San Francisco."

"That's not funny." The elegant Detective Rubens shook herself like a dog coming out of deep water. "I know, I know, it's not supposed to be, but really. Jesus wept, was that real? Did we actually just see that?"

"I feel sick." Elena's skin had gone the color of dirty ash. "I think I'm going to—I have to go—excuse me—"

She made a noise in her throat; then, a hand to her mouth, she fled. Hsia and Takamita, both clearly unsettled, stared at Cass as if waiting for a command that would make the reeling universe right itself.

And Cass, the leader, steadfastly predictable, was unable to react or even think. Bewilderment, anger, and above all the cold recognition of some truth beyond his own endurance, had wrapped him in a cocoon of blankness. Water, he thought dimly, water and trees, hiking shoes, heavy socks, a back in black.

A back in black...

He had seen that back before. Hours earlier, he had told Chris Winter that the human back is virtually impossible to disguise, and Meg Winter had agreed with him. They had both been right. He knew those movements, that jerk of the left shoulder that came when Nemo was startled, the momentary stillness that was like an animal caught in the glare of headlights. All of it was known, familiar, infuriatingly distant. He knew the shell, but the label would not come.

And Cass, the man responsible for acting on the evidence, was immobile, paralyzed, unable to cope. He blinked, swallowed, and knew that, if he was going to deal with the situation, he would have to do it alone. He was aware of a single desire: to empty the place of distracting presences, and concentrate.

His head was pounding, threatening to explode, and his chest seemed wrapped in bands of steel. He ignored the coldness in his stomach, the intuition that the answer he'd looked for so hard was one he might not be able to live with. He couldn't discuss those formless feelings with the group, not yet.

"Lieutenant?" Hsia exchanged a troubled look with Anne Rubens. "You want us to make copies for the networks? And what about scream capture prints, hard copy, for the papers? They'll be yelling for them."

"No." Every word was a lump of ice. "We can deal with that crap in the morning. Right now I want you all to go home. I need...I need to do some thinking. Home. Go. Everyone out."

"Say what?" Takamita was gaping at him. "But—I mean, that's— department regulations say we can't—what about Shansky, Soufriere, they're on duty—"

"Goddamn it, no!" Cass heard his own voice spiral out of control, and swallowed hard. Oh Christ, he thought, I'm going to have hysterics. It was the last thing he needed. What the hell is wrong with me? "No, everyone's relieved, as of right now. On my order, my authority. Go on home, all of you. If I need help, I'll call. Good night."

His tone forbade argument. The group left in silence, a silence which would be shattered by a flurry of furious discussion the moment Cass was out of earshot.

Delgado was the last to go, and he left alone. He, too, had been infected with Cassy's premonition of something very wrong; in Delgado's case, however, he knew the cause. For a split second, in his superior's rigid face, he had seen the echo of his sister's expression. It had taken only a moment to remember when he'd caught that look on Leo's face. It was at Joseph Ching's bedside, at her recognition that Nemo was someone she'd seen before.

He shot his superior officer a single considering glance, and went silently out into the night.

Cass, left alone, sat quietly for some minutes. He found that he was trembling, bit his lip hard, and waited for his hands to steady. Then he picked up the remote and began the longest night of his life.

He started by watching the scene on the cliffs all the way through. After the first time, having oriented himself, he rewound it and began all over again; this second pass gave him a sense of timing, of color, of settings. A third time helped him step into causes and effects. After that, the scene having become as familiar as a television rerun, he watched it through in slow motion, once, twice, three more times. Then again, twice, at normal speed. Two more times at a snail's pace. Now, the events on the hillside firmly imprinted on his memory, he began to dissect it.

Forward, forward, freeze.

He clicked the remote's pause button, focusing on the first indication that something unusual was happening. Carla Morisco's foot, in its sensible hiking shoe, protruded from between the trunks. He could see the thick sock, the bottom of a pair of jeans tucked neatly inside the sock. The leg, in fact, was visible nearly to the knee.

Forward, slowly forward, freeze.

Nemo's first appearance. It was like some cheap, crappy Hollywood B-movie, Cass thought bitterly; the damned thing was almost too theatrical. Enter the murderer, stage left; bring the camera in for a tight shot, a close-up.

He slowed the replay to a crawl, keeping his eyes on Nemo, watching the movements of shoulder and back, memorizing the way the hands moved, the knees bent. That achieved, he backed it up and ran it through at normal speed once more.

For the first time that night, he became aware of sounds coming from the television. Up until now, the visuals had so absorbed him that his ears had turned off in sympathy. The camera was a top-of-the-line model, and it had a powerful microphone. It seemed to have picked up everything within a sizeable radius. The traffic noise from Lincoln Way was steady and soothing, its dim indistinguishable humming broken by the occasional blare of a car horn. Another sound took a moment to identify as the timeless hush of the Pacific Ocean, slipping under the Golden Gate. Cass, concentrating, could even make out an irregular wheeze that sounded like a kitten's mew. After a moment, he realized that it was Meg Winter's asthmatic breathing.

The only thing left in silence was the act itself, the tableau taking place under cover of trees and coming darkness. The noiseless presentation of murder was both fitting and horrific. He backed up and began again, this time in slow motion.

Forward, forward, freeze.

Nemo, still and poised as a stalking lion, the thin back showing awareness of impending danger. Where in hell had he seen that precise motion before, *where*? Cass felt the cold lurch of his stomach, his senses registering a shock before his mind could adapt, and felt a hot, bitter bile rise in his throat. He opened his desk drawer and pulled out a bottle of antacids, stalling, willing his mind to work.

Okay, Lieutenant Chant. Take it easy, slow. Don't push it. You try and push, the memory starts playing hide and go seek and you lose, baby. Be logical, be cool. Let's do this the smart way, one step at a time.

He gulped down two aspirin, lay back in his chair and began to think.

A man, someone he knew. Someone Leo knew, too. Someone capable of causing that iceberg in his belly.

Leo's pictures. No telling how old they were, she'd said so herself, but they were in an older sketchbook and the memory, the recognition she'd felt, wasn't a fresh thing. Someone she'd drawn and someone they'd both known, probably many years ago.

Illogically, intrusively, a picture of his daughter popped into his mind. Irritated, he tried to blink it away; this was no time to be dwelling on Mara.

That's what you think.

He shook his head, weary and baffled. This thing was wearing him out, getting the best of him. He was tired, that was his problem. Lack of sleep could turn a person's brain into mush. He needed to sleep, without pain or worry or distraction, put his head on something soft, something welcoming.

Like a wife's breast.

He shuddered, his eyes open and staring. Now, what sadistic corner of his soul had produced that nasty little thought? A wife meant a husband and he was no husband, hadn't been for years and years and...

Someone you knew, someone Leo knew. A long time ago. What did old Ching say? "You would at least know the killer's race."

Someone Leo had drawn as a compact, a microcosm, of everything she felt that was bad and twisted and spoke of rejection. Chinese geomancy. A twisted spirit, a twisted lip. And Mara's face...

"Jesus," he said dully. The dusty office swallowed the sound of his voice. "Oh, Jesus."

It was ridiculous, what he was thinking. He was tired, spent, played out, and his own exhaustion was betraying him, playing cruel tricks on his memory. Besides, it was impossible. Almost every serial killer in history had been a man. Nemo was a man. He had to be a man. His brain was messing with him, if he was thinking even for one moment that...

Forget it, pal, you can't escape it that way. You're the top dog, the man in charge, and you can't afford denial right now. Not on this one. Work it out.

The dichotomy was too much. Cassy's conscious mind gave up the struggle. As it let go, the memory came clear.

A girl, slim as a reed, lying in his bed in the early light of dawn. He had been making love to her as only a man who has achieved the object of his greatest desire could do. In his soaring tenderness, his feeling of emotional translation, he had paid no mind to her reaction.

Lovemaking over, he had settled down beside her. Her black hair coursed down the pillow like a waterfall. She was beautiful, perfect. He had never loved anything as he loved this girl. He loved her so much it hurt.

He had reached out to touch her, to reaffirm what he had attained. She had stiffened, frozen, refused to acknowledge him. Turning away, presenting her back, her shoulders jerking as if to underline her rejection and distaste.

Blindly, slowly, Cass reached a fumbling hand and took up the remote. The TV screen was blank. He managed to find the rewind, to bring the DVD back to that moment when a monster, an animal, understood its own danger. He watched it, his face masklike and impassive while his heart cracked and bled out. His pitiless memory and his waking eye transposed the two images, and found them identical.

Three times, four times, five. The floodgates were open, and with a vengeance; every time he watched it, another memory of the woman he had lost nearly fifteen years ago re-surfaced and bit. This was no delusion, no waking nightmare of sleeplessness and self-pity, and Cass knew it. This was the truth, and it meant the end.

Things began to make sense: the small footprint, the agility, Nemo's estimated age. No wonder no one had made the obvious connections; who, after all, ever heard of a female serial killer who preyed on pregnant women?

The words of the psychiatric evaluation came back with clarity and precision. "It is reasonable to extrapolate that this killer has at some time in their lives been exposed to a negative experience involving pregnancy or childbirth..."

I don't know what to do.

This thought took hold of his mind and repeated. It showed no pity, it refused to let go or make room for reality. *I don't know what to do, I don't know, I don't...*

The *feng shui*, the perversion of ancient geomancy into necromancy, when had that happened? Had Tam Lin always been mad, and her husband, in the madness of his own obsession with her, never noticed?

Thoughts, fragments of terrible immediacy, moved in and out of corners. He would have to resign, or at least relinquish control of the case. This would probably mean the end of his career. The law would call it a conflict of interest, and the police commissioner's political enemies would have a field day. And his family, what of them?

Leo would suffer horribly, hurt in the way she would mind the most. Cass remembered a British case; the killer's wife was an artist. After the trial and the conviction, the public started buying her work in masses, greedy, scavenging, wanting a souvenir of the woman who'd slept with a serial killer and lived to create again.

Leo would burn every drawing, every painting she'd ever done, before she submitted to that. She would never be able to deal with that kind of fame. It would drive her mad, extinguish her creative spark. It would eat her alive.

And Mara, his darling child, light of his world. Her life would not be worth living once the Dogs of War got hold of the truth. She would be unable to set foot out of doors, unable to go to school without being treated like some kind of leper. Cass could see the tabloid headlines, the drooling, vicious articles that would be ghosted by a staff writer without conscience or pity. *Abandoned At Birth: The Story of a Serial Killer's Daughter.* It was intolerable, unbearable. And there was nothing he could do.

Cass sat with his hands over his face, never moving, while the strength of the overhead lights eased with the first signs of morning.

Chapter Twelve

"**D**id I ever tell you about the car your grandpa built?"

Rhea Chant and her granddaughter had eaten dinner, watched a program about dolphins, and listened to music. Mara had done her homework and helped with the dishes. She was feeling lazy, calm, replete in more ways than one.

Mara turned her head, which was settled on the back of the sofa, and regarded her grandmother. Rhea seemed restless, as if in some way she felt the need to amuse and entertain. Maybe, Mara mused, it was because the two women were rarely alone together. Or maybe it was a generational thing, a deep-rooted belief among older women that, whoever the guest in one's house, they must be provided with entertainment.

"Yes," she said simply. "You did. But it was years ago, Christmas when I was about seven. I don't remember too much about it, except that I laughed a lot. Tell me again."

Actually, she remembered the story well. Still, telling it would make Rhea feel better, and Mara could let her mind drift even while asking appropriate questions and offering comments.

It suddenly occurred to her that Rhea wanted not to entertain, but to distract. Rhea didn't want to discuss whatever the cop shop had told her when she'd called Cassy earlier. It made Mara wonder. Had something happened?

"...looked at all these cars and decided the only car worth the metal it was made from was a Rolls-Royce, and a blue-collar working man wasn't buying a Rolls, not in those days, especially not a black man... ."

"They're not exactly breaking down the dealership doors today, either." Mara smiled at Rhea. "Be reasonable, Grandma. This is still a blue-collar working-class neighborhood, and it's still mostly black. You see a Rolls in any driveway around here?"

"No, honey, I do not." Rhea aimed a gentle swipe at Mara's head. "But I'm talking about nearly forty years ago, and people thought different then."

"We're not talking about attitudes, are we?   We're talking about money."

"You telling this story, or am I?" Rhea demanded. "Because if you'd rather tell it, I'll sit back and let you talk." She caught Mara's grin, her graceful gesture of capitulation, and the asperity died. Really, the child was too beautiful to be out loose. Smart, too. She picked up the thread of the story; Mara listened, relaxed and amused.

"So he said, honey, we need a car. I haven't seen but one worth buying and there's not enough money in heaven for that one. So I'm going to build one." Rhea snorted. "If it had been anybody else, I would have called for the men in the white coats, but I didn't argue with him. There was nothing he couldn't build, or at least design on paper. If he'd decided to build a moon rocket, the Eagle would have landed while Eisenhower was still president. Tom would have done it better than NASA. Cheaper, too. He would have made it out of old tuna fish cans. And it would have worked, without any O-ring problems and whatnot."

"Is that where Aunt Leo gets it from?" Mara couldn't remember that Rhea had put all this detail and feeling into the story the first time around; the tale somehow felt new, a bare sketch on a napkin that had got transformed into a tapestry. Maybe she felt more like she was talking to an adult. Maybe it was permissible to allow the adult nuances of feelings to show, now that Mara was older. Or maybe she had a hidden reason for telling this story at this particular time.

"Honey, I don't know. All I can say is that if Leo got her talent from Tom, it must have got all twisted around when it mixed with whatever she got from me. Because he could draw anything, but it was all real things, science and design and product." Rhea struggled to make her meaning clear. "He wasn't interested in anything out of his imagination, even his imaginary things were just versions of real things."

"Ah, a left-brain type. Like his own handmade car?"

"Just like that. Anyway, that's how he made as much money as he did, a lot of money for a black man back then. He didn't have the college degree, of course not, so he couldn't call himself an engineer or an architect, but he could call himself the best draftsman in San Francisco, and he was."

Mara straightened. This part of the story was new to her; Tom Chant had died of pneumonia before she was born. She knew very little about him; Rhea had never spoken at length of her husband. Everything Mara knew about her grandfather came from Cass and Leo. She knew that those memories were bound to be colored by shades of rebellious phases and changing times.

"Tell me more about Grandpa. Where did he work?"

"For a shipbuilder over at Hunter's Point, a man named Joshua Goldman. The shipyard's gone now; Mr. Goldman died the year Nixon resigned, and he was a bachelor with nobody to leave it to. And the economy had no place for it anymore." The fierce brown eyes had gone soft. "Mr. Goldman always said your grandfather could do anything he put his mind to. Oh, he was a nice man, Mr. Goldman. A little chubby bald Jewish man from the east coast. Did you know I worked for him, too? That's where Tom and I got to know each other."

"Really?" Mara was caught, fascinated and charmed by this look into another life. "Did you draw—I mean, were you a draftsperson, too?"

"Me?" Rhea laughed, a rich easy chuckle. "Baby girl, I couldn't draw my way out of a paper bag. No, I was Mr. Goldman's secretary. And he paid me pretty good, too. We're talking about the late fifties. This was before civil rights got going. Back in those days, a woman made maybe half of what a man would get for the same job, and black women were mostly maids."

"Well," Mara said drily, "that hasn't changed very much, has it? The man-woman salary thing, I mean?"

"True. But if you worked for Mr. Goldman you got paid what you were really worth, and he didn't give one inch about whether you were a man or a woman or black or white. How do you think we were able to buy a nice house in a decent neighborhood? I held off having a baby for a couple of years, and we both kept working. When we had enough for the down payment, Mr. Goldman co-signed for our mortgage."

"He sounds like a saint. No, maybe not a saint, not if he was Jewish.

Does Judaism have anything equivalent to a saint? Tell me more about the car."

The story proceeded. Tom Chant had researched the question meticulously, decided that every affordable model on the market was overpriced and inefficient, and promptly designed his own. He had spent weekends buying scrap metal, decent glass, spare parts; those he couldn't find, he built from scratch. Joshua Goldman, fascinated and amused, had lent him a welding set-up from the shipyard. The new house, on a pretty street between Potrero Hill and Bayview, had a good-sized garage. It became his workroom, and the homemade car had taken shape.

Rhea continued, her memories flowing easily now.

"At first I thought he'd gone clean out of his mind. You never saw anything so awful. That was before he smoothed down the bumps and edges. Mr. Goldman came over for dinner a couple of times, and I remembered to never cook him pork or shrimp. Afterwards he and Tom would disappear down into the garage and I wouldn't see them for hours. Cars back then were big ugly things—my goodness, early sixties, the first really nice little sports cars were out there, but Tom knew there'd be a baby or two on the way when we could afford it, so he said, a sedan."

"With tail fins? Did Grandpa's car have tail fins?"

"It did not. He said they were 'aerodynamically unsound' and that he wasn't putting them on any car of his. He also said a car didn't have to be the size of a Pacific Fleet destroyer to be safe, it just had to be made right. So this car was smaller than other family cars from that period. And gas mileage, would you believe it? He found an old V-6 in a junkyard and he took that thing apart, learning it, reading it like a magazine. Then he changed a bunch of parts around, cut them up, redesigned them, and when he put that engine back together he put it in the car and told me it would get over twenty miles a gallon. And you know what?"

"Let me guess." Mara was staring at her grandmother, seeing a younger woman, softer at the edges, a realistic woman with a deep capacity for laughter. For a girl who had never had a mother, this glimpse of the ghost behind the living flesh was unsettling. "He was right?"

"Twenty one point three five three miles per gallon." The ghostly echo of her pride, forty years behind her, was alive in Rhea's face. Perhaps it had always been there, hidden, waiting for a reviving trigger. "And Cadillacs,

Rolls-Royces, all the fancy cars that took up so much room and cost so much money, they got maybe twelve, if you were lucky. Wasn't that something?"

Mara was silent, absorbing the shadow of a woman she hadn't known existed, the accomplishment of a man who'd died before she was born. Something stirred in her, a feeling which, had she known it, was common enough to people in their forties but rare for an adolescent. The flicker astonished her; she was aware of a yearning, a need to know more, the realization of roots and ancestry and genetic connection. On an impulse she moved forward, gathered her grandmother in her arms, and held her tightly.

It lasted only a moment; Mara, self-contained by nature, had never been comfortable with prolonged displays of affection. As she let go, something wet brushed against her hand. She knew that Rhea was crying and she knew, too, that any acknowledgement or even mention of those tears would be unwelcome. She said nothing. Rhea untangled herself and stood, her face averted.

For a moment Mara wondered just what had triggered those tears. Had it been Mara's unusual gesture, Tom Chant brought to life for a few moments, a combination of those things and maybe others? It didn't matter, anyway; all that mattered was that Rhea should feel better. Mara hurried into speech.

"Do you have any pictures, Grandma? Of the car?"

"Um." Rhea, already moving, headed for the oversized buffet cabinet against the dining room wall. The upper half, glass-fronted shelves, displayed the good dishes; the bottom, five drawers, held everything from rubber bands to napkins. Most homes have a cabinet or a dresser that fulfills this duty. Memories live in the drawers and sometimes on the shelves, gathering dust, taken out on holidays or when the tribes gather, lovingly brought to life for the benefit of the present day. Then the memories, bound in leather or tied with red ribbon, are carefully put away again. It is sad, joyous, completely human.

Mara knew that yearning again, a brief poignancy, sharp and bittersweet. Understanding that her youth left her unequipped to handle it, she pushed it away. It occurred to her that the likeliest home for those memories, Rhea's photo albums, had never been offered to her. Again, she wondered why.

"Here." Rhea dropped three oversized photo albums on the sofa. "I think it's the first one, but I'm not sure. You have yourself a good look. I'm going to make some tea. You want a cup? Peppermint, maybe?"

So the tears were still too close to the surface, and Rhea needed the privacy of her own kitchen. Mara made a noise of assent, opened the first of the albums, and buried herself in it.

A past not Mara's own rushed out of the pages at her. There was not a single photo in Cassy Chant's home. As he put it, when your job means looking at pictures of mutilated corpses, you lose your taste for photography. Fascinated, she studied the faded relics with a lump in her throat.

There were no baby pictures of either Tom or Rhea; the earliest picture was a wedding portrait in black and white, as if their existence had begun with their bonding. Rhea, in a simple white dress, looked regal and alert. Tom Chant, a full head taller, held Mara's eye.

She'd never really looked at him before, and was surprised at his size. He had a broad chest, a strong neck, a powerful body altogether. It was his children's bad luck that they'd inherited their size from their mother. Mara wondered if Leo had ever drawn him.

She flipped the pages slowly. The newlyweds in Golden Gate Park, out at the beach, Rhea in the awful clothing of the late fifties against the vivid backdrop of a racetrack. Her skirt, caught by the wind, had blown up around her thighs to reveal a pair of sensational legs. Mara grinned to herself, deciding that her own superb legs must be part of the Chant family legacy. She heard the rattle of china in the kitchen; vaguely soothed, she continued her exploration.

The shipyard, the new house. A small round man with worried eyes and a generous mouth, standing dwarfed beside Tom Chant; this must be Joshua Goldman. Spread over three pages, several pictures of the legendary car in various stages of development. Rhea had been right; only an engineer would have thought it anything but ugly in its early stages. It looked like some fabulous monster out of a bad science fiction movie.

It had improved, though. The later shots showed a sleek machine that might have been designed yesterday. Why on earth hadn't her grandfather gone to Detroit with this finished product? He might have ended up a millionaire...

Mara turned the leaves, and found herself looking at a baby girl with strong muscles and dusky pigtails, with a multiplicity of cheap plastic barrettes. Leo, she thought with amazement, it had to be Leo. She peered at the faded ink below the portrait: *Leontyne, December 1970.* From newly born to two years old, her aunt romped, kicked, played with a small tabby kitten. In a few shots she had faced the camera head-on, and Mara was so surprised that she nearly dropped the album. Leo's eyes met hers, the same vital, intelligent energy that marked the woman staring from the infant's rounded face. The effect was uncanny, like looking at a familiar soul in the wrong body.

Another page; a baby boy, by himself and with his sister. Mara smoothed the plastic cover. If Leo had been fully herself from birth, Cass had not; there was nothing in this giggling chubby infant to indicate the small worried man that had raised her. Mara found nothing familiar in this ghostly manchild. He could have been anyone.

"Here you go, baby. Tea before bed."

Hearing the finality in Rhea's voice, Mara accepted the cup and glanced at the clock. It was past eleven, and she had school in the morning. Not without regret, she closed the albums, drank her tea, and kissed Rhea good night.

She slept badly. She was uncomfortable in any bed but her own, missing the familiar things she herself had chosen. Rhea's grandfather clock, chiming the hour from the hallway, seemed indecently loud. And the albums, the old ghosts calling to her from those pages, permeated her sleep. At four in the morning she was staring at the dark ceiling of the room that had been her aunt's twenty years before.

Rhea was a creature of habit; she would sleep until just before seven, and would not appreciate being roused before then. Quietly, Mara went out into the living room and settled on the couch. She turned the lamp on, angled it, and resumed her study of her family's history.

The photos of Tom Chant ceased around the time of Leo's college graduation photos. There were many shots from those years, Leo looking like an extra from *Flashdance,* Cass unclear and vulnerable, still somehow not yet completely formed. There were also pictures of pictures, done by Leo, which surprised Mara and charmed her; while they lacked her aunt's adult skill with a brush, the visions were there, beautifully distilled. They were full of light and energy. Yes, Mara thought, Leo had been Leo from day one...

Mara had reached the end of the second album. Her hand turned the page, found the last photo. Her eyes widened, then squeezed shut in shock and horror. She heard her own breath, ragged and quick. She opened her eyes again, making them focus on what they had rejected, hoping it had been a hallucination, hoping it would be gone.

Damningly clear, as unmistakable as the face of hell, the photo was still there.

Cass, barely out of his teens, carrying books under one arm. There was a girl beside him, a slender exquisite girl, a piece of antique Chinese carving that had somehow found its way into the world of the living. The heaviness of pregnancy only enhanced her fragility. She wore a white maternity dress, and her fine black hair blew loose around her face.

Cass was looking down at her with an expression Mara had never seen on his face; besotted, adoring, obsessed. The girl, rejection written in every small line of her, had been captured in the act of turning away from him. The camera had caught three-quarters of her face.

It came to Mara, a picture that was not a photograph. She saw herself and Leo, shoulder to shoulder, comparing an old sketchbook and a new photocopy. She closed her eyes, knowing that she was a moment away from blacking out. Instead of clearing, the pictures intensified and clarified. Her artist's eye would not permit self-deception.

She whimpered, a small exhale of sound. Her chest was throbbing. She opened her eyes and stared at the photograph.

There was no mistake.

Mara saw the smooth thick skin, the color of old porcelain; the touch of color in the girl's cheeks was the tint of wild roses. She saw the small upward tilt to the nose. High cheekbones, their gaunt effect softened by the rounded curve of the skull below them. Long sweet brackets around the mouth. The mouth itself, its full lower lip etched into a painter's memory by the odd twist.

"No." The tiny whisper could not have been heard a foot away. "No oh no, *no...*"

Tam Lin Chant, beautiful and terrible, heavy with the burden of the unborn Mara. No wonder Leo had drawn her, Mara thought dully. Such beauty, such oddity, so many contrasts. She wondered when those damning sketches had been made, those devil faces that would later shock the people of San Francisco over their morning coffee. She wondered why her father had said nothing, when he must have recognized the face that had altered his life.

Or had he? Had fifteen years of denying his wife's existence mercifully blocked his memory and blanked his eye?

And what of Rhea? She had certainly placed that photo where it was, had probably taken it herself. Yet she, too, had remained silent. Had she forgotten its existence, wiped Tam Lin from her awareness? It was possible. When had she last had opened this book and looked at these photos? Ten years, twelve? The day it was taken?

Mara's breath was flaming painfully in her throat. *I'm fourteen years old*, she thought concretely. *Fourteen. This isn't fair, it isn't, it isn't. I can't cope with this. I don't know what to do. I need someone to tell me what to do. Oh, God, help me...*

The grandfather clock whirred and bonged, chiming six times. Mara bit back a cry of terror, dropped the album, and knew that her nerve was gone, shredded, blown away perhaps forever by her first look at a mother who was also a monster, a lunatic, a murderess.

In less than an hour Rhea would wake, fuss around her beloved grandchild, insist on cooking breakfast. Mara swallowed a surge of hysterical laughter that rose like vomit in her throat. The idea of facing her grandmother with this dreadful new knowledge was beyond acceptance. She couldn't do it. She must get out of here, now, before Rhea woke and saw the abyss reflected on Mara's face.

Mara gathered the rags of her wits. She slipped the photo free of its plastic covering and jammed it into the pocket of her pajamas. She had to get dressed, make a plan, get out of here. She would make up some lie that would seem true and reasonable to Rhea, and be gone before that acute woman woke and saw the truth.

She found a message pad beside the phone. Without thinking too much, she wrote rapidly.

Grandma: forgot to tell you, I've got a project with a classmate and we're getting together to study before school. Her mom's picking me up at 6:30. Thanks for having me over, I'll call you later. Mara.

She stuck the note to the bathroom door with unsteady fingers. Breathless, she threw her clothes on. The words, *have to get out leave go have to have to*, ran continuously through her mind. Panicked, choked by her own urgency, she slipped the photo into her purse and went out into the first light of morning.

She checked her purse. Eleven dollars. Good; more than enough for a cab. She had always taken her father's insistence that she carry enough for a taxi with her for granted; this morning, she offered an inchoate silent thanks to whatever might be watching over her.

It was only then that her brain clicked into gear. A cab to where? Certainly not home; if she couldn't face Rhea, how on earth could she face Cass?

Leo. Go to Leo. She did those drawings, she'll understand, she'll know how to handle this thing and what to do. If she's with a guy that's too bad, he'll have to leave. Leo will understand. And, besides, there was nobody else to go to.

An hour later, having taken two buses because not a single cab had come by, Mara finally arrived at her aunt's warehouse. Later, she would be unable to recall a moment of that cross-town trip; her mind had turned itself off, refusing to function, admitting its inability to cope on its own. Leo had become a beacon, a haven of comfort, the only sanctuary on earth for a child with a dreadful secret.

She ran the two blocks between the bus stop and the warehouse, panting, unaware of the world. The security gate that guarded Leo's safety became, in her niece's imagination, a hedge of magical briars from a fairy tale, keeping her out, shunning her, knowing she was tainted...

She stood with her finger on the bell for a long time, unwilling to believe her own bad luck, to accept that there was nobody to hear the bell pealing through the building.

She had missed Leo by precisely eight minutes. There was nobody home.

That same first light of day saw Jim Delgado awake, worried, and reaching a decision.

He had slept badly, in fits and starts. The events of the previous evening, though dramatic enough to worry most people's rest, had not really affected him; Delgado was a pro, a veteran cop of eighteen years. Fifteen of those years he'd specialized in homicide. As a realist, he'd understood long ago that convincing his subconscious mind to ignore what he saw at work was the only way to remain sane. Let violent death follow him into sleep and he'd never survive.

Tonight his subconscious had let him down. He'd dreamed, not of Carla Morisco's foot sticking out from the trees, but of Cassy's reaction to it. Cassy's behavior had been totally out of character; his silence, his demand to be left alone, his suspension of all normal routine, all these things. There had been something uncomfortably like panic beneath that impassive facade. And Cass Chant was not a man to panic.

More than anything else, Delgado was disturbed by his own moment of recognition, that the look on Cassy's face was the virtual shade of the look on his sister's, at a moment when she had drawn a face she knew.

Five times, six times, Delgado found himself tugged from sleep to the edge of awareness by a mind whose activity refused to be stilled. The feeling, which he personally referred to as "busy brain," was infuriating. As the day broke, he sat up and rubbed grit from his eyes. Grumpy and tired, he had done with rest for the night. He couldn't lie here anymore. For the fondness and respect he bore Cass and for the feelings he had for Leo, he must get up. Some action must be taken; something had to be done. If he couldn't approach Cass—and Cass had made it very clear that he was not to be approached—then only one alternative remained.

He rejected the idea of calling Leo out of hand. There was urgency beneath the fretful annoyance of showering, shaving, making coffee hours earlier than he would normally have done. Perhaps, on some level, there was fear as well; Cass had blocked himself away and turned himself off to overtures from the outside world. And Cass and Leo were very much alike. If he called her, told her what was on his mind, she might just do the same. If he was going to take the initiative, it was better to take her by surprise.

He phoned for a cab, finished his coffee, and went outdoors to wait.

Delgado had been born in the Bay Area and he knew its weather. The Sunset district was still fogged in, but a single glance to the east informed him that the downtown area had already cleared. When the cab arrived, Delgado climbed in, gave Leo's address and closed his eyes.

"Here you go, pal. Seven dollars even. Looks like someone got here before you."

"What?" Delgado, who had been dozing in the back seat, opened his eyes. There was someone standing on Leo's doorstep, a young girl; even at this distance, with nothing to see but her back, he caught the slumping despair she was feeling. Hastily, Delgado paid off the driver and hurried across the street.

"Miss? Hello? Are you okay?"

Mara had been leaning her face against the wrought iron gate for what seemed an eternity. So absorbed in her misery was she, so lost in confusion, that she hadn't heard him come up behind her. At the touch on her shoulder she cried out, flinched, and whirled away from him.

Delgado's mind reeled. It was Mara Chant, Cassy's daughter, but what in hell had happened to her? The girl he had met a few times before was a calm, self-possessed creature with the kind of beauty that could stop traffic. What had caused those streaky tears, the trembling lip, the agony that disfigured her face like a jigsaw puzzle made of broken glass? And what in sweet hell was she doing on the street, at this time of day?

Even as he asked himself these questions, he knew the answers would have to wait. This was no adult suspect, it was a fourteen-year-old girl, and a very scared one at that. "Hey," he said softly. "Hey, it's okay. Don't you remember me, Mara? I'm Jim Delgado, I work with your father. We've met a bunch of times. I didn't mean to startle you."

"Startle me," she whispered, and knuckled her wet eyes like a small child. "*Startle* me? Inspector Delgado, oh god. There's no one home."

"Call me Jim." Her face was shocking, a ravaged mess that made her look fifty years old. Instinctively he made his voice calm, normal, as unconcerned as possible. "What is it, honey? Did you want to see Leo? Won't she wake up?"

"There's no one home," she repeated wretchedly. It was almost as if she was talking to herself. "I've been here forever and I rang and rang and there's no one home. Damn her! Damn her, I need her! Why isn't she home?"

Her voice splintered into tears. Without thinking, Delgado put an arm around her, pulled her tightly against him, crooning nonsensical words of reassurance. He felt her break into wrenching sobs. For a minute she stood, her face buried against his jacket, her shoulders shaking. Then she pulled away, mopping at her face. The sobs had become a tiny exhausted whimpering.

"Okay." By this time, Delgado was thoroughly unnerved. Don't push her, he thought, go easy, careful. "Look, Mara, there's a bar, Sam's Place, around the corner. It's dark and quiet and this time of morning they'll just be opening up and it ought to be pretty empty. I'm going to take you in and buy us both a cup of coffee. But look, you're way too young to go into a bar and your father would probably cut my liver out and feed it to the cat if he knew about it, so you've got to promise me that you won't tell him. Okay? Promise?"

"Whatever. I guess." The whimpering had stopped, but her breathing had an irregular, ragged edge that promised hysteria just below the surface. Delgado's small joke had produced not even a faint smile. "Sure."

"Then let's go."

Sam's Place, just opening, was completely empty of customers. The owner, who knew Delgado, lifted an eyebrow, got a tiny shake of the head in return, and went back to polishing the countertops. The air was redolent with the smell of fresh coffee. Delgado ordered two cups.

They sat in a booth at the back. Delgado looked at her hands, clenching and opening in small convulsive movements, and made up his mind.

"Mara," he said quietly, "something has obviously scared the hell out of you. I'm not your father or your keeper or your guardian. You don't owe me anything, not even an explanation, so I'm not going to ask you what you were doing out here or if Cass knows about it. I'm pretty sure I know the answer to that one anyway. But I will say this: it looks to me as if something happened, something you don't know how to handle. If you want help from me, you've got it. Your father and your aunt are both my good friends. I don't know you very well, but I care about them and I think that makes me your friend, too. Still, it's your call."

The beautiful swollen eyes, which had been fixed on her untouched cup, came up and met his. Delgado got the impression that she was reading him, gauging him, stripping him to the bone in her effort to assess his honesty. He sat very still, waiting.

She let her breath out in a soft whispering sigh.

"It's in my purse," she said, and her voice was dead. Her eyes had not once left his face. "I took it and put it in my purse. I didn't know what else to do with it, I couldn't just leave it where it was. You said you were my friend, that you'd help me. If you don't, if you use this wrong and hurt me, hurt my family, I'll never forgive you, never, not for as long as I live. I'll kill you if you hurt us with this. I swear I will."

"I'll help you."

Her eyes still holding him, she fumbled with the catch of the handbag. One hand disappeared inside, and came out holding a photograph. She put in on the table between them, snapped the bag shut, and dropped it on the seat beside her.

Delgado reached for the photo and took it up.

He had worked with Cass Chant for eight years, and he knew the boy in the picture at once. At first he was so beguiled by this younger Cass that he ignored the rest of the scene. Then his eyes found the girl at Cassy's side, and he recognized the model Leo had used so long ago.

The initial shock was like a vicious kick just below the heart. Once that subsided, Delgado was oddly unsurprised; whatever had caused Cassy's reaction last night, whatever had driven this haunted lovely child to a desperate search for help in the small hours of an October morning, it had to be something like this.

Leo's voice sounded in his mind, talking about the past, echoes of a conversation on a Saturday morning that seemed a thousand years away. *Tam Lin Chiu...a pretty exchange student...he met her at Berkeley...All the little hairs at the base of my neck stood straight up and sounded the alarm...three days after Mara was born, Tam disappeared from the hospital...maybe vampire would be a better word for her than vamp...Tam Lin...*

"I couldn't tell my father," Mara told him urgently, willing him to understand. His reaction, whatever it had been, had obviously reassured her. "I thought Leo could help me, tell me what to do. She drew those pictures, she knew my mother, she'd understand. But she wasn't home. So I was sunk. I mean, totally screwed. I couldn't tell my father. Could I?"

"No. No, you sure as hell couldn't." Delgado was amazed at how even his voice was. "Where did you get this, Mara?"

"It was in an album at my grandmother's house. At the very back of an old photo album. I don't think she'd opened that thing in maybe ten years. It was dusty."

"Did she see it? When you spotted it, I mean?"

"No. It was early; she was still asleep. I had to leave."

"Christ," he muttered.

This was hell, pure and simple. It was unbelievable, nightmare stuff. No wonder she'd had gone out into the night to find help. The flimsy picture must have felt like a live grenade, a millstone, a thousand-pound weight draped around her neck. It was too much for her to carry alone; it would have been too much for anyone. Poor beautiful brat, he thought, and his heart ached for her. What a way to get a first look at the woman who bore you and then abandoned you.

"Okay," he told her. "I said I'd help you, and I will. But first let's get some more coffee."

She waited for him to come back, balancing two steaming cups. "Jim, what are we going to do?"

"I don't know yet. But we're sure as hell going to do something. I need to think about it for a minute. It's tricky. And you drink that; there's milk and sugar and you need it. You've had a shock. This will help, physically, I mean."

The consequences that had haunted Cassy all through the night were there for Delgado to see. A career gone, lives ruined, political ramifications, the Dogs of War getting the story between their teeth. Hell, complete hell.

Had Cassy recognized his wife all along? Delgado rejected the idea at once. No way, he thought fiercely. Cass was the best, aces, a complete pro. He was too good a cop to have done such a thing. And not nearly a good enough actor to have hidden it that well. No, he'd been as clueless as everyone else.

But last night, watching the DVD? Delgado was almost certain the truth had triggered then. Maybe not the full truth, maybe just enough to make him break every basic departmental rule and order them all out. There was going to be hell to pay. And, running through these thoughts like a hot wire, another question. Where in heaven's name was Leo?

"It's a mess, isn't it?" Mara's eyes were full of adult comprehension. "I had to take it, don't you see? If I'd left it for my grandmother to see, she might have had a heart attack. And my father! This is going to ruin his career, if it doesn't actually kill him. So how could I tell him? It isn't his fault."

That it would ruin her own life, had perhaps already done so, she left unsaid. This generosity brought a lump to Delgado's throat as nothing else had done. He turned his full attention to the immediate problem of Mara herself.

"Listen," he said. "Like I said, I've got to think about this one. It's the toughest situation I've ever been in. But right now, I'm worrying about you. You're in a jam. Hiding out at Leo's would be perfect, but she isn't there. I don't have a key, unfortunately, or I'd let you in myself. It's too early for school, and you don't want to go home, do you?"

"Go home?" She stared at him, astonished. "And do what? Try and pretend to my father that everything's nice and normal? You think I could hide this, that he wouldn't see it in my face? Even if I could hide it, he'd only send me to school anyway. I can't go home. I can't!"

"Then there's only one thing to do." *This is nuts*, he thought clearly, completely nuts. *What the hell am I thinking here? The photo is evidence. I can't just stuff it in my pocket and hang on to it. I'm sorry for Cass, for Leo, for the kid, but I can't do it. I'm a homicide cop, and I'm holding evidence that puts a name to a killer. If I don't do something about it I'll have to explain why later and that will mean the end of my career, not just Cassy's. Cass, Leo, Mara, seven pregnant women, seven babies about to be born. How many more fallout victims from Tam Lin's bomb do there have to be? I must be out of my damned mind.* "Your father probably spent the night down at the Hall of Justice, or most of it. Something about that DVD worried him—"

"DVD? What DVD?"

He blinked at her for a moment before the truth sank in. She didn't know. She'd been with Cassy's mother and that tough old lady had probably kept it from her. Trying to protect her, he thought bitterly. Well, as nice a thought as that was, it had just become irrelevant.

He filled her in completely, omitting only his own interpretation of Cassy's reaction. That was probably unnecessary, anyway; the girl was acute enough to analyze her father's reasons. She must have known he'd guessed.

"...so he thinks you're with your grandmother," Delgado finished. "Is he likely to miss you before school lets out for the day?"

"No." There was a faint hope in the almond-shaped eyes. "Not before three o'clock at the earliest, because he'll think I'm in class."

"Then we've got an option. Here's the plan: I'm going to phone in, tell them I'm coming in late, that something personal's come up. You're staying with me until we can deliver you to Leo."

Chapter Thirteen

Homicide Inspector Malcolm Soufriere, kicked off duty with no explanation given, was disoriented. He'd left with the others, wondering what was going on; he'd stopped off for a burger and gone home, as ordered. He'd kissed his wife, fallen sleep, and done everything else he would normally do.

As the youngest and newest of the Homicide staff, Soufriere was still feeling his way around. He didn't like deviations from routine. Routine made sense, and made him feel secure. Cassy's behavior had unsettled him. He'd even lied to his wife about why he was home eight hours early. He said nothing about the DVD, or about being sent home.

If he expected a restless night, he was wrong. While the veterans tossed and turned, Soufriere climbed into bed, shut his eyes, and plunged into a comatose sleep.

"Mal? Wake up."

"Huh?" He opened his eyes. "Jackie? What time is it?"

"Seven. Your lieutenant just phoned. He wants you to come in. Coffee?"

At just past eight, Soufriere walked into Room 450 and found it empty. For a moment he was flustered; it had never occurred to him that Cass would leave the office before he got there. Now what was he supposed to do?

The note on his desk made him feel better. His feelings about Lieutenant Chant were mixed, a muddy soup of hero worship, awe, and resentment. Sometimes he wondered if Cass even knew his first name. The note settled that question.

6:30 AM Malcolm: I've ordered ten copies of the Winter DVD and two dozen hard copy prints of the clearest shots of the killer. They should get here about half past eight. If they're not here, call and raise hell. We need them ASAP. Put the whole pile in my desk drawer. These are not, repeat NOT, to be distributed to any media people until I give the okay. Sorry to get you up so early, please apologize to your wife for me. See me later regarding duty roster rescheduling. C. Chant, Lieutenant.

At eight-twenty, as Cassy's note had promised, the package of prints and copies arrived. Just as Soufriere was signing for it, Leo Chant poked her head around the half-opened door.

"Ms. Chant! Nice to see you. Hang on a second, okay?"

"Yeah, I guess so," she said listlessly. "Take your time. Whatever."

Soufriere opened the bulky package and checked through the contents. Then, waving the delivery man out, he ushered Leo in. "Sorry, I had to make sure the lab had sent us enough copies of those shots. Did you want to see the lieutenant? Because I'm the only one here right now."

"Actually, I thought he might want to see me." Her voice was dull and colorless. Soufriere thought she looked terrible, like an unwanted child, abandoned and left out in the rain. He couldn't figure out where the difference lay; physically, except for the slump of tired shoulders, she looked normal. Yet the impression of the little girl lost, confused and needing guidance, was unmistakable. Usually her smallness was terrifying, edged in energy and a kind of power. This morning, she seemed almost fragile.

"Damn," she muttered. "He's not here?"

"Afraid not. Here, have a seat and let me get you a cup of coffee. I just made some." He led her inside, wondering at her lost, vague look. The few times he'd seen her before, he'd thought she was too dynamic. As she dropped limply into the chair beside Cassy's desk, he set a cup of black coffee beside her. She took a sip and blinked.

"Good coffee. Usually what you get up here is more like toxic waste."

There you go, Soufriere thought, maybe she's just tired. Good coffee will fix that little problem every time. "My pleasure. Now, is there something I could help you with?"

"I don't know." She raised her eyes. Seeing the disconnected look, he knew he'd been wrong. "I don't know what the usual procedure is. Carla Morisco is a friend of mine, and Jim Delgado told me on the phone last night that Cass would want to ask me questions, about her associates and lovers and all that crap. He said Cass would probably call me, after he checked out that DVD. But he never called."

The reference to Delgado was not lost on Soufriere, but he decided to ignore it. "I don't think you need to worry. If the lieutenant thought you had any information he needed right away, I'm sure he would have called."

"Probably. But I kind of wanted to see him anyway, I'm not sure why." She gave a tiny shrug. "Maybe I just needed some inspiration. So I came down. Did you say those are pictures from those tourists? Delgado told me all about it on the phone."

"They sure are. We haven't said anything to the press yet, your brother's orders. Later on we'll distribute them to the media, but not until he says so. Something about it really bothered him. He kicked the entire staff out for the night. Completely against department procedures."

She stared at him. "That doesn't sound like Cass to me."

Soufriere flushed. He was talking too much and to the wrong person, and he knew it. He bit his tongue and hoped she wouldn't rat him out to her brother. "Yes, well. It was nice of you to come down. I'm just sorry it was for nothing."

"Oh, I don't know." For some reason, she was looking more alert. "Can I have a look at those pictures?"

"Well..."

"I'm just curious." She flashed a smile at him, a smile which held patience and good humor, and showed nothing of the bright light that had suddenly gone off in her head. *Bingo*, she thought. *Got it, got it, and about time.* "You know, I did the original sketches. I'm just wondering how close I got to the real thing."

Soufriere looked from the bulky package to the woman in the chair. He was very young, and recently married. Women like Leo Chant were beyond his limited experience. But he wasn't stupid, and something of Leo's inner burn came across to him. "Artist's curiosity?"

"You could call it that."

What the hell, he thought, she was the lieutenant's sister. If Cass trusted her enough to take her to Joseph Ching's bedside, who was he to throw his weight around? He handed her the package without another word.

She slid the stack of enlargements free of the envelope, keeping her hands steady. There were multiple prints, and multiple copies of each print. Each print was enlarged to eight by ten inches.

She riffled through them, taking her time, trying to seem casual. This nervous rookie looked like grabbing the whole pile back again at the first sign of anything he didn't understand.

She sorted through them, keeping them in order. The bright light of inspiration was flickering behind her eyes, but it was only a flicker. What she wanted, needed, would ignite it, send it flaming as bright as an Olympic torch.

There. That's it. That's the one.

The chimera had been caught for all time in the act of jerking its head toward the camera. One shoulder was hunched, one hand outstretched. The face was at once clear and blurry. Leo felt a tingle of warm blood, a tremendous deep satisfaction in her stomach. For a few moments she stared down at what she held.

Got you, got you, got you. Oh yes. Now I know what I did wrong. Now I know why I came here.

With a strong effort, she got control of her excitement. She looked up at Soufriere, hoping the smile she produced was not the feral hunter's grin it wanted to be.

"I see you've got multiple prints here. Can you spare me a copy of this one?"

"A copy?" He'd known this was coming, known it from the moment her hands on tightened around the edges. He was badly shaken; right now, Leo looked crazier than Nemo himself. But she was Cassy's sister, and she did occasional work for the police. "Cassy didn't want these given out to the media..."

"I'm not the media." The thought that he might refuse was intolerable. No toffee-nosed little rookie was going to get in her way, she thought fiercely. If she had to whack him over the head and smuggle the print out of the building, she'd do it. "I'm Cassy's big sister. I'm the lady who did the originals, and I want a copy of this print. I won't give it to the Dogs of War, I won't even tell anyone I've got it. But I want it." She saw hesitation on his face, and played her trump card. "Look, why don't you just give my brother a call and ask his permission? I don't mind waiting."

And you'll probably sit there until I do what you want, Soufriere thought bitterly. Damn. It was too early in the day for this kind of thing. He looked up, saw a chilly inflexibility that reminded him unnervingly of her brother, and mentally threw up his hands in defeat.

"Sure, what the hell, take it. But you'll have to sign for it."

"Where are we going to go for the next seven hours?"

Delgado, buttoning his coat, glanced down at Mara. The day was unusually cold for November in San Francisco; there was a crisp frosty tang to the air that reminded him of a trip to New York, one January long ago. The girl's leather jacket, while useful for a normal autumn day in the city, was inadequate for prolonged outdoor exposure.

"Damn," he said aloud, and Mara nodded in complete understanding. He spoke ruefully. "I was wondering about that myself. The ideal thing would be to wait until Leo got home, but she may not get home for hours. I don't know about you, honey, but personally I'm freezing my ass off. Too bad there's no cafe on this street. We could hang out inside and watch for her. As it is..." He trailed off with a shrug.

"I know. I've been out here forever anyway. I don't think I can stay warm too much longer."

He gave her a closer look. Her skin had a cold blue tinge, and her breath, as she shivered, came in little puffs. It was worse than he'd thought; the temperature must be right around forty degrees. If she hung out here too much longer, she'd wind up with pneumonia and her father would have Delgado's neck. Explaining all this to Cassy was going to be tough enough as it was. He came to a decision.

"I see two choices. We can hang out here and freeze, or we can go someplace where there's a phone and a heater. I vote for the phone and the heater. That way we can stay warm and call Leo every fifteen minutes until she answers."

She nodded, her arms wrapped around herself for warmth, and spoke through chattering teeth. "Your house?"

"Makes sense, if you don't mind."

"I don't mind, unless—will anyone else be there?"

"Nope. I'm a bachelor."

"Good. Then let's go."

They walked toward Market Street, Delgado praying they wouldn't run into a beat cop. Mara broke the silence.

"Jim," she said hesitantly, "I have to ask you about something. It's personal. Okay?"

He glanced down at her. "Ask away."

"Are you having a thing with my Aunt Leo?"

Delgado had been listening with half an ear, scanning for a vacant cab. The question jerked his head around.

"Who wants to know?" The absurdity of the phrase, one he habitually used for pushy adult relatives, didn't occur to him until the question was out.

Mara took it literally, and answered in kind. She looked him squarely in the eye. "Her niece, that's who. Also someone who has to trust you. We're about the same size, but I'm not dumb enough to think you couldn't break my neck with one hand if you wanted to. Do I need to ask you again?"

"No, you don't." A cab swept around the corner, its sign lit up, and Delgado waved it down. As it pulled over to the curb, Delgado spoke to Mara. "You're entitled to ask. Yes, I am having a thing with your Aunt Leo. At least, you could call it a thing. I care about her, and I also like her, which by the way are two different things. If that constitutes a 'thing,' then there's your answer. And I agree with you that she'll be able to handle this better than your father will."

"Of course she will. She's stronger than he is."

Mara scrambled into the cab, with Delgado right behind her. She waited for Delgado to give the address before she spoke again. "Have you got anything to eat, Jim?"

"In my pocket, or at my flat?"

This surprised her into the elegant snort that, with Mara, passed for laughter. "Well, I didn't think you carried pizza around in your wallet!"

"Considering my schedule, it might not be a bad idea," he said darkly. He was relieved, both at her tact and at her laughter. Talking to this child about the fact that he was involved with her aunt was weird enough, without having to do it in front of a nosy cabbie. All things considered, of the many bad days Nemo had saddled him with, this morning took the prize for worst. It was turning into any cop's idea of a surrealistic nightmare, the original day from hell.

When they reached Delgado's neighborhood, Mara offered to chip in on the fare. Reassured that Delgado had enough money, she waited quietly for him to settle up.

Upstairs, Mara wandered around the flat while Delgado turned the heat on and filled the kettle. Like Leo, she found Delgado's living quarters pleasing; something about them reflected directly on the man who lived there, and reassured her.

Mara, no fool, was aware of the chance she was taking by her presence here. She was too sophisticated not to know that walking alone into a man's apartment, even a man who worked with her father, was foolhardy at best and dangerous at worst. Somehow, she couldn't seem to make herself care; the universe was on the verge of caving in around her, fracturing and shattering, beyond all hope of fixing. If Jim Delgado turned out to be a rapist or a murderer, there was nothing she could do about it, not even worry.

Her own instincts, so long trusted, had been badly shaken by the morning's discovery. Still, if those instincts were working at all, Jim Delgado was completely trustworthy. The flat was a visual proof of it.

She heard the kettle whistle and was vaguely surprised to be given, not coffee, but a cup of instant hot chocolate. Sipping at it, feeling the rush of glucose through her blood, she realized for the first time how drained she was. She'd been running on pure adrenalin for the past few hours. This sense that she'd walked into an evil fantasy, her belief that Delgado was a trusted friend and not a mad rapist—were these things just wisps of nonsense, as tenuous and fragile as her own personal strength and security had proved to be?

The thought was despairing, terrifying. Could she ever trust anything again, as long as she lived?

The flat was warming up rapidly, and Mara took her coat off. Then Delgado, who seemed restless, walked over to the sound system and spoke to her over one shoulder.

"I'll give it until half past nine, and then I'll try Leo again," he said. "In the meantime, would it bother you if I put on some music?"

"Not at all," she said. "Whatever you like."

Delgado considered the pile of compact discs. After a moment, he pulled one free of the stack and punched it in. The high, pure notes of a trumpet filled the room.

Miles Davis. *Sketches of Spain.*

For a minute Mara was very still, her eyes on him. He stared back at her, wondering what he had done to bring the color rushing back to her cheeks, and the life back into her eyes.

"Hey," he said uneasily. "Is this okay? I'm a jazz guy."

"Yes," Her face alight with something that Jim Delgado could not understand. He could understand nothing, in fact, except that somehow he had passed some unwritten test that he hadn't known had been imposed.

"You're sure?"

"Oh yes, yes, this is fine." Mara's voice was full of inexplicable relief. "Listening to it will make me feel a whole lot better."

The print of Nemo, blown up to obscene menace by use of the Hall of Justice's enlarging photocopy machine, sat pinned to Leo's second easel.

She'd made it home at half past nine, print and copy both hidden in the depths of her bag. She had turned the heat on, and the overhead spots; she had dragged the second easel from the storage cupboard and set it beside the first. A stretched canvas, fourteen by twenty inches, sat blank and waiting.

She knew what she had to do. She had her voodoo totem now, the artist's equivalent of the sorcerer's fingernail clipping, or lock of the victim's hair. The print held Nemo, all of him, shoulders and back and hair and hands. This morning she had chased a painted devil. She had failed to catch him, and hadn't known why.

Now she knew. Her first attempt had been incomplete because its source had been incomplete. She'd had no sense of the real Nemo; she'd tried to work from caricatures, cartoons, pale encapsulations of her own feelings. Those long-ago sketches were not Nemo, they were merely the artist's interpretation of Nemo. Leo understood why the canvas had remained spiritually empty; while guesswork on a creative attempt might have borne fruit, she hadn't been going for creativity. The problem was simple. She'd tried to paint a brutal reality from an unreal source.

Now, thanks to a pair of tourists with powerful consciences and an expensive camcorder, that problem was solved. Leo stared at the enlargement, studying it, learning it. She felt a deep satisfaction. This time, it would be different. This time, it would work.

As she straightened up, it occurred to her that she hadn't checked her messages. For a moment she wavered, indecisive, wondering if it would be better to wait until her job was done. But she knew that, the awareness once having come into her mind, it would remain there, distracting her at a time when distraction was the last thing she could afford. Impatiently she tore her eyes from Nemo and went to the answering machine.

Three messages. She rewound the tape, listening to the first one.

Beep. Click. "Yes, good morning, this is Susan Ortiz. I'm sorry to bother you so early, but there's a problem with the artwork for Peter Casper's story. Apparently the author has some definite ideas about what he wants as a review illustration, and he's been giving us a hard time about it. I know it wasn't part of the original agreement, but I was wondering if you could come in this afternoon and talk to—"

Leo punched the "off" button, her forefinger jabbing so hard that the machine nearly skidded off the table. Muttering a couple of vicious expletives, she fast-forwarded the tape until it had reached the end of the recorded messages, set it back to the record function, and turned the volume all the way down to zero. After a moment's further consideration, she turned the ringer on her telephone off, as well.

Then, effectively cut off from the outside world, Leo went back to her canvas and took up a tube of acrylic paint.

She knew what she was going to do. Her original concept had been the correct one; make it as close to reality as possible. The problem had not been with her work, but with the available model.

Now she had a photograph, a real picture of a real monster. The photo was in black and white, and the painting would be in black and white. She would paint the photo, dot by dot, fleck by fleck, inch by inch, scaled to the last centimeter and deepest shade of grey. There would be nothing in the finished product that wasn't in the photograph. If only a passionless rendering of Nemo's world would bring her face to face with Nemo, then so be it.

Black paint, white paint.

She began with the backdrop, treating the perspective as she would have treated any landscape. The bulk of the Marin headlands, the curve of the bay. Her head moved back and forth in a machine-like rhythm, from photo to canvas, taking in everything. Her hand, perfectly attuned to this rhythm, took its cues from her detachment, working swiftly and accurately. In what seemed like a few minutes, the backdrop was completed.

She took a break, letting the acrylic dry. Street sounds, the hum of passing traffic and the occasional yell of a car horn or a big truck shifting gears, washed vaguely through the studio. She ignored it all, including her answering machine. Had she bothered to glance that way, she would have seen that four more calls had come in. But she never even considered it; right now, for what she had to do, the outside world could only distract.

Black paint, white paint.

The towers of the Golden Gate Bridge, shadowy spires at the right of the photo, were easily done. The fog-dimmed glitter of bridge lights, almost surreal in black and white, took longer. Back and forth her eyes went, finding every splash of colorless light, every reflection on the moving gray water beneath the bridge itself, every echo of muted brightness in the misty sky.

Another break, while the fresh paint dried. Still Leo ignored the turned-off phone, the answering machine. The message indicator now indicated eleven calls.

Black paint, white paint.

The treetops, normally innocuous enough, were now frightening. The photo showed them as a looming mass of darkness, punctuated by the spikes of empty branches pointing like accusing fingers toward the canopy of sky. Leo felt a superstitious chill run down her back, stopped at once until it was gone, and returned to her work. Inch by inch, the treetops took their place in Leo's voodoo charm. After them, the trees themselves.

The scrub, bristling and amorphous, that covered the hillside. She took it slowly, checking every plant in the photo for individuality and variance in texture. What her eye saw, her hand recorded; when the dark mass was done, the painted hillside, steep and unmanageable because of the camera angle, was a virtual twin of the hillside Chris Winter had recorded.

Stop, break, allow for drying. Leo, drinking a glass of water without tasting it, wondered that her wrists were not aching and swollen. There were now sixteen messages on the muted answering machine. She never glanced that way.

Half past one. Back to work.

Black paint, white paint.

Carla's foot. A well-made hiking shoe, a heavy sock, a leg jutting from between the trees at a sickening angle. Leo's pace had slowed now; she painted the rough texture of the sock, the bumpy weave, with slow and careful precision.

And now it was done, the entire stage, all but the master puppeteer himself. It was a quarter past two.

Leo took up a brush and began the reproduction of the chimera.

⁂

Thirteen times. Over the past five hours, he had called Leo's number thirteen times.

Delgado was getting worried. Luckily, since he had a low opinion of his acting ability, he didn't have to worry about the effect of communicating this feeling to Mara. She had succumbed to emotional stress and lack of sleep and stretched out on his sofa. From the occasional whimper, Delgado knew that her sleep was uneasy, haunted, punctuated by bad dreams.

Thirteen calls made, thirteen messages left. Where the hell was Leo?

Moving quietly so as not to wake Mara, he slipped into the kitchen and poured himself some juice. He was longing for a beer, but a kind of delicate awareness of the unusual situation he was in, kept him from drinking alcohol while the child was under his roof. He drained the glass, set it down in the sink, and ran his fingers through his hair.

The timing was terrible, and he knew it; it was one of his main worries. The need for secrecy, the very fact that Mara could not be expected to face her father until she had spoken to Leo, put a nerve-wracking timer on the fuse of this whole miserable situation. In another hour, Mara would be rightfully expected home from school. Delgado didn't know whether Cassy was even at home; the only thing he knew for sure was that he hadn't been at Homicide when Delgado had called in this morning. And Mara couldn't call home to check in. He knew Mara had a cell phone, but he hadn't heard it ring. She must have turned it off.

Delgado, usually so quick-witted, couldn't think of one good reason to phone Cass at home. If Cass was home, things would reach critical point in about an hour, and Delgado didn't have a clue as to what he should do about it. He felt like he was trying to walk a tightrope with a blindfold over his eyes.

Another soft whimper from the sleeping Mara brought his head around. Briefly, he allowed himself the unfair luxury of blaming Leo for the current situation. If she'd been home, they could have had a head start on this whole mess hours ago. Damn it, he'd told her last night that Cass might need to question her about Carla Morisco. He'd told her to stick close to home, or at least to leave a message where she could be reached. She'd agreed, she'd understood, she'd promised to do just that.

So why the hell wasn't she home? Where was she?

He picked up the cordless phone and punched the redial button. Attempt number fourteen resulted in Leo's voice, explaining that she wasn't available right now and asking him to leave his name and number.

He got himself another glass of juice. Goddamn it, where could she be?

Delgado forced the Chant family dilemma to the back of his mind. He had a little problem of his own. He'd left a message with Elena this morning that he had personal business to attend to; he'd said he'd be in late. But how late was late? He'd been scheduled for duty today, and his shift was two-thirds over. It occurred to him that calling in could take care of two problems. He could cover his own rear end and, at the same time, find out if Cass had come in today.

There was no point in waking Mara; let her get what rest she could. Taking the cordless into the bathroom and closing the door behind him, he punched in Homicide's number.

"Homicide, Soufriere speaking."

"Malcolm? Jim Delgado. How's it going?"

"Jim!" Soufriere sounded unexpectedly relieved. "Boy, am I glad you called. Things are kind of weird right now."

"Weird, huh? Sounds dangerous." Delgado was not too disturbed; Soufriere, Homicide's pet rookie, was notorious for being thrown off balance by anything not strictly conforming to routine. "Look, Mal, is Lieutenant Chant in?"

"No." Now that he considered it, Soufriere sounded more worried than usual. "Hasn't been in all day, and that's part of what's worrying me. We got a call from him hours ago, telling us not to do anything about that DVD until he'd spoken with the commissioner."

"With the *commissioner*?"

"Yeah." Soufriere was beginning to sound downright unhappy. "His sister was in, though. And I think maybe I blew it."

Delgado's hand tightened on the phone. "Leo Chant was in? When?"

"This morning, along around eight-thirty. Cass left me a note, said he'd ordered copies of the Morisco DVD and a bunch of hard copy prints. His sister stuck her head around the door just as I was signing for the package. She asked me what it was, and I told her. I guess I should have kept my big mouth shut, huh?"

"I wouldn't worry about it. If Cass trusts her, I'm sure you can. Did she say why she'd come down there?"

"Yeah, she said she knows the intended vic, the Morisco woman, and she thought we'd want to take a statement. She looked really played out. At least, she did until I let her look at those prints."

Delgado's heart had begun to jump erratically. He managed to keep his voice even. "What do you mean?"

"Well, she asked for a copy of one of them." Soufriere sounded unhappy. "Maybe asked is the wrong word. Demanded is more like it. It was like she came in looking like her head weighed too much to hold up straight. Then she looked through the stack, and wham! It was like some big bright light went off somewhere. I could *see* it, Jim. It was almost like she'd recognized something."

Delgado's palms were wet. "Did you give her a copy?"

"Yeah, I did. And now I think I screwed up, Jim. Because the lieutenant left me a note telling me to sit on those copies until further notice. So you see..."

Leo. Leo, did you recognize her? Is that why you wanted that picture so badly?

"Look, Mal, don't say anything." Delgado spoke quickly and decisively. "Not to anyone about anything, you got that? Not about Cass talking to the commissioner, not about his sister, not about her wanting that print. Not a damned word. I'll handle it from here. You just stand by until you hear from me. Okay?"

"You bet."

Delgado punched the phone off and thought furiously. So Cass was talking to the commissioner? That added up to one thing: Cass had figured it out. The poor bastard.

As bad as Cassy's situation was, Delgado couldn't help him. The question of Leo was something else again.

She'd been at Homicide this morning, long before she was usually out of bed. She had demanded that print. Why? What in hell did she think she could accomplish with it? Even if she had recognized Tam Lin, that print wouldn't help her.

Unless she thought she knew where Tam Lin was. Unless she was planning to hunt her sister-in-law down.

The warm room suddenly felt cold. No, Delgado thought. No way. Leo was not enough of a fool to go chasing after a homicidal maniac without a word to anyone. If she knew where to find the killer, she'd say so. Wouldn't she?

He didn't know. It was humiliating to have to admit it to himself, feeling as he did about Leo, but he didn't know her well enough to guess. And he could hardly ask Cassy; that was out. But there was one person he could ask...

The hand on her shoulder woke Mara from a dark dream of death and abandonment. For a moment she stared through terrified, uncomprehending eyes at the man leaning over her. Then her senses snapped into place, and she sat up.

"Leo? Have you gotten through to Leo?"

"No." She'd never seen such intensity on a man's face before. It frightened her. "Listen. I just found out that she stopped off at Homicide this morning. The inspector on duty let her go through some hard copy prints from the DVD and she demanded one."

"So?"

"Soufriere, the inspector I mentioned, said she took one look at those prints and lit up like a bonfire. She recognized it, Mara. She recognized it, took it, and now she's gone, we can't locate her. Talk to me, girly. You know your aunt a whole lot better than I do. Why would she want that print? What in hell would she be doing with it?"

Through his concentration he thought that her face suddenly became kaleidoscopic. He couldn't tell what was going on behind those long, heavy-lidded eyes. It was obvious, however, that something was. She knew the answer, or believed that she did. He could see the precise moment when the truth clicked into place.

As for Mara, Delgado had faded out. In his place were a hurricane of memories, tiny sharp vignettes.

Canvasses in Leo's studio, some dusty, others, as old or older, bearing the unmistakable imprint of constant handling.

Herself in a darkened bedroom, drawing through instinct while music soared behind her.

Her aunt, knowing without asking that Mara herself bore the same gift of vision and facility.

Two evil cartoons of the woman who had been the turning point for the Chant family.

Mara saw these several things, recognized them and acknowledged them, in a heartbeat. Yet her mind insisted on returning to one thing, understanding somehow that it held the answer to Delgado's question.

Old works, constantly handled. Why?

She got to her feet. After a moment she became aware that Delgado, sitting on a vast burning impatience, was watching her silently. She spoke with an authority beyond questioning or disobedience.

"We have to go over there, right now. Call a cab. And I think you'd better bring your gun."

"I intend to." The strangest part of this strange day, Delgado thought dimly, was that it never occurred to him to question her command. He went for the phone, stopping just long enough to pick up his .38 and slide it into his shoulder holster. "We don't have a key to her place."

"We'll find a way in. Now call that cab, please. I don't think we have any time to waste."

Chapter Fourteen

The necromancer Tam Lin was on the street.

She was hungry, starved, in a terrible angry fashion. She knew she must feed. Her protection against infinity, that shadowy landscape of hatred and death she had made for herself, had been robbed of Carla Morisco and her unborn child. This theft was the source of the monster's hunger. Feeding the place she had created nourished her. It was the only thing left that could.

The food had grown scarce since the earlier meals. Media coverage made everyone cautious, except those young enough to believe it could never happen to them. Finding a pregnant woman walking the streets alone, especially since the Ling Ma killing, was difficult. Carla Morisco had been a stroke of astounding good fortune. Tam Lin would not have defined it that way; at the extreme of madness, luck was righteous and inevitable. Her logic was closed. The food, the walking fertile dead of her kingdom, was there. What she had found before, she could find again.

Tam Lin had taken an ancient female survival art to a new extreme; she had cultivated a self-effacing invisibility, walking the streets virtually unseen. Invisibility lay, too, in the mind-set of the world around her. The phenomenon was an old story. Many of the London police hunting Jack the Ripper had believed the faceless serial killer to be a woman. They felt that the Ripper had escaped because the public would not believe that a woman could do such a thing.

Another safety net, another protection, this one more prosaic; none of Tam Lin's victims knew her.

There had been no contact with them until the ultimate moment, no attempt to cultivate them personally. They were slain at random, killed as they were spotted and as they coincided with Tam Lin's need. Homicide had wasted endless hours trying to connect the victims by some common thread. They had investigated husbands, lovers, brothers, friends, hobbies, jobs, and religious affiliation.

They had found nothing. There was nothing to find. Tam Lin required only pregnancy as an initiation fee into the dreadful ranks of her elite.

As mad and reckless as Tam Lin was, some survival sense still remained to her. The small, heavy pipe she thought of as The Sleeper rested in her jacket pocket. As the police scientists had noted in a report to Homicide, the business end of The Sleeper was kept wrapped in a handkerchief.

There was also a three-foot length of nylon cord in Tam Lin's pocket, cut from a good-sized spool of the stuff. Even the cord posed no threat to Tam Lin, for she had not bought it. She had found it in a box of trash outside a house where the residents had obviously moved away. Cass Chant and his underlings could check out every possible source on earth for that cord, and never come up with the answer.

Cass Chant, Cass Chant. A distorted smile contorted Tam Lin's twisted mouth, and then was gone.

Cass Chant.

She never thought willingly about him, or about the long months of pregnancy. When she remembered that time, she still contracted into hatred. Fourteen years had not dulled the memory of her fear, her belief that the thing growing in her, nourishing itself on her, thriving as she weakened and grew ugly, was alien and demonic.

Those months, which had culminated in long hours of feverish pain, had produced a far nastier scar than the one left by the episiotomy. They had produced a vision, a dream, a hunger. Most importantly, they had made her aware that she had the power to feed that hunger.

Cass Chant, Cass *Chant*... .

She hadn't touched the newborn creature Cass had named Mara, not even to feed it. She had let the milk dry in her breasts without a qualm. Tam Lin had never once looked into the infant's face. She had known what she would see. It would wear the disguise of a human baby, the cuddly seductive helplessness with which demons of that kind disguised themselves so well.

It was a trap, a snare; it had deceived women throughout the ages, but Tam Lin was not deceived. The creature was a nightmare leech, taking its life from the woman forced to host it. This one had sucked the beauty and strength from Tam Lin. She would not give it milk or anything else.

She saw nothing contradictory between this attitude and her obsessive belief that her chosen ones should consider the health of their unborn. Tam Lin wanted the babies kept safe in their mothers' wombs for one reason only, that the demons she brought into her necromancy might be perfect in all ways. No one, after all, eats a scarred apple when an unblemished one is available.

Her own pregnancy, nine months of possession by that demon alien life in her body, was the only thing she had ever feared. Cass Chant had caused that fear, suffocated her with his feelings and desires, planted the parasite in her and been proud of it.

Cass Chant.

Tam Lin allowed herself one clear thought of the would-be lover, the man who had dared to consider himself a keeper and owner. She had remained in San Francisco all these years, learning the tools of her magic. She had stayed here, in his hunting ground, and he had never known it.

Now he was forced to hunt her. She knew he would fail. She hoped that failure destroyed him.

From the bell tower of a local church, three soft peals rippled into the afternoon.

Tam Lin turned into Mission Street. The barrio was a good hunting ground. The Latinas here were Catholic, and Catholic women were often pregnant; their religious leaders demanded it. The drawback was that religious people also tended to be superstitious, and that meant an almost hysterical caution.

She passed down the colorful street like a ghost, barely seen by the jostling crowds. The barrio was dirty, loud, fascinating, and sometimes very beautiful. Mostly it was alive, pulsing in an urgent emphatic fashion that constantly echoed the prevailing culture. There seemed to be no corner of the endless avenue that did not throb with motion and voices and the sound of inner city life.

All this activity coursed around Tam Lin like rainwater parted by a small stone. She was unseen, and unseeing. Her eyes and spirit were tuned completely to what she needed. Except for those things, the food and the best way to acquire it, the rest of the world was the merest distraction.

There were fewer pregnant women than there had been a few months ago, and none were alone. Yet they were here. Tam Lin saw two of them together, and felt the familiar heat of recognition. It registered in her pulse rate as an erratic surge. She moved slightly closer, watching without seeming to watch, keeping her breathing even and regular.

They had paused to examine produce at a tiny fruit stall. One was young, barely out of her teens. She showed the contradictory mix of blurred edges and focused concentration so common during pregnancy. Tam Lin knew that the growth in this girl's belly had devoured the bloom of her youth. The bulge was hugely sentient, very close to term. The girl was faded, dull, irrelevant; she had been defeated by the enemy inside. Tam Lin dismissed her without a second thought.

The other woman was something else entirely. Tam Lin scanned her, read her, and identified what she was with the precision of a coroner's report.

She was older than her companion, closer to thirty than twenty. Tam Lin, obliquely fascinated, knew that she was seeing something special, something unique, something worthy of a place of honor in her collection.

The woman was small. The softening impact of pregnancy had had no effect on her; possibly it had been defeated by the strength of her resentment. Her whole posture was harsh, snapping, expressive of a rage she would not admit to herself lest it consume her. She ignored the unborn child, refusing to display by a single gesture that she had been invaded.

The necromancer's pulse fluttered. This would be the shining star of the magician's landscape, its glory, its crown. The woman was furious, hating, undefeated. Tam Lin had never seen anger to match her own in a pregnant woman.

Tam Lin, trembling with starvation and need, loved her and hated her and knew she must collect her. This was the one. This was the food she craved, this defiant resentful angry woman who was a gourmet's banquet.

The two women walked on, the younger one chattering in nervous bursts, the chosen one listening with sullen concentration. They stopped, stalled, moved on again; they were momentarily swallowed by the crowd, and reappeared. Their pace was slow, aimless.

A short distance behind them, invisible among the eddies of moving humanity, the monster kept them well in sight. It was thirteen minutes past three.

Anna Mendez, just short of thirty years old, knew all about God's personal spite.

She'd always known that God had an attitude problem toward her. From the time her mother died and left her in the custody of a bitter aunt and a worn-out uncle, Anna had realized that the deity, whoever He was, hated her fucking guts.

She'd never known why God would have it in for a little kid. By the time she was old enough to apply logic to the question, she was past caring and smart enough not to risk trouble by sharing her views on God's spite with anyone else.

Anna had learned the hard way that sharing that particular opinion brought trouble in truckloads. The one time she'd tried, she'd told her cousin Johnny. The vindictive bastard ran straight to his mama. The old bitch had jumped at the excuse of blasphemy for yet another reason to beat the shit out of the orphaned niece she didn't like and still resented being saddled with.

That was the last time Anna had been dumb enough to trust anyone. As she bitterly acknowledged to herself, a person didn't have to be a rocket scientist to figure out how not to get her ass kicked.

Besides, she had plenty of proof that God hated her guts, especially these days. All she had to do was to look in the mirror at her swollen belly.

Before this pregnancy, Anna had given up thinking about God's spite. The rage and resentment against a god of love who had no love to spare had become a constant background reality, like emotional white noise. Of course God wouldn't let her get away with that; what fun was tormenting someone if they tuned you out?

Her condition, the unwanted result of a one-time encounter she hadn't even enjoyed, was typical of God's attitude toward her. First the doctors told her she couldn't even have kids; then they told her the baby was a malignant tumor. By the time they'd figured it out, it was too late to get an abortion without risking her own neck.

They'd been nervous about that at the clinic, scared that she might sue them. She didn't, because there was no point. It wasn't their fault that the pregnancy tests had come back negative until she was nearly six months gone, any more than it was their fault that she hadn't started showing until that late in the pregnancy. It wasn't medical incompetence, it was God giving her just one more dose of shit in a long, long cycle of shit-giving. What the hell, you couldn't sue God.

That, no doubt, was why He'd saddled her with this baby, making it impossible for her to ignore Him, forcing her to think about how much He hated her. Well, it had worked fine. She thought about it all the time now. She'd been thinking about it after lunch, when the phone rang and her little cousin Sophy asked for company to do some grocery shopping.

She'd gone because she liked Sophy, born to that same hated aunt just after Anna had been moved to foster care. Sophy had adored her big cousin from babyhood. The fact that Sophy's birth had killed the bitch aunt was a big reason to like the kid. Sophy was scared to go out by herself, even in broad daylight. She was a nervous little thing, easily spooked by small stuff, and Anna had to admit that these killings weren't small.

Anna walked the five blocks to her cousin's tiny, spotless apartment. Sophy thought her cousin was either brave or crazy, but Sophy was wrong. Anna wasn't crazy, and she wasn't afraid of the Maternity Murderer getting her. She just didn't believe God would let His favorite punching bag be grabbed away from Him by another mean kid. If you're God, no one gets to steal your lunch.

She saw right off that Sophy seemed even more spooked than usual. Her cousin was one of those dainty females who should have been radiant during pregnancy. She sure as hell didn't look radiant. There were black circles under the big soft eyes, and an ominously distended vein pulsing on her temple.

Sophy caught Anna's look, and flushed.

"Sophy? What's the matter? Are you sick?"

"No, not sick. Just...I haven't been sleeping too good." She sounded strange, Anna thought, her voice was too high-pitched, all stressed out. "Something in my diet, maybe."

Anna raised an eyebrow. Sophy thought every order her doctor gave was a royal command; if he told her to eat kitty litter for the fiber content, she probably would. "What, didn't Doctor I-Know-Everything give you a diet sheet? Yeah, I thought so. Come on, honey, what's the matter? You don't look hungry, you look scared. Talk to me."

The color ebbed, leaving Sophy as pale as she had been flushed. Anna saw her cousin's hand move to the crucifix that always hung around her neck, and sighed. It was too bad the kid wasn't tougher. "Come on, Sophy. What scared you? Did something happen?"

"I told you, I haven't been sleeping. I've been having bad dreams." Sophy's unconscious grip on the silver cross tightened. "It's really one dream, the same dream, but I have it all the time now. It wakes me up, and then I can't get back to sleep."

Anna was aware of a flash of protective feeling. It surprised the hell out of her. Sophy cast her eyes down. Anna saw the vein in Sophy's temple accelerate its pumping, and regarded her cousin with genuine worry.

"This must be one nasty, nasty dream," she said gruffly. "Sometimes it helps if you talk about it. You tell Joey?"

"No. He works so hard, he needs sleep. And he worries about me enough as it is." Sophy sat down. "It's just a stupid dream. Forget it."

"No," Anna said. "I think you'd better tell me, and get it off your chest."

Sophy glanced at her. She should have jumped at the excuse. Instead, she was reluctant.

"I guess," she muttered. "I guess, okay. There's me and my baby, a girl baby who looks like you, and I'm in bed, and someone comes in and tries to steal her, hurt her. I can't move, I can't get out of bed and it wouldn't matter even if I did. I wouldn't be able to stop him, because he doesn't have a body or even a face. There's just something—I don't know what, a devil maybe, something awful. It just wants to hurt."

She hadn't wanted to explain; every word had been a form of torture. Sophy was really scared.

Anna felt the skin prickle along her bones. "Ugh! You poor kid, no wonder you wake up. But I can see where the dream comes from, why you keep having it."

"You can?"

"Sure. Worried about this Maternity Killer guy, worried about a new baby, about not being able to protect it. Look, let's do your shopping. If a devil or anyone else gives you a hard time, I'll kick his ass and let you watch. Okay?"

The day was sunny and crisp, holding the first real bite of oncoming winter. It was perfect weather for a walk in the real world. In a detached way, Anna was pleased to note that her cousin's mood had lightened, even if it wasn't enough to make her stop glancing over her shoulder. It was too bad that her own mood had gone so dark and edgy. While Sophy dawdled over the items on her diet sheet, Anna was aware that her own irritation was mounting toward boiling point.

Damn being pregnant, anyway. What in hell good was putting more people in the world? There were too many people as it was. If Sophy hadn't been pregnant, she wouldn't be feeling half as vulnerable. As for Anna herself, there were times recently when she thought she'd just have the abortion done, no matter the risk to her own safety.

Sophy bought tomatoes and spinach. She bought milk and bran cereal; she bought a chicken. Anna took one of the heavy grocery bags and carried it; Sophy looked exhausted, as limp as a dead flower. Anna's mood, grudgingly concealed, got worse with every passing minute. By the time Sophy was ready to go home, Anna was almost hoping that someone *would* hassle them. Kicking some ass, even with the handicap of pregnancy, would make her feel a whole lot better.

At half past three, Anna waved good-bye to her cousin and headed home. With her hands jammed in her pockets, she allowed herself a few minutes to indulge in the luxury of sheer bad temper. Her mind, refusing to cooperate, spiralled back through year after year of God's sadistic little tricks on her.

Anna came out of this annoyed reverie to find that she had reached her own apartment building. The downstairs door was propped open, the usual procedure during the hours when the tenants' kids, just getting home from school, might find their parents at work. The lobby was poorly lit and needed a paint job. Anna, who had lived on the third floor for five years, never saw the forty-watt bulb and peeling walls without a nasty reminder to herself to tackle the slumlord who owned the place. Not that he'd do anything; hell, the greedy bastard probably worked for God.

Tired and generally furious with the universe, Anna walked into the deserted lobby and made for the stairs.

Behind her, a silent shape slipped into the hallway. Hugging the shadows, the necromancer became part of the dim interior. One sinewy hand, encased in a black cotton glove, slid into a deep pocket. The hand found The Sleeper, and took it up. Soundless and quick, the killer moved forward.

Okay. Ready, done, it's show time. Do it.

Leo stared at the completed canvas. One corner of her mind was astonished at what she had made. Using acrylic paint and no single of touch color anywhere, she had produced what was essentially a photograph. There was no single spark of her own creativity to be seen anywhere. This was not art, but something at once lesser and greater.

Scaredy-cat. Quit stalling and do it.

"Oh, man..." She spoke to the familiar room, her eyes on the canvas. She wasn't scared, and she didn't believe she was stalling. It was just that she couldn't think about anything except what fun it would be to douse the damned thing with kerosene, set a match to it, and watch it burn. She'd never seen anything so horrible.

Okay, so you're not scared. The sooner you're in, the sooner you're out. Then you can burn it. Get in there and get it done.

She acknowledged the truth of this thought by dragging the straight-backed chair to its place before the canvas and settling herself into it. A rueful, ironic thought flashed through her mind: this was what she usually did to relax.

She stared at the painting.

Black and white and gray, the muted thunder of water moving under the Golden Gate, the twinkle of lights on the bridge diffused by the incoming fog...

A tiny, distracting thought nagged at her. Why had Cass slapped a gag on those prints? His first priority should have been to get them to the media. Why had he hidden them instead, delaying the vital warning to the frightened city?

Later. Not now. Look at the painting.

She looked at the painting.

Alarm captured forever in a killer's hunched shoulder and outstretched hand. It was a very small hand, all things considered. Carla Morisco, a wounded question mark on the damp scrubby ground, partly hidden by the shadows of the trees and the deepening twilight...

Something moved in Leo, jerking at her awareness, nearly pulling her loose. She hardened herself, ignoring the twitch in her legs. Ghostly fingers fumbled for the life-colored cord that connected her to herself, and found it. She moved towards the painting.

The smell of salt in the air, wind soughing through the treetops, unseen traffic along Lincoln Way behind the hand that had recorded this horror and frozen it in time...

Leo's small body relaxed on its throne. Her eyes were wide and sightless. Lightly, easily, her spirit slipped free of its confining shell and drifted toward the canvas.

She was aware of a tremendous resistance. She tightened her grip on the cord, willing it to lead her, pushing hard against this unknown defense system that wanted so badly to keep her out. Then the resistance gave way, and she was in.

She knew at once that something was different, very right, very wrong. Hovering like a puzzled, uneasy shadow, she tried to pinpoint where the difference lay.

One thing became obvious immediately. Unlike her earlier attempt at painting Nemo's killing ground, this place was not empty; the smells, the sounds, the impact on her senses were all present. In fact, they were too much present, for what should have been no more than suggestion was harshly overmastering instead. The surf was not muted, but a heavy immediate pounding; the fog was not merely damp, it was cold and clammy and plastered Leo's hair against her skull. She thought that the place was too much, too real. The only indistinct thing on this damp chilly canvas was the limp shape of Carla Morisco, blurred in outline until she might have been nothing more than a smear of darkness.

That was one difference, but it was not the only one.

Something here, something hiding, something watching.

Yes, she thought distantly, *that's what it is. I'm not alone in here. There's someone else here with me, someone awake, aware. Not Carla. I've done it, I've made it work.*

But the watcher was hidden, and would stay hidden unless Leo forced the issue. She didn't know how she understood this, but the knowledge was certain. It was her game to call. Her sense of power was exhilarating, almost too much to bear. This was why she had come. She was in control.

She drew herself inward, concentrating all of her energy and awareness into command.

Come out. Come out and face me. You can't hide from me now. It's time to meet your maker.

Nothing, only a breathless silence. It seemed to Leo that she was godlike, omnipotent, in this scene of oncoming darkness. The hidden one's emotions were impossible to read, but Leo labeled them. He was scared, unable to face Leo's power. She had never felt such confidence, such total control. She savored it, feeding her own strength on the sensation.

I said, come out.

There was a flicker of something Leo couldn't identify; it might have been amusement, or agreement, or perhaps something more alien. She knew a vast surging impatience in herself, and gave it rein.

I order you to show yourself. I command you. This is my place. I control here.

(no you don't)

What the hell!?

(not control, no, not you, your mistake)

The painting shrank and contracted around her. Leo, with no corporeal lungs, found herself fighting for breath. She was dizzy and confused, but not yet frightened. She was not the only sentient presence here. Someone, something, had replied to her demand, replied in a high, thin tone that was unpleasant and not quite recognizable.

Yet it was familiar, distantly known. Whoever she was, the woman who had spoken, Leo had heard it before.

The realization hit Leo like a slap to the mind.

She. Female. Nemo is a woman.

⟡

With one foot on the first step, Anna stopped cold. She didn't know what had set off every psychic alarm bell her nervous system possessed. She knew only that someone, something, meant to give her grief; her instinct on that one subject was sound and sure. When you are convinced that God hates you, you learn to keep your warning system at full alert.

Anna was also conscious of a certain glee. Not ten minutes ago, she'd been thinking that kicking a little ass would ease the pressure. Whoever this jerk was, would-be mugger or somebody's adolescent kid with a sick sense of humor, he was going to be *muy* sorry when she got done with him.

Mindful of her pregnancy-impaired balance, Anna took her foot off the step. She heard the soft rush of footsteps behind her, the quick flurry of motion, as her attacker closed in.

Faster than she thought herself capable of moving, Anna whipped around. Even as she turned, she felt the disturbance in the air that meant an arm being swung. Instinctively, her own arm lashed out in self-defense. It connected, struck hard against the attacker, and slid away.

"Wrong move," she whispered. "Wrong move this time, pal. Way big-time wrong. That's the breaks. So sorry."

Before the words were fully out, a blow connected painfully against the side of her neck. She understood, as she reeled backward, that her attacker meant business. She had deflected a blow aimed with deadly force, and straight at her skull; if he'd hit true, she'd have been knocked cold. She mustn't take a clean hit, and she mustn't fall. If she did, she was dead.

These thoughts went through Anna's mind in less time than it took for her physical reactions to kick in.

She reached out, grasping a wiry wrist that felt hot and repulsive. She wrenched at it, trying to twist it away from her, and found it immobile against the pressure. Sickly, Anna realized that, although her attacker was really no bigger than his potential victim, he was as strong, maybe stronger, than she was.

She thought briefly about screaming. But there didn't seem to be enough air in the world to power her lungs to that potentially life-saving action.

Instead, she lashed out with her free hand, slapping her assailant across one ear. The blow was a solid hit, strong enough to stop most people. It had no effect at all.

The bastard's face was averted, invisible. It was almost as if he had some special reason for not wanting Anna to see his face. But that made no sense, not if he was planning to kill her anyway...

I can't move, I can't get out of bed and it wouldn't matter even if I did. I wouldn't be able to stop whoever it is, because he doesn't have a body or even a face...

There was pain in her belly now, short sharp cramps that stabbed unbearably. She was frightened, close to panic. Through it, Sophy's explanation of the dream that had been haunting her cycled like a litany.

...he doesn't have a face... .

The terror was spreading now, taking hold like a hungry fire. It had suddenly become imperative that she see this creature's face. Sophy's words ran with terrible clarity.

I don't know, a devil maybe, something awful...a baby girl who looks like you...a devil, something awful... .

Anna reached out with her free hand. Instead of aiming a blow, she caught hold of the black cap the killer wore, and wrenched it loose. A cascade of fine black hair swung free to her attacker's shoulders.

Anna heard a tiny hissing breath, a quick cascade of words in a language she couldn't identify. Slowly, like someone in a trance, the killer turned around. The averted profile became long eyes, an upturned nose, a full twisted mouth with long brackets. It was a travesty, a living cartoon, and it had stared at Anna from the front page of Monday's morning paper.

The dimly lit hallway, the electric terror that the confrontation had pumped into the air, pulsed like an open wound. Everything became gray, then an angry reddish-black. *I'm going to faint*, Anna thought dimly. *Jesus H. Christ, I've never fainted in my whole life and I have to pick now to do it. Of all the shitty jokes God ever played on me, this one takes the cake...*

The evil mask was very close now. On the edge of unconsciousness, Anna realized that the strength in the Maternity Murderer's arm was fading into limpness. With her eyes locked on the killer's own, Anna thought she saw a look of surprise, something part shock and part recognition and part agreement.

Instead of closing in for the kill, the hunter had frozen in place. Something had stopped him.

Anna's final thought, before she slid into the accepting sleep of unconsciousness, surprised her.

Maybe God had a kind streak after all.

A shift, a pull, a vicious imperative command.

Tam Lin, at the edge of absorbing Anna Mendez's life, heard the voice of the sorceress on the other side of the shadows. This time, she recognized it.

The strength there was tremendous. The woman she had known had never been so strong. This was power incarnate.

Tam Lin hesitated, feeling her own strength ebbing as she was pulled. She fought back briefly, her own surprise shielding her from the enemy. To stay and feed, or to go and bury this hated ghost? The pull was very strong, almost as strong as the memories she had tried so long to conquer.

Temptation, fed by the knowledge of who was trying to best her on her own ground, was too great to resist. With a tiny shrug, Tam Lin let go of the physical world and fell into her sister-in-law's painting.

(i know you, you are leo chant, i should have known when you called to me this morning but i didn't, i only knew that you were female and familiar, did you think you could meet a sorcerer on her own ground and win, you fool, you conceited little woman, you have pushed me and you will pay)

The river of words, cold and contemptuous, washed over Leo. She felt them, heard them, and winced away. The power in the adversary's voice was staggering. Immersed in the crushing darkness of the painting and the situation itself, Leo struggled to pull herself back to the strength she had felt in herself only moments before. Still unaware of real danger, she honed her thoughts and made them into words, hurling them like stones at the taunting unknown.

Okay, so you know my name. I know your voice, I know your face, but I can't put a name to you. So why don't you put a name to yourself? Scared of me, maybe?

(i am afraid of nothing, as you will learn, you have pulled me from my pleasure and you will pay, you will pay)

There was a high, vicious gloating in this torrent of hatred. It faded into a charged silence that seemed full of shadowy echoes.

Leo felt herself tighten, pulling into herself. Even as she understood what she was doing and why, a question formed in her mind.

What am I doing? I'm getting ready for a fight, a physical fight. But there's nothing physical for me to fight here. Is there? And behind that question, the root and source, running insistently: *Who in sweet hell is she? Who?*

The beat of the wind was changing, becoming more like a human heart heard through a doctor's stethoscope. Between one beat and another, the fog ceased drifting, taking on the substance of a thick wet blanket. Through it, Leo heard Nemo's voice, high and cold, rasping the nerves like a tenpenny nail dragged over slate.

(you wanted me, here i am, yes here i am, we'll see who is master here now, yes)

The wind that had sounded like a heartbeat was painfully loud now. Crazily, Leo found herself concentrating on the rhythm: *thump-THUMP, thump-THUMP.* Soft-loud, soft-loud. There was something hypnotic about it. She had told herself that she wasn't scared. She was scared now.

Okay, she thought, *so I'm scared. Maybe I ought to be scared, maybe I bit off more than I can chew. Let Cass find his own killer. I'm getting the hell out of here.*

She reached out for the life-colored cord, the thread of connection to the physical world. Feeling with all psychic antennae, she ordered her fingers to tighten, grasp, take her out and away.

There was nothing to find, nothing to hold. The cord was gone.

Chapter Fifteen

"Try the bell again."

Three peals, four peals, five. While Mara jabbed at Leo's doorbell, Delgado rattled the security gate until his wrists ached. It would have given him a real if unworthy satisfaction to have wrapped both hands around Leo's neck instead. He was going to kick her ass seven ways to Sunday when he got his hands on her. Why was she frightening him this way? Why the *hell* wouldn't she answer the door?

He never questioned Mara's insistence that Leo was inside, and in some kind of trouble. He might not be the psychic type himself, but he wasn't insensate, either. Something was happening, he could feel it. Urgency beat through his blood like jungle drums, a warning of invaders, intruders, danger just beyond his visual range. He shook the gate once more, remembering with a sudden wretched clutch around the heart how he and Leo had seemed to catch echoes of each other's minds, that first day they had made love.

"This is useless." Mara took her finger from the bell and faced him. "We're wasting time, and we don't have any time to waste. Can't you pick the lock? I thought all policemen knew how to pick locks."

"You're confusing the cops with the crooks. Well, let's see. I could pick the lock on the gate, but the problem is the door. We're talking two standards and a deadbolt here. Even if I could get it open, it would take forever. The windows are out; those shutters would take a blowtorch." Delgado gave the gate a resounding kick. It hurt his toe; the pain was reassuring. "Besides,

I'll bet you the security alarm is on. Unless I can get all three locks open within about thirty seconds, it'll go off and we'll have half the force down here inside of two minutes, including your dad, most likely. And we don't know the alarm code."

"I do."

"You're kidding."

"I know it," Mara said tightly. "I memorized it when Leo had the system put in, in case of emergencies. She asked me to, because she was always forgetting it back then; she's got an attitude problem with anything that smells like math. But by the time we managed the locks, we might be too late. And those steel shade things on the windows might as well be protecting Fort Knox. What about the skylight? I could get through that."

Delgado stared at her. "Yeah, you probably could. And once you were in, you could turn off the alarm and let me in through the door. But how would you get down? It must be a fifteen-foot drop to the floor."

"I'll manage." The girl looked bloodless, Delgado thought uneasily, bloodless and boneless and past caring about whether she got hurt or not. He cared, though. Cass would never forgive him if Mara came to harm, and he'd never forgive himself, either. Besides, she'd been hurt enough already.

"I won't hurt myself, it's okay." Delgado gave her a startled glance at this apparent mind-reading, and she managed a fleeting smile. "Don't look at me as if I were a witch-doctor. Your face shows a lot of what you're thinking, that's all. Look, we'd better move it. There's a small alley on the back side of the warehouse. I'm pretty sure there's a fire escape. You'll have to give me a boost up."

The alley, fifteen feet wide and blocked at the far end by the wall of a neighboring building, was larger than Jim had expected. Of course, he thought. This place had originally been used as a commercial warehouse. You can't have a warehouse without some way of unloading goods. There must be a cargo gate somewhere. Maybe they wouldn't have to risk that flimsy-looking fire escape after all.

"Forget it." Mara was scanning the outer walls of the warehouse, her eyes gauging height, distance, and possible footholds. "If you're thinking about the old service bay, it's been plastered over. I helped Leo do it myself."

The dark echo of some long-buried superstition moved down Delgado's spine. Mara had said she could read his face, but nobody could read your features when they weren't even looking at you. And that meant she'd read his mind, not his face. The kid seemed to be functioning like some kind of human antenna, receiving inaudible signals from some distant, alien source.

"I think I can grab the bottom rung of the fire escape, if you'll lift me." Mara turned to regard him, and Delgado's throat closed for a sickening moment. Her eyes were completely detached, too bright, too focused. It was like looking into the eyes of a hundred-year-old holy woman. Even her voice no longer matched up. "No offense, but I wish you were bigger. Are you sure you can handle my weight?"

"Um, yeah." Delgado croaked the reply, and knew that he was completely unnerved. He felt a jolt of annoyance, and with an effort of will pulled himself together. Okay. So this teenager had suddenly turned into Buddha or Confucius or some damned thing. He'd cope with it later. The important thing was Leo, Leo inside this damned warehouse with its eighty billion locks that were supposed to keep her safe and obviously hadn't done their job. "Yeah, I can hold you. No problem. But you realize you'll probably have to smash the glass. The minute you do, the alarm will go. So I'd suggest you check out what's going on inside before you get in."

"Of course. I'll tell you what's happening, assuming I can see anything."

The girl felt as light as a bird in his arms. And the lowest rungs of the fire escape were just within reach of her stretching fingers. Delgado held her ankles as she grasped the steel ladder. For a moment she tensed, straight as a ballet dancer. Then she pushed off against his hold, her arms locking to take the brunt of her own weight as she hoisted herself up and began to climb.

He stood back, sweating and trembling with relief, watching as she moved up the fire escape and swung herself easily onto the roof. As she disappeared from his view, the knowledge that he'd acted like a maniac hit him right between the eyes.

What in God's name was he doing, sending her up there alone? It made no difference if he went through the door or the skylight; she could turn the alarm off with him already inside. What if there was a killer in there, someone awful and deadly, carrying a weapon, meaning to hurt. His brain must have turned into tapioca pudding, for him to have even considered sending an unarmed child into that. He should have gone up with her. He was the one with the gun. Suppose Nemo was in there...

Nemo. Tam Lin Chant. Her mother.

"Mara! Mara, come back! *Mara!*"

To his endless relief, her head appeared at the edge of the roof. "What is it? What's wrong?"

"Whew." His breath blew out in a cloudy gust; the day seemed to be getting colder. He realized with dismay that in less than two hours night would settle on the city. The idea of crawling around on that roof in darkness was very scary. "Nothing's wrong, except that I nearly screwed up beyond belief. I can't let you go down there by yourself. What I mean—"

"What you mean is that if anything happens to me, you'll still be stuck out here and the whole mess would get even worse?" At this distance, her features were a pale blur. He could feel her frustration like an insect's bite. "Damn. You're right, we can't risk it. So now what do we do?"

"What we do is, you wait there and I come up." The pulse of awareness hit him again, letting him catch a throb of impatience from the child on the roof. He spoke sharply. "I mean it, Mara. You stay where you are, you don't do a damned thing until I can get up there. Don't even get near the skylight. That's an order. You got that?"

"Okay, okay. Just hurry."

It took ten precious minutes to find a box strong enough to withstand his weight, and he had to go back to Sam's Place and flash a badge to acquire it. When he got back to the alley, his first action was to jerk his head upward to see if Mara had obeyed him. She greeted him with a wave.

"What's that, a milk crate?"

"Yeah. Okay, here I come."

With a snap of muscles that sent a jab of pain down his back and shoulders, Delgado caught hold of the ladder and scurried up. Shaking his head to Mara's outstretched hand, he pulled himself up on the pebble-strewn roof and sat for a moment, trying to catch his breath.

Beside him, Mara had turned to face the west. Delgado followed her gaze and saw what she saw. The sun was slowly losing its hard bright edge. It was clearly farther down in the sky than it been only minutes earlier.

Mara moved her eyes to his face, and Delgado, hearing the unspoken message, nodded. Sunset was coming, and full dark was dangerously near.

It was time to get moving.

He led the way to the glass camel's hump that was Leo's skylight. Even from this distance, he could see where the trip-wires for the alarm system had been carefully laid in to ring the glass. Closer scrutiny revealed that the glass itself, all twelve sections of it, was laced with the tell-tale trip-wires.

The trick, he thought, *is to look but not touch.* Keep your weight off the wires and the alarm stays off; put weight on them or break the glass and all the pretty flashing lights heat up down at the security company's office. It was a good system, a well-designed system. Only this time, somehow, danger had gotten in anyway.

Mara, crossing the roof at his heels, touched his shoulder. "Come on," she said quietly. "Let's do it. You want to check it out, or should I?"

"I will. You stay behind me."

Carefully avoiding the wires, he dropped to a crouch. The loose gravel bit against his knees, and the breeze was sharp and cold, seeming almost to hum. For a few seconds, he sat without moving, listening, feeling the sense of trouble gather around him. *Jungle drums, jungle drums, intruders approaching, barbarians on the way, warning...*

He shook off the momentary paralysis, wondering why his heart kept thundering against his ribs. Carefully avoiding any contact with the alarm wiring, he stretched his neck to full extension and peered down into Leo's studio.

Track lighting and one soft spotlight, focused on the easel and chair. The automatically operated metal shutters were down over the windows; they seemed to peer into the room like blind, dysfunctional eyes. The stacks of canvasses, the butcher's block table, the coffeepot, the barstools.

Delgado took in the normalcy of the big room. Then his eyes found Leo, the only living thing in this setting for a still life, and the rest of the room was forgotten.

Alone in the room, she sat in the chair before the easel. The pose of her body was unnatural; although her lower body was tense and ready, her torso and neck were limp and terribly, inexplicably helpless. No part of the woman in the chair showed any sign of movement. She might easily have been dead.

"Jim? Is she there?"

He was so intent on the oddity in the room below that he'd actually forgotten Mara's presence behind him. He jumped a little, but his eyes, pinned and captured by the woman below, never wavered.

"She's there. She's alone." He wondered why the absence of material threat should not have eased his belief that Leo was under some kind of siege. *Danger, danger.* He held hard to his self-control. "But there's something wrong, something about the way she's sitting."

He was vaguely aware of Mara kneeling beside him. Copying his posture, she stretched and peered. He heard a rasping intake of breath, a whisper of recognition and comprehension, a bitten-off exclamation that smothered whatever words had wanted out. Then she grabbed his arm and pulled him forcibly away from the skylight.

"Listen," she said rapidly. "Listen to me. You've been giving the orders and that's cool, that's right, because so far this has all been up your alley. But now you've got to listen to me, to trust me. Will you?"

"Yes." It was getting darker on the roof, the air growing shadowy and dense in a manner almost as unnatural as the scene framed by the skylight. *Leo,* he thought, *Leo, what is happening down there?* "Yes, I will. You know what's going on down there, don't you? You want to clue me in?"

"Not yet. But I'm going down first." The smooth drawl was incisive as a laser beam. "I'll turn off the alarm and then you come down. If anything goes wrong, the code is 6063. Got it? When you get down, *don't touch anything.* No matter what happens, don't touch a damned thing. Don't touch me, and don't touch Leo. This is important, I know it sounds weird but I can't explain it to you, not now. There's no time now. But you've got to promise me. You've got to swear."

"I swear." The trite, hackneyed words, spoken with a solemnity that made no sense even to the speaker, were nearly blown away on the chilly wind. "I promise."

"Good," she nodded. "Because if I'm right about what's happening down there, and you break that promise, Leo could die."

"What?"

"Die," Mara said over her shoulder. "Touch her before she wakes up, and she could die. You remember the code?"

"Yes, 6063. Mara, for God's sake!"

"You promised. You swore. And heaven help all of us if you interfere."

Mara brought the heel of her shoe down hard on the skylight, once, twice. The third blow shattered half the glass, sending a cascade of sharp slivers into the studio. Then, without a backwards look, she reached for the metallic rim of the skylight, lowered herself into position, and dropped.

On the grimy floor of a Mission district hallway, Anna Mendez lay unconscious. At the junction where dreams are produced, she was contemplating the possibilities of death.

Knowing that she was about to die had certain twisted satisfactions attached to it. Not even the terror of confronting the faceless devil of her cousin's nightmare could smother the knowledge that finally, at long last, she was going to get a chance to confront God and tell Him what she thought of Him. Hell, if she was dead, she didn't have one single damned thing to lose. What was He going to do about it? Kill her? Send her to hell? She was booked for that one-way anyway.

Except I think that maybe I'm not dead. As a matter of fact, I think I'm still alive. Maybe I ought to wake up, and check out the situation.

As if in confirmation, her body stirred, producing a soft whimper. The whimper became a cough as her open mouth inhaled dust. It tasted lousy.

The thought brought her a few centimeters closer to full awareness. If her sense of taste was functioning, maybe she really *wasn't* dead. Of course, it was possible that you kept your five senses after death. Typical, she thought hazily. God called your number and you still had to cope with shit like tofu and pickled beets...

Living muscles contracted, to produce a stab of pain in her back and thighs. The baby, she thought dreamily, the little whats-it, Jehovah's Revenge. It-he-she is getting squashed. Eyes closed, wits wandering, Anna let that percolate through her mind and realized that it proved the utility of yet another sense: touch. So life after death meant dust and cramps and food she didn't like. Swell.

There was a dull ache in her shoulder, an echo of the blow from a weighty iron pipe. Her arm, which seemed to be pinned down by something heavy and inert, sent a message to her brain. Irritably she twitched the arm free, feeling it brush against a rough, heavy fabric. My nervous system still works, she thought. That pretty much settles it. No point in going against the odds. I'm not dead. Three to one says the pissed-off pregnant lady is still alive.

Anna opened her eyes.

The hall, which faced north and never got much natural light anyway, was almost completely dark now. There was no way of knowing how long she'd been out, but it must have been quite a while; the sun, knife-bright before her encounter with death, had lost its potency.

She pulled herself slowly to her knees, one hand on her belly. The other hand, briefly supporting her unsteady weight, moved until it found the fabric she had touched on her way back from purgatory.

The contact was enough to complete the process. It stamped the truth into her mind. Astonished through her detachment, she accepted an unarguable fact. She *was* still alive. She hadn't died. Not even close.

The rough fabric was the sleeve of a jacket worn by the Maternity Murderer. He had followed her, snuck into the hall and attacked her. He'd tried to bop her over the head with a tire iron or something, but she'd fought back and the blow hadn't connected on target. She had seen the killer's face, and recognized it; then she had fainted, like some dumb-ass *chica* in a romance novel or something. And the Maternity Murderer was still here on the hall floor. Maybe, just maybe, *he* was the one about to bitch to God in the Great Hereafter.

Anna heard a mad little giggle, jumped, and realized that she'd been the one giggling. It occurred to her that she was probably on the verge of hysterics. Obviously, that wasn't going to do any good. She controlled the insane desire to laugh by forcing her mind to list the facts.

They were simple enough: She was alive, and the killer was still here. And, now that she thought about it, those two items just didn't add up.

Sitting in the dark, not realizing how deeply in shock she was, Anna puzzled over the conundrum. He had not killed her. She, Anna Mendez, had fainted without stopping him, but he had not killed her. Something else had stopped him, and hard enough to knock him out. The question was, what?

It occurred to her that maybe he'd had a stroke, or a heart attack, or an aneurism or something. Maybe he was dead. And, even if he wasn't, she probably ought to get off the floor and get her pregnant still-alive ass in gear and tie him up like a chicken, before he got any bright ideas about waking up and trying it again. Obedient to the logic of all this, she got to her feet.

It didn't occur to her to walk up the stairs, ring a doorbell, and summon help from another tenant. She felt, obliquely, that the time for that was not yet; this little matter was between her and God. She tried the hall switch and swore as she remembered the dead bulb. That fucking slumlord, she thought hazily. Collect the rent but let the building fall apart before he'd change a bulb. Prop the door open and let murderers wander in and out. Asshole.

There was no sound of breathing to be heard except her own. Carefully feeling her way to the foot of the stairs, Anna squatted beside her attacker. Her hands found a face. The skin was chilly, but not cold. She felt a breath, caught her own, and waited for another intake of air from the killer on the floor. It came, but only after a long time.

Okay, she thought, *okay. Whatever the hell got him, he's out like one of the landlord's bulbs. Which, now that I think about it, gives me a couple of options. One, I can stand here and kick him to death, which would be fun and satisfying but not very useful. Two, I can go outside into the street and yell for help until someone comes. Three, I can go upstairs and get someone down here to watch him while I call the cops.*

As she got back to her feet and headed for the stairs, the reason for the killer's failure came to her. It was so simple that she couldn't believe she hadn't figured it out before.

She'd been right about God. He wasn't going to let His favorite plaything be snatched away by another schoolyard bully.

~~~~~

Weeks later, Delgado would sit down and examine his belief that something screwy had happened to the normal workings of time that day. No amount of self-examination, no attempt to clarify or rationalize his memories, ever shook that belief. Every action, from Mara's last words on the roof to what happened in the room below, seemed to have taken place in the middle of some kind of temporal sneeze. No matter how often he reconstructed the sequence of events, or tried to convince himself that everything had moved normally, he couldn't get away from the facts.

Mara had smashed the skylight with her heel. He remembered that; it had seemed normal. Yet when his memory tried to follow her movements directly afterward, it produced only a blur of motion; there was no Mara, no supple young girl in motion. He remembered only a few strange flashes of color and what looked like the contrail of a plane in the distance. Yet the icon of her fingers, gripping the jagged frame as she prepared to send her body into free-fall, remained clearly in his mind. And he was prepared to swear that he had followed her progress with his eyes.

Yet he never saw her actually land on the studio floor, or run to the control box, or enter the alarm code. He knew she had done these things, but only because he could hear them; if his vision had gone wrong, his hearing had sharpened to compensate. He heard a good hard thump, knew that she had landed safely, and was twisting his body into position to follow her down even as his ears registered and acknowledged her light footsteps running the length of the room. He let go, stifling the panic that comes with falling, and heard the electronic beep of Mara punching in the digits that would keep the warehouse private. He hit the floor with a jarring pain in every muscle, bit back a yelp, and pulled himself upright.

His eyes went immediately to Leo, and he understood how criminally irresponsible he'd been in sanctioning the use of the skylight. The damned thing was almost directly over Leo's chair. While he hadn't seen Mara land, he could measure by his own position, a bare yard from the still form in the chair. It was pure luck, he thought, that both of them hadn't fallen on Leo's head, or that she hadn't been slashed by flying glass. As it was, there was glass in her hair. He could see splinters, sparkling like ornaments...

"Don't touch her!"

"I wasn't planning to." Delgado, who had taken an involuntary step forward, made himself stop. Stopping was almost as difficult as controlling the superstitious panic that was shuddering through his mind. He turned his head and regarded Mara. "She's got glass in her hair. We're lucky the goddamned skylight didn't cut her to ribbons. Are you hurt?"

"No."

It was a lie, Delgado thought, a gallant lie. A streak of blood down one cheekbone showed where she'd been caught by the glass. And something had happened to her right foot; she stood stiffly, hunched to the left, favoring the opposite ankle. But it was just possible that Mara herself was unaware of any injury.

"I'm okay. Jim, you promised not to touch her—"

"I don't break promises," he said harshly. "But I'm a grown man and a cop, and I don't like working in the dark. And frankly, honey, I'm sick of this shit. So tell me one thing. *What in hell is wrong with her?*"

The girl glanced up at him. "You wouldn't believe it, not unless you see it."

"What the hell does that mean? I am seeing it!"

"No, you're not. Look at the picture."

Totally exasperated, Delgado obeyed one more time. He turned his attention back to Leo, Leo who seemed to be in some kind of trance, a Sleeping Beauty surrounded not by the briar hedges of an evil fairy tale, but by oddity and threat and the dark hypnosis of something that she herself had apparently painted.

"The picture," Mara said softly, inexorably. "Don't look at Leo. It's all there in the picture."

Delgado's gaze moved to the picture on the easel. The shock of what his eyes took in was a slap to everything real.

He saw a perfect reproduction of a bad dream. He recognized the setting, taken from the camcorder's evidence. The bridge, the onrushing foggy night, the victim on the ground, the killer. All of these things had been painted, frozen, casting an enchantment amounting to a sorcerer's spell on the painter herself.

But they aren't frozen, he thought. *It's moving, changing. Oh my god I'm going blind, I'm losing my mind, it can't be moving, it's only paint and paint can't move.*

"That's why she wanted those prints." Mara's voice sounded muffled, distant, regretful. "I was right. Oh, Leo, you idiot, you stupid brave idiot."

"But—" Jim swallowed, his hand closing painfully on Mara's shoulder. The black-and-white horror danced and slipped, losing definition, gaining it again. Tam Lin Chant, a body on the ground. And something else. A shape, a form, that was sometimes there and sometimes not. A painted presence, as mutable as the night air. It was there, he was seeing it. Or was he? *Was* he?

This isn't real, he thought madly, *it can't be real, it can't.* "The picture— it's *alive.*"

"Painted devils." She stepped toward the easel, her words appropriate and strange. He had heard them before but couldn't place them; yet, they were perfect. "The sleeping and the dead are but as pictures; 'tis the eye of childhood that fears a painted devil."

"Oh, Jesus," he moaned. "What are you *talking* about?"

"Lady Macbeth said it. We're doing the play in school. And it's true, it's true." She took another step. "It looks alive, because there's life in it. Leo's inside. But something's gone wrong. I don't think she can get out."

"This is nuts," Delgado said reasonably, or so he thought. "Leo's trapped in that thing? You're saying she's stuck inside it, and that's why it's moving?"

"Painted devils," Mara told the easel. "Painted devils."

"Stop it," Delgado whispered, "stop saying that." He cast a desperate look at Leo's face. It was as shuttered and blind as the warehouse windows. A sudden image filled his head, like something out of a bad horror film; Leo, tiny and distorted, a cartoon lost in a nightmare, wandering through a black and white comic strip, pounding on each frame with her fists, searching for a way out, screaming without sound...

"The sleeping and the dead are but as pictures." Mara hadn't heard a word he'd said; she was speaking to something, someone, that Delgado couldn't see, speaking as if she expected some kind of acknowledgment. "Leo, you arrogant pushy heroic moron. How could you think you could possibly call the shots in someone else's world?"

She limped forward, her eyes fixed on the painting. It pulled at her. Through the distraction of the living world around her, through her own physical discomfort and Jim's barely concealed panic, she felt the pull.

Delgado stayed where he was. On a level well beneath his rational mind, he understood what had happened, and what the girl was going to do. Yet he had to speak; in a situation beyond reality and sanity, he had to say something. "What—what are you going to do? Tell me you're not even considering doing what I think you're considering. Please."

"I'm going in."

He exploded, his temper shredding. "You're going in? What the hell, kiddo, you think this is some kind of buddy movie? Next you tell me to cover your back? You're going in where? How?"

She ignored him; it was possible she hadn't heard a word. "Don't touch her, Jim. Don't touch me. I think I can end it, right here. Maybe I can't. But I've got to try. If I blow it, it won't hurt anyone but me."

She dropped to a sitting position beside Leo's chair, tucking her legs up into the familiar half-lotus she used when painting. Bridge lights twinkled, distorted now by more than the artist's brush. Trees loomed, twisting in the wind of a struggle Mara could sense but not see.

I've never done this before, not with someone else's work. I didn't know anyone else could do this but me. The eye of childhood, a painted devil? Oh, Leo. I can't believe I didn't realize that you, of all people, could do it, too. Maybe all painters can do it. But with someone else's work? I'll do my best. If I can't do it, forgive me.

Her body relaxed, receded, faded to unimportance. With a soft sigh, her blood pressure dropped to the minimum level necessary to sustain life. On the shadowy highway between the corporeal and painted worlds, her fingers found the cord that was herself, her link, her ticket to the universe. She took hold of that cord, which pulsed hard and bright. It was herself, her safety net. Nothing could harm her.

Easily, painlessly, Mara followed that cord into Leo's painting.

(run away, you can't run away can you, no place to go)

Thump-THUMP. Soft-loud. The heartbeat of mania, louder than anything Leo had ever heard, filled the universe.

Leo had thought she understood fear. There had been moments, episodes in an otherwise powerful life, when something had gone wrong and frightened her out of the easy control she'd been born with. Some were recent, fresh scars without enough time to form healthy scar tissue. The most recent, her foray into a painting of France, that lovely woodland landscape that she'd wrongly believed to be harmless, was still vivid enough to frighten.

But she'd never known anything like this. This was heart-stopping, mind and soul-destroying. It was outside her experience, and beyond her ability to handle.

(leo chant leo chant, this is my place, you should have stayed safe away)

The life-cord was gone. Leo knew that she could dodge that high clear hellish voice for eternity and beyond while she fumbled wildly for her safety valve. The cord was gone, missing in action. Until she could locate it, there was no way out. She was caught in a limbo of acrylic paint, with a murdering sorceress who knew her name.

There was another way to escape, painful and dangerous and always avoided. She considered it, only to reject it. Breaking her concentration to force herself back to the real world was not an option this time. Instinct remained to her, and she clung to it; it told her, loud and clear, that to weaken her concentration for one second of Nemo's time would be fatal. For right now, at least, that road was closed.

No way out, no way out...

The unreal body occupying this painted hell sucked in cold wet air, and coughed. Leo forced the dampness out of her lungs and tried to focus. She faced the issue squarely; it was possible that only one of the combatants in this war she'd initiated could emerge back into the real world. If that was true, she had one chance. She had to beat this woman, this necromancer who knew her name, beat her down until there was no spark left. The realization gave Leo a jolt of confidence. In a one-on-one, she'd never lost yet.

(hiding, stop hiding, you wanted me here and now you've got me here, leo chant, i always hated you, hate, hate)

The poisonous litany, meant to scare, failed in its object. The spark of confidence surged a bit higher.

I don't give a damn for your hatred, bitch. Why should I? Why should I be frightened of someone who hits women over the head? Someone who wants to play games but won't show her face? You have no power, none at all, and do you know why? You're worthless, that's why. You're garbage. You're dead useless cowardly scum. You're unworthy of my fear. I wouldn't waste my hate on you.

She aimed the words like an archer with a long-bow. They came without thought, taking the form of her personal contempt. She felt them rip through the drumming tension around her. And, like an arrow sent true, they hit their target. Her adversary's recoil, a wordless wincing that sent tangible ripples through the fog, was brutally satisfying. Leo pressed her advantage.

Go ahead and hate me. Go right ahead. I want you to. No wonder I thought you were a man. That's what you want to be, isn't it? No woman would twist the way you twist; everything about you is the wrong side of masculine. I despise you, do you hear me? I don't even hate you, you're not worthy of my hatred, you with your pointy little chin and your fat little lip and your ignorance. You can't even play at feng shui without getting it wrong, you couldn't even get your own magic right. You're an amateur, not a sorcerer. You're not even a woman, and you probably never were.

(shut up shut up, you will pay for those insults)

Something brushed her groping fingers, something vital and bright. The cord, Leo thought, and clutched at it. It slipped away, tantalizingly out of her reach. She felt herself weaken, her concentration wavering as that living pulse flickered away, and fought wildly to regain it. Words came out of her, an unfamiliar phrase that sounded like the tag end of someone else's poetry. They were perfect, utterly appropriate.

Infirm of purpose, give me the daggers.

(what, no, who are you, not leo chant but i know you no i don't, who?)

The sleeping and the dead are but as pictures.

I didn't say those words, Leo thought. I didn't say them and neither did the devil I called. Who...?

The sleeping and the dead are but as pictures.

Light, as bright and mobile as a streaking comet, filled the lowering clouds and changed their color. Leo blinked and inhaled, commanding her bewildered mind to understand.

Something had happened, was happening now, that made no sense to her. It made no sense to the shadow demon she fought, either. She could feel the adversary's fear and confusion. And, with every passing fraction of time, the air of the battlefield grew brighter and more alive.

'tis the eye of childhood that fears a painted devil. Do you know me now, my mother? And you, Leo. Can you put a name to me?

Mara?!?

Warmth, light, power. It felt good, it felt fine. The core, the strong potent reality that was her brother's child, washed over Leo.

But it wasn't possible. How could it be possible?

(no it isn't you lie not Cass Chant's child liar)

There was rage in Nemo's voice now, and a terror that belied the denial. Mara's answer was as serene and as final as the voice of omnipotence.

Cass Chant's child. And your child. Enough, mother. It's over. The only lies that can be told here are the ones you tell yourself. And there's no point in telling yourself that one; I am the child you had. I'm strong, stronger than you. You can't defeat me, mother. You can't even seriously challenge me. So let it go. It's finished, and so are you.

(not true not true cannot be true you lie no not you)

Leo Chant, forgotten by the travesty of a family in this seamless place, listened and understood. She was no longer a combatant in this test of will, and no longer at risk by letting her mind move freely. Knowing this, her memories opened like cracks in the spring earth, the sealing ice melting and running off, letting the past in.

In the flood of remembrance, she saw too much to retain when the waters had subsided. Herself with a number two pencil, sketching trees and faces, capturing what they were, painting the singing of flying birds. Cass, new and raw and crumbled from the rigors of birth, squalling his protest, and her own welcome to the newborn.

Images streamed past, some unique, some as parts of a larger puzzle. Her father's funeral, her mother's grief and recuperation from that grief. Paintings moved past her opened mind, and people; her first lover, brief roseate flashes of everything that had ever gone into the making of Leo Chant.

Finally came the memory that she had tried so hard to unearth, the memory that had pushed her like a strong wind down the road to this moment when she knew who she was, who Mara was, who Nemo was. A painting class at Fort Mason, ten years ago. She'd been having a brief fling with a male model named Jimmy, a man who suffered from narcissism to a grotesque degree. Leo had finally had enough of it and told him to go to hell. The model, that day at Fort Mason, had been Jimmy's friend Lothar, another conceited louse with pectorals as big as his ego.

So long ago, it seemed to have happened in another life. Yet it came to her now with the clarity of this moment; her headache, her anger, her final furious decision that the gods were screwing around with her by dumping a naked friend of Jimmy's on the makeshift wooden platform. She could even remember the smell of the oils.

She remembered. She'd needed to vent.

And she had slammed down her brush and reached for a sketchbook and occupied the remaining time in the best way she could conceive of: exorcising a demon. She had drawn the purest conception of evil that she knew how to draw: her brother's vanished wife, Tam Lin.

Now that the memory was whole, Leo understood several things that had eluded her. The confusion over Nemo's eyes became clear, remembered with full detail. She had drawn one rendering with Jimmy's eyes, round and smug and certainly not Asian. And small wonder, too, that she had drawn the head without hair. She'd been trying to exorcise concentrated evil, not to portray sex or fashion. So clear, so clear.

And Mara, the mystery child, the enigma that her brother had made with this dark and tainted creature. How had she known, and how had she come into this place where only the painter and the painted should be able to go? What was happening in the world of flesh?

With the thought, Leo's fingers tingled. She recognized the sensation, a precursor of physical agony in that other world, with relief. A moment more of this, and the lock would be broken. A little more and she would be back in her body, twisting with cramps, sweating and sick.

But she couldn't leave Mara here. She couldn't take the escape route which her niece had miraculously provided, not if accepting the gift meant stranding the donor.

(go away go away get away from me hate i hate go)

Tam Lin's voice was spiralling out of control, higher and higher. It reminded Leo of a wasp, of some stinging insect which, in search of prey, found instead a trap of tar paper and poison. And all the time the tingling in Leo's fingers grew sharper, and the fog grew lighter and warmer.

(Let her go, mother, just let her go. You have no hold over her anymore. You can't hold her here. Or me either. She has safe passage out of here, safe under my protection. You can't keep her here. You can't do anything if I don't choose to let you. You know that, don't you? You know.)

(why do you protect her, who is she that you should protect her?)

The words were lucid enough, but uneven, choked. The demon sounded short of breath, as if gasping for oxygen. Yet Leo knew how impossible that was. How could a shadow, lacking a body, be short of breath?

(She is my father's sister, the blood of my blood. She's my family. She was there for me, real and vital and alive, when you were nothing but a dirty word in a dark place. And I love her.)

Oh, Mara, Leo thought, and felt the weight of spectral tears stinging. You don't have to do this. And do you think I would you leave you here, with her?

Thump-THUMP-THUMP.

The heartbeat pulse was suddenly faster and louder. Something was happening, changing; the difference was almost tangible. Leo had a fleeting vision of an explosive device set to a timer; when the clock struck the hour, the bomb would go off. But something had gone wrong with the timer. It was out of control, working on its own, no longer willing to wait for the clock.

(*I don't do anything because I have to, Leo. I only do what I want to do. You don't have to worry about me, not now. She can't hurt me, she can't touch me. The cord is real and solid, I have it in my hand. But you have to go, right now. You must get out. Please.*)

(hate, no, not my child, never had a child only a demon I was not fooled demon)

Tam Lin was screaming now, screaming in a horrible piercing whistle. She exuded madness and fear.

(devil sucking away life and beauty face north and sleep no stop you can't do this hate)

Thump-thump-thump. Too fast, too strong.

The tingling in Leo's fingertips spread rapidly. It moved to her legs, her back, her belly. She gasped, feeling the two worlds she had spread herself between wavering in a cold grey confusion. The tingling became pain. Her chest contracted, shrinking away, fighting her lungs. *No air,* she thought madly, *oh god there's no air I can't breathe I can't breathe.*

The light was intolerably bright, and the pounding pulse threatened to deafen her. She felt a shudder, a pull from her sleeping and abandoned body, and managed to squeeze out Mara's name.

(*Go. Just go. This is between my mother and me. No one else can do this. I'll be safe, I swear.*)

Everything stopped and hung, suspended and frozen. Leo felt a wracking agony. It brought her gorge up in her throat. She didn't know whether the pain existed in her living body or her struggling spirit. She was beyond caring.

"Mara," she whispered, and the painting collapsed around her.

Chapter Sixteen

Jim Delgado saw it all.

He stood between the two unconscious women while the sun sank over the western horizon. He had virtually forgotten their presence. His eyes were locked on disconnection and death, the history of the Chant family, playing itself out in a place beyond his reach. All his attention was focused on the dreamscape that would decide the outcome.

He saw it all, saw and understood. Yet it should have made no sense. There was no small painted Leo to inform, no visible transference of Mara to take its place in acrylic when the spirit left the girl's living body. Everything was subtle, suggested, unreal. There were only the flashes of light, the impression of hard-dried paint that still seemed to flow and drip like running lava.

Darkness, light. He saw it all.

He knew the precise moment when Mara Chant met the painted surface and gained a painless entry. The warmth, the golden pulsing life of her entrance, was reflected so strongly that it came back at him from the canvas to touch his skin. A sudden surge of heat, caught, trapped briefly and improbably in the shards of splintered glass on the studio floor.

It brought in its train the memory of a long-lost Christmas when the child Jim had found himself less interested in the guests and presents than he had been in the flickering fireplace, the reflection of fire twinkling benignly on the curved surface of glass tree ornaments.

Darkness, light.

He pinpointed the instant when Mara took control of the shadowland, a moment less visual than sensed. Her conquest came suddenly and powerfully, registered in the calm that relaxed his spine, the return to near normalcy of his dilated pupils, the easing of atavistic gooseflesh on his arms.

Darkness, light, more light.

Tam Lin fought back, and he felt that, too. He felt the battle being waged in that distant reality as a soreness, stabbing deep in his bones and muscle. There was no way for Delgado to hear what was said there; whatever truths and confrontations were exchanged among the three women were known to them alone. All he could do was watch, and trust his own intuition. Nothing was left to the man of action but passivity and hope.

Darkness, flaring suddenly into a huge, silent explosion of triumph. Delgado whispered under his breath, a wordless denial and an incoherent prayer.

In the space of a heartbeat, the prayer was answered.

Light like a solar flare, bringing heat with it. It surged wildly, dominant and passionate, smelling of sunlight and summer. It consumed the blacks and grays, running into Delgado's eyes like a vast pyroclastic flow of something that came straight from the heart of the earth itself. He cried out, moving without knowledge or coordination, his hands flying to protect his eyes from the conflagration.

Leo, he thought, *Leo, Mara, oh God, what did I do? You couldn't survive this, nothing could survive it. Why did I let you go into this alone...?*

To his left, the body in the chair twitched. The movement was slight, and Delgado was too wrapped up in the enormity of his own fear to see it. The second twitch was stronger; the third, immediately afterwards, was a full spasm. The chair rocked under it, seesawing, threatening to tip. The blank unseeing face contorted with agony; the muscles of her throat tightened with effort.

Delgado turned around.

Life poured back into the abandoned shell of Leo Chant. Watching helplessly not two feet away, Delgado thought that what he was seeing was the equivalent of childbirth, as seen through the eyes of the newborn. To Delgado, there was something indecent about this fierce animal agony. He felt that his eyes were catching a ritual never meant for him to see.

Leo arched her back, sending the chair flying. The writhing body hit the floor, twisted, and arched once more. Both arms flailed, windmilling in a wide arc. Her lips parted just enough to allow a high, whistling exhale.

She rolled, stopping inches from Delgado's feet. As he stared, paralyzed, she curled up on her left side and clutched at her stomach. It took Delgado no time at all to grasp that this final action, showing control and decision, could only mean one thing.

Wherever she had been, she was there no longer. She had come back.

His own muscles unlocked. Everything was forgotten, his promise to Mara, the insanity of the day that was ending, the consequences still to be faced, the prolonged fear of the months that had led to this moment. He dropped to his knees and pulled her into his arms.

He knew at once why Mara had compelled his promise. The body he held was hot, and oddly repulsive to the touch. Delgado felt as if he'd laid hands on a nest full of burning writhing snakes; the shock of touching her made his stomach lurch. He fought off the desire to drop her. Instead, he carefully shifted her so that she faced the shattered skylight.

Leo gasped, swallowed, and began to retch with long dry shudders that wracked her entire body. He held her loosely, letting the seizure run its course, whispering her name under his breath. A fierce desire to protect her welled up, amazing him. As the shuddering slackened, he felt her body temperature dropping closer to normal.

"*Mara..*" The torn whisper was barely audible.

"It's all right," he crooned, as if comforting a child. *She's alive*, he thought exultantly, *alive and aware and undamaged. She's going to be fine.* "Relax. Take deep breaths. Everything's all right now."

She opened her eyes and stared into his face. "Jim."

"The one and only." He kissed her hair. "It's all right, it's okay."

"Nemo." She blinked up at him, her body limp. Her voice was a thread, and her eyebrow was furrowed. "I went in after him and he wasn't a him. Tam Lin. Mara's mother. Nemo is Tam Lin."

"I know." He kissed her again, first one eyelid and then the other. "I know all about it."

"I tried to get out and then I couldn't and then I could. Mara got me out. She followed me in." Abruptly she pulled herself upright, out of his arms. "Mara!"

As if replying to this cry, the girl on the floor sighed. It was a soft, light sound, expressive not of pain but of something more subtle.

As they watched, Mara came back. There was nothing of the wrenching sickness that had marked Leo's return; this was as easy and graceful as if she'd been dozing on a warm beach somewhere. She moved her arms, her neck, her head; she stretched and shivered, once, as if adjusting to some drop in temperature. At the point of transition, the uncanny beauty which had been hers from the day she was born swelled, expanded, and became supernatural. She was almost blinding. Then it faded and was gone, and she was herself once more.

"Mara?" Leo dropped her knees beside her niece. "Mara, honey, it's Leo. Are you okay?"

"Um." Mara opened her eyes. "Fine. Are *you* okay?"

"I've never been better in my life, because of what you did for me." There were tears in Leo's voice. She took the girl into her arms, wrapping her tight and safe, searching the beautiful face as if afraid she would find the marks and scars of Tam Lin's sorcery there. "You didn't have to do it. Mara, I'm so terribly sorry."

"You don't have to be sorry about anything. It's over." The girl's eyes were dreamy, peaceful. She let Leo hold her, accepting the proffered warmth. "It's all over now. She's gone."

"Are you sure, baby girl?"

"No." Delgado sounded strange. "It's not over yet. Look."

He pointed to the canvas.

In the fierce heat of Tam Lin's final struggle, the brutal realism of Leo's rendering was becoming an abstract before their eyes. The hard dry finish of the acrylic seemed disobedient to natural law. The trees ran together, melting into each other until they were formless, unilluminated blobs of shadow. The bridge lights, so meticulously painted, streaked and melted, running into the dark curve of the Golden Gate.

(no, lost, lost and gone, no, dark darkness lost, what did you do to me why, monsters, no, no)

They all heard it, a wild screaming in the choked high pitch of a wasp's death agony. A cold wind ripped through the studio, sending the splinters of glass from the violated skylight dancing like fairy dust.

Delgado staggered back, crying out and covering his eyes. Leo tightened her hold on Mara, and buried her face in the girl's neck.

So, in the end, only Mara was watching. Her eyes alone recorded the final spasm of her mother's ending. It was fitting. It was just.

A tiny hole appeared in the center of the painting. Like an acidic ulcer turned malignant, it spread through the fractured world Leo had recreated. Cold came from the mutation on the easel in sickening waves, daring those who lived in the world of sanity to watch at their peril.

Over Leo's bent head, Mara watched.

The cold became searing heat. It flashed out at them, a white-blue impossibility accompanied by a roar that the earth might make when continents collide. Then it shifted to a crackling serpent's hiss as the canvas burst into flame.

At ten minutes to five, as the afternoon dwindled, Cass Chant sat in a comfortable leather chair. He had been in the commissioner's office for three hours; the commissioner, after hearing what the head of Homicide had to say, had turned the color of dried putty and put in an emergency call to the mayor's office, requesting His Honor's immediate attendance. The mayor, after a brief recap of the facts involved, was looking even sicker than the commissioner.

Cass finished the detailed report of his conclusions in a voice that held nothing but emptiness. At the end of the worst day of his life, emptiness was all he had left.

The graveside monotone, however appropriate, had gotten on the commissioner's nerves. He liked Cass, and he honestly sympathized with what he must be going through; after all, he'd watched him come up through the ranks, and had appointed him to his current position. No two ways about it, the whole thing was a horrible mess. But, hell, Chant had to know that they couldn't just accept his resignation and let him fade out. There might yet be a way out. He glanced at the mayor, saw similar logic in his eye, and cleared his throat.

"Look, Cass," he said carefully, "you don't want to be too hasty here. If you resign, you're dumping your entire career. We still don't have all the facts. And didn't you say you haven't heard from this woman in fifteen years or something?"

Cass looked up, and the commissioner winced. Graveside was the word, all right. The poor bastard looked like he'd been dead for a week and was just waiting for someone to tell him to lay down. As the commissioner fumbled wildly for something to say, the phone rang.

Grateful for the reprieve, he snatched it up. "Barnes speaking."

The excited quack of someone with big news nearly made him drop the phone. The others watched as his jaw tensed and his eyes grew wide. He listened for less than ten seconds before hanging up.

"This may do it," he said. "One way or another, this may just do it. They've got Nemo, unconscious; another attempt that didn't come off, down in the Mission this time. The would-be victim just phoned 911. Nemo's being guarded by a neighbor with a handgun. Homicide's on the way there, with full backup and an ambulance. They've got a squad car downstairs, ready and waiting. Let's move it."

Dave Aguilera, who lived in the apartment across the hall from Anna Mendez, was the only eyewitness to Tam Lin's physical ending.

He stood under the scanty illumination provided by a new sixty-watt bulb, staring down at the killer who had been terrorizing San Francisco for, in his opinion, way too long. The killer in question hadn't moved a muscle.

Aguilera hadn't touched the shape on the hall floor, not even to check for signs of life. He saw no reason to touch the crazy son of a bitch. He didn't know what was wrong with the guy, or what had stopped him from wasting Anna Mendez. He didn't particularly care. All he knew was that the Glock he was pointing at the killer's head was going to make one major hole if the nutjob on the floor woke up and got any bright ideas about leaving.

His wife Suzy had replaced the light bulb while Anna herself had been calling the police. Listening to the wail of approaching sirens in the distance, Aguilera realized anew how amazing Suzy was. She could have panicked, screamed or fainted or something useless like that. Suzy had made sure that Anna was okay, pointed her toward the phone, and accompanied her well-armed husband downstairs to change the bulb in the hall. She was something special. He was a lucky, lucky man...

The body on the floor twitched, jerked, twitched again. Aguilera, unworried, stepped back to give himself room to fire if the guy tried to get up. What the hell, he'd have some official help any minute now. The sirens, and there were plenty of them, couldn't be more than a few blocks away. From the sound of it, the cop cars and ambulances and whatever else they'd dispatched were already bottling up traffic down on Mission.

He was right. Five minutes later, four police cars and an ambulance screeched to a halt, cutting off all means of entry and escape from the little side street. When Cass Chant burst through the door, his gun at the ready and six officers at his heels, Aguilera was kneeling over the slight shape on the floor.

He lowered the .38 to his side. Glancing up at the stone-faced cop in charge, he thought that he'd never seen a look like that on a grown man's face before. He never wanted to see one like it again, either. It wasn't decent. The guy looked like he'd just lost a relay race where the second prize was hell.

From outside came the sounds of the law's machinery, cordoning off the street, keeping the curious back. Aguilera cleared his throat.

"Too late," he said, and straightened up. "He's dead."

"What?" Cass Chant's voice was as lifeless as the killer on the dirty floor. The tortured eyes never moved from where the body had fallen. "What did you say?"

"He's gone, man. Snuffed out, finito. I watched it happen. Heart attack or something, maybe two minutes before you guys got here. He gave a couple of twitches and that was it. Save the state some bucks, anyway."

"Two minutes, you said?" A police paramedic had come up beside them. "I may be able to revive him. You want me to try it, Lieutenant Chant?"

"No." Maybe it was just the uncertain light, but Cass Chant seemed to have tears on his cheeks. "No, there's nothing to revive. Maybe there never was."

"I got a postcard from Mara yesterday."

"You did?" Leo, who was blurring a too-dominant edge on her sketch pad, glanced up in surprise. "Turn your head a bit to the left, will you? Thanks. Postcard? I got one about three days ago, a shot of some mariachi types on a beach. It didn't say much. She's not a talker, my niece."

"Neither did mine." This posing stuff was trickier than it looked, Delgado thought. This was the third sketch she'd done of him. "Just the usual stuff you get on a postcard. They're both fine, the flight was smooth, Mazatlan is very sunny. Not too personal, you know? But pretty reassuring."

"If I know Mara, that's probably just what she was trying to do." Leo peered at him, swept the charcoal pencil down the paper, and set the pad down beside her. "Done for now. Thanks, baby. You're a good model."

He grinned at her. "Yeah, and I cook, too."

Her crack of laughter echoed around the studio. "Among other things. You can move now, if you want to."

He got up and stretched his cramped legs. "You know, Leo, we got off very, very lucky. The commissioner and the mayor, they could have let the whole story out. If she hadn't died..."

"I know." Leo walked into his arms. He could feel her shivering. "If they'd had to try her, it would have been as Tam Lin Chant and the whole damned world would have been on top of us. I'm just glad that all her papers listed her as Tam Lin Chiu, spinster, legal alien. Wiping out every trace of her marriage to Cass was probably the one considerate thing the crazy psychobitch ever did."

The rasp of naked hatred in her voice was as strong as it had been since Tam Lin's death. Would she ever get completely over it, Delgado wondered. For that matter, would any of them? He tightened his grip.

"It's over, Leo." Delgado spoke softly, meditatively, to the top of her head. "It's as much over as it's ever going to be. I know how much damage she inflicted, don't think I don't. I was with you, there at the finish. But it could have been much worse. Cass doesn't have to resign, and Mara can go on living. The bitch is gone now, gone in every sense of the word. Cass can bury her ghost, and Mara already has. It's been nearly six weeks, and in a few days we'll be looking at Christmas Eve. Okay, so it's a cliché, but that's supposed to be the time for burying the dead and healing old pains. Don't you think you ought to move past it?"

"Easy for you to say." The fabric of his old cotton shirt felt soft against her cheek. It occurred to her that Jim's quiet good sense was remarkably comforting. "No, well, maybe it isn't that easy for you to say. You're right, you were there. I'm sorry, Jim. I just can't stop thinking about that last day. And when I think about that, it opens up all the old wounds. I'm trying, you know. I really am."

"Well." There didn't seem to be anything left to say; besides, they read each other too well to make superfluous words necessary. "So, are you hungry?"

She leaned back against his supporting arm, offering up a ghost of her old grin. "Depends. You talking about food or about, uh, non-culinary delights?"

"Your call." He smiled back. "I'm easy."

"That," she said, "makes the *choice* easy."

For a sneak peak at Deborah Grabien's next novel
from Drollerie Press, ***And Then Put Out the Light,*** turn the page.

And Then Put Out the Light

Emily turned the corner that led to the bus station in time to see the Stonehenge bus disappearing in the distance.

Typical, the thought bitterly, this was typical. If the trip down was anything to go by, this sort of thing probably happened four times a day. First there had been ice on the tracks, then a two-minute stop at a small country town had mysteriously become twelve minutes. And now there was no bus for another two hours. Considering the distance between the train and bus depots, you'd think they'd hold the damned bus. Considering that the train was the only London connection, you'd think...

"Miss your bus?"

Emily's stomach contracted in shock, but only for a moment; even before she turned around, her mind had registered that this voice, female and strangely accented, was not the one she'd been waiting for.

The girl, small and round-faced, smiled up at her. She looked to be no more than twenty. Wisps of corn-gold hair slid from beneath the hood of a down Parka and waved in the cold air; light blue eyes watered a bit in the wind. Her face held humour, and a good deal of intelligence. Emily found herself smiling back.

"By about one minute. The train from London was late. I hate to sound critical, but wouldn't you think they'd let the bus people know?"

"Well, that's the Poms all over, talk big and screw up on the small stuff. Whoops, there I go again, being parochial about the Motherland." The girl stamped her feet and hugged herself. "Cold, isn't it? We don't see this kind of cold in Sydney. Damn, I left my gloves on the bloody train."

"I know, I'm freezing my ass off too. We don't get much of this in New Mexico or California, either." The depot was filling up with people now, probably all passengers of the London train, and all looking disgusted or dismayed. "So you're from Australia. I couldn't quite place the accent. Did you come down from London, too?"

"Oxford, by way of London. I'm doing history there, and today was a lecture on British colonialism so I thought I'd give it a miss." The girl grinned suddenly. "Bad for my blood pressure, revisionist history. I'm Judy Waite, by the way."

"Emily Moon-Bourne." Emily glanced around her, noting the black clouds, the iron-grey sky, the tourists wandering aimlessly in disconsolate little groups. Overhead, casting a stark shadow, a solitary bird wheeled and made off toward the west. It was going to snow again; Emily could taste it in the air. "You know, the next bus isn't for two hours. Let's go find a hot cup of tea."

The town itself was extremely pretty, lovely in fact. Emily, who had seen nothing of Salisbury but the starkly dirty section by the railroad tracks, was surprised and pleased. The streets wound and curved, the older buildings were interesting and inviting, and near the centre of town a kind of gazebo caught the eye and held it. Women with woven shopping bags stamped and blew and made their way in and out of greengrocers' and haberdashers'. The entire town, in fact, managed to pull off an effect of old-world charm, while avoiding the usual pitfalls that would have led to it being labeled picturesque or, worse, quaint.

They found a tea shop near the centre of town. Judy, peeling off muffling layers of down and wool, was revealed as an exquisitely made little creature, full-breasted and slender-waisted. For all the liveliness of bone and smile, her body possessed a certain stillness, an inner calm. She slid into the booth opposite Emily, caught her companion's fascinated look and raised her eyebrows.

"Something wrong?"

"I was just wondering if you've ever sat."

Judy blinked. "Beg pardon?"

"Sat. For a portrait. You've got the bones for it, and the contained expression. You'd be wonderful to paint or, even better, sculpt."

"Oh, I see. You're a painter?"

"A sculptor. I don't usually do people, though; mostly things that fly, birds, insects, the occasional dragon if someone commissions it."

The people at the next table were spooning clotted cream on hot scones, and steam rose in fragrant gusts from their white mugs. Emily's mouth watered. "God, look at what they've got! Whatever that stuff is, I want some."

"Isn't it gorgeous? It's called a cream tea, and it tastes as good as it looks." The waitress set a pot of tea down on the table, took their order and rustled away. Judy brushed the hair back out of her eyes. "You know, that's interesting, I mean about what you do. The last statue I saw that made an impression on me was an insect. And do I mean an impression? No worry!"

Emily gulped down the scalding tea; it sent warmth and life through her system immediately. "Sounds interesting. Was it that good? Whose work was it?"

"Haven't got a clue, mate. As for good, that might not be the right word. I mean, it was well done, but it was the ugliest thing I've ever seen, too right it was. I actually had a nightmare about it."

Emily laughed. "You may not know this, but you're paying the artist a huge compliment. Was it that scary?"

"Too right it was." Judy shuddered and wrapped her hands around her teacup as the front door opened and shut, sending a blast of cold air moving around her head. "I kept dreaming it was trying to sting me."

"Sting you?" Emily looked up suddenly, her teacup suspended. "What do you mean?"

"Well, that's what wasps do, isn't it? Sting people? What's the matter, see a ghost or something?"

"Maybe you did." Emily shook her head slowly. "A wasp. Koa wood, on an ebony stand? Head and tail forward, back arched? A stinger like something out of a blue movie?"

"That's the one. Must be, there could hardly be two of those, could there?" Judy was watching her closely. "You see it too?"

"I carved it. I'll be damned. That's the most...look, Judy, where did you see it?"

"In France." Judy was staring at her. "South of France, Nice. A little gallery in the old town there, near the tower. Damn, what's the place called? Oh, right, the Tour Bellanda. Huge place on the hill by the port, beautiful mosaics, Phoenician I think. There's a maritime museum there, too. But I honestly don't remember the name of the gallery. Sorry." Judy moved the teapot aside, making room for the waitress; who set scones, jams, cream on the table and moved on. "You carved that thing? Sorry, I didn't mean to criticize your work or anything. It was just..."

"Ugly as hell? It was meant to be. I sort of based it on my ex-husband, at that time my not quite ex-husband." Not thinking, she spread marmalade on a scone and put it down again. "Goddamn. In France? I never knew who bought it, it was an anonymous buyer. That's crazy, the most absurd thing in the world. That's nuts."

"I don't see why. Must be nice, knowing your stuff's getting a wide look-in." Judy snapped her fingers suddenly. "Solferino. That was it, the Galerie Solferino. Rue des Something or other."

"By the tower, you said, The Tour – what was it?"

"Bellanda. The street leads right up to the door." Judy hunted in her backpack for a pencil. "Here, where's my napkin, I'll write it down for you, draw you a map - Emily? Are you all right? You've gone all white."

"Another ghost, that's all." Emily swallowed hard. Here it was again, images superimposed over images; a young girl with a pencil, sitting at a food-strewn table, scratching away. All that was needed was Kirstin across the room, right about where the front window of the tea shop was. I'm being followed, followed, followed...

She glanced up at the window, frightened, unable to help herself. She knew that her mother's small white shade would be watching her, waiting to meet her eyes. The glass was frosted, interior warmth meeting exterior cold, clouding and obscuring. Her breathing was harsh in her threat.

There was someone out there, peering in. Hands pressed against the glass, and a face. A man's face. A tall man's face, lips familiar even through the white mist that clouded the panes, the red mist that clouded Emily's eyes...

She got up so quickly that Judy spilled her tea. "I have to go. I've just seen someone I know outside, and I must catch him." She fumbled in her purse, threw a five-pound note on the table. Why was she moving so slowly, her legs felt like rubber, the air itself seemed to have turned to an ether-like substance designed to hold her in place. "I'll be back or else I'll see you at the bus depot before the next bus goes, this shouldn't take long. Here. Bye."

"Take the napkin." Judy, oddly, seemed unsurprised by Emily's urgency. "You may need it later. Happy hunting."

Emily fought her way to the door, wrenched it open and pushed past an incoming couple and out into the street. She stood there, her own breathing too loud in her ears, straining her eyes through the softly falling snow.

He was gone. Of course he was gone. Whatever his reasons, whatever game he was playing, Emmy Deer had called it right; she would see him when he chose to be seen, confront him when he chose to be confronted. Nothing would happen before that moment. She could do nothing but wait, passive and frustrated. Tears sprung to her eyes, chilling her.

Had he even really been there? What, after all, had she seen? A pair of palms pressed against a window, lips that had looked familiar because she wanted them to, needed it that way. Maybe she was losing her mind, cracking up, having some kind of midlife breakdown. Maybe her need and her loneliness and her shattered ego had come together in a touch of madness...

A passer-by looked at her curiously, and she dashed the tears away, ducking her head. As she did so, her eyes fell on the pavement and her breathing shortened, stopped and started again in painful jerks.

Footprints. They were disappearing under the fall of new snow, but there they were, unmistakable, the imprints of a man. Her eyes moved upwards, finding the outer glass of the tea shop, seeing the smears there, where a pair of hands had tried to clear the frost away.

What are you waiting for, you coward, an invitation? Follow the damned footprints. Win the grand prize. X marks the spot. And you'd better hurry, chiquita, because in about six minutes there's going to be a nice fresh layer of virginal white snow to look at, and nothing else. So make like a St. Bernard. Track him. Find him.

"No.' She spoke softly, hearing her own small voice carried away on the moving weather. When she spoke again, it was in her thoughts. 'No. I'm not going to chase him. I won't play that game. I can draw him when I choose and see him when he chooses, but I can't catch him and I don't want to. It isn't time yet. Aren't you the one who said that I wouldn't see him, connect with him, until he decided it was time? So I won't follow the footprints. No."

And Then Put Out the Light
by Deborah Grabien

Coming in June 2008
from Drollerie Press

Printed in the United States
96268LV00007B/358-363/A

9 780979 808104